All the Lonely People

ISBN: 1-4801-0006-4
ISBN-13: 9781480100060

All the Lonely People

A Novel

Jess Riley

Riley

10.98
6/14/13
NRN.

Dedication

For Mom, Dad, Jake, and Maddie … if I could build a whole new family, I'd pick you all over again

Critical Acclaim for Jess Riley's debut novel, *Driving Sideways*:

" ... alternately hilarious, humiliating, and heartbreaking, often within the same sentence. Smart and funny without being forced, sentimental without being maudlin ..."

—Booklist

" ... a gorgeous novel—I LOVED it!! It's enjoyable, uplifting, and so so so funny and sparky. I found it hugely entertaining and very touching. Jess Riley's voice is irreverent and wonderful, and her writing is genius."

—Marian Keyes, internationally bestselling author

"A hopeful and hilarious debut. Jess Riley may well be my new favorite author."

—Jen Lancaster, New York Times bestselling author

It's Not a Prologue. It's More a Disclaimer

I suppose I should begin with a disclaimer of sorts.

When you meet someone for the first time, you're supposed to put your best foot forward. Be charming and light and positive and warm and fuzzy and hip and subtle and sweet. And utterly, completely, infinitely, and wholeheartedly full of shit.

I'm supposed to say my job is a real barrel of monkeys, filled with wacky coworkers who take advantage, sleep their way to my promotion, and fill our work days with petty gossip, malicious games, and one-upmanship that beggar belief. Actually, I don't mind my job. It comes with the latest technology, a biohazard spill kit, and young people who keep me informed about pop culture as well as the current state of the juvenile justice system.

I'm supposed to have a meddling, fussy mother and a beloved, beleaguered father. I wish I did but I don't, so let's get that out of the way right off. Just in case you were expecting that sort of thing.

I don't live in an exciting metropolitan area. I don't summer at the beach with old friends, I don't fall in love with the guy who was under my nose all along, and I won't be attending a single wedding at which I secretly wish I were the bride. I don't learn a valuable life lesson from a precocious child or a sassy senior citizen. I won't be opening an organic bakery you can only get into with a secret password after a donkey ride through a mountain pass. There are no recipes in the appendix. I'm a horrible cook with damaged taste buds because I was too greedy to let a piece of my grandmother's cinnamon apple strudel cool before I shoveled it into my cake-hole when I was nine.

You didn't come for any of that. You came to hear about the worst year of my life, to see the emotional car wreck in which it culminated. The plane plummeting to earth in flames. The mangled bodies, the crumpled metal, the older brother who was once thrown out of a minor league baseball game for fighting with a twelve-year-old over a free T-shirt. So now that we're clear on a few things, let's start with Thanksgiving. Because isn't that where you usually find the turkey?

Chapter 1
"Take a joke already."

If ever a face deserved to be splattered with a spoonful of hot mashed potatoes, it was the one belonging to my older brother Clint.

He's the kind of person who elevates common household bullying and paranoid delusions to the realm of performance art. When he says something awful you first think, *There's no way he really means this.* Then, *Is he trying to charge me up?* Or, *What if it's all actually a front for a host of deep, aching insecurities—what if he's really just brokenhearted about humanity?* Scratch a cynic and you'll find a disillusioned romantic, the saying goes. Later you wind up angry at yourself for reading too much into things, but you simply can't help it when you're trying to figure out whether or not your brother actually believes that water fluoridation is part of some New World Order plot to take down the government.

Here are some of his greatest hits from the Clint Stewart Zinger-a-Day Calendar: "You know those kids you teach probably don't belong in school, with the normal kids. Think about it! Public education for everybody is pretty much a failed social experiment anyway." *But wait, there's more! Remember* "What the fuck did you do to your hair?" *And* "Are you stupid or something?" *Featuring classics like,* "I'm not racist or anything, but——," *Order now and we'll throw in this fertility conversation favorite, free!* "So what's wrong with your husband's junk? Or is it you?"

Whenever he cuts too close to the bone, his standard response is, "Jaime, you know I'm only kidding!" Sometimes it's, "You're too sensitive." Or the perennial favorite, "Take a joke already."

Most of the time I take the joke, turn the other cheek, accept the undercooked apology, forgive and try to forget. Because that's what you do with family. Accept them as they are, or cut your losses and walk away.

Such warped statements and stunts on the part of my brother are not new to me, but they have grown progressively more cynical. Years ago, he'd once basked in the misguided applause from every soul on an airplane who assumed his crew cut and ARMY t-shirt meant a recent return from Iraq or Afghanistan. "Let's all take a moment to thank the veteran on this flight for his service to our country," the flight attendant said over the PA system. I began clapping along with the rest of the passengers until it dawned on me that I was clapping for Clint. I elbowed his ribcage. "You never fought in a war! You were stationed in Hawaii the whole time!" He just beamed and shrugged, and I leaned over to retch in my complimentary barf bag. This happened during a family trip to Las Vegas, after our father left but before our sister Gwen did, before Mom was diagnosed with cancer, long before Clint and compassion parted ways. "He's only trying to get a rise out of you," Mom used to say. "It's how he shows he loves you."

"He nearly killed us because he swerved to *hit* that cat!"

Mom would always sigh, giving Clint the benefit of the doubt. *Oh, you know how boys are.* If our mother had one flaw, it was her steady belief that her children were incapable of saying or doing anything ugly.

It's hard to pinpoint a spot in the timeline of Clint's life as the moment his heart calcified, the moment he shuttered his worldview and put his benevolence on lockdown. Instead, it has been as slow and sneaky a transformation as aging. I can no longer tell if his crass bravado is armor against real or perceived slights inflicted by the world, or if my brother really and truly is a major dick.

And now here we all are at Thanksgiving dinner, the turkey glistening in the candlelight, the room laced with the scents of cinnamon and nutmeg and sage browned butter sauce … and there I am, fork paused in mid-air, staring at Clint in disbelief. "How could you say that?"

"What? You know it's true."

"That's a pretty crummy thing to say, even for you." The entire table falls silent, chewing and listening. The conversation began innocently enough, about the meal and the Packers and Hannah's latest piano recital, but two things quickly warped it: vodka and the recent death of our mother. She died of ovarian cancer six months ago. The amber prescription bottles still line her kitchen windowsill, her brush still bursts with gray strands of her hair, her closets are still filled with shoes and dresses and a lifetime's worth of trinkets and photos and letters. I haven't cleaned any of this yet because doing so would feel like throwing pieces of her away. I'm not ready. I was never ready for any of this. It's not like you can take a class that prepares you to deal with the premature death of a parent: *Losing Your Mom to Cancer 101*. Although I think I could write a pretty damn good syllabus at this point, and one for the companion course: *Sibling Rivalry in Difficult Times (Or is Your Brother Just a Huge Asshole?)*

"Come on, Clint," my husband Erik says. "Be fair."

Clint ignores him. "Well, was she there when Mom died? No! You were at a bed and breakfast getting *massages* and *mud wraps* and eating *scones* with your fucking *pinkie* in the air."

His words make my cheeks burn. Erik and I don't point out that we actually did none of these things at the Sandpiper Inn, because when Clint adopts his "Well aren't *you* the Queen of Sheba" tone, there's no reasoning with him.

Still, he rattles me. I *hadn't* been there for her when she needed me most. I try to say, "It happened so fast," but nothing comes out. Because my mother's death really didn't happen so fast—it had been a painful, awful, extended mess that went on and on until one day, the end that never seemed to be in sight suddenly arrived. And I wasn't there. The one weekend I'm not with her, she dies. I didn't want to go away, but I knew I was losing myself in the care of my mother, withering away along with her, and part of me began to wonder what I'd do with myself after she died. On some level, I knew I needed to reconnect with the world: my husband, my friends, rooms that didn't smell of sickness, appointments that didn't involve blood draws or co-pays or more bad news. So I reluctantly booked the trip.

On my bitter, angry days I suspect Clint timed his phone call so I'd show up right after she died, so he could always say he was the one holding her hand when she took her last breath. The ultimate pre-emptive adult shout of "Shotgun!" before our next journey together, through the Valley of the Will to the Land of I-Think-Mom-Would-Have-Wanted-Me-to-Have-This-Bureau/Antique   Umbrella   Stand/ Set of Vintage Milk Glass Dinnerware. A land visited only by tourists, never cartographers. Once there, I lost track of how many times I rolled over and said, "Just take it."

Clint's wife, Joy, clears her throat. "Sweetheart, please don't use that kind of language at Thanksgiving dinner." She gives me a plaintive look, which is easy for her because she tends to look somewhat plaintive and pinched at any given moment. "Jaime, you have to understand. This has been such a difficult year for us." Her blonde eyelashes flutter with emotion.

Perhaps this, more than anything, unscrews the lid on my fury, and I feel it pinball through my veins like a shot of adrenaline. I feel my pulse beating in my eyelids, in my fingertips. "I *know* it's been difficult. Who lived with Mom for the past year? Who prepared her meals, bathed her, cleaned her house, ran her errands, drove her to the doctor?" I take a ragged breath. My throat is constricting and I will myself not to cry. *Who didn't spend years bitterly blaming her for Dad's leaving only to morph into the Perfect Son when she got sick, just as she might be revising her will?* I don't say this, of course, because the well has already been poisoned. Also, I'm afraid to.

Clint, violently chewing a hunk of turkey, swallows and looks at me pointedly. "Well, some of us have to work two jobs. So our mother can make her mortgage payment."

"So your mother *could* make the mortgage payment," our Uncle Harry helpfully points out. He downs the rest of his gin and tonic, ice cubes clinking in the glass, and turns his attention to the creamed corn. His wife Yolanda refills her wine glass to the brim, pulls out her phone, and begins texting someone. My Aunt Carol, sitting next to her, bares her teeth at a mirrored compact.

Clint spears another hunk of turkey. "Speaking of which, when are you moving out? Are you cleaning before showings?"

"No, I'm leaving dirty underwear strewn around the bedroom and piles of dishes in the sink."

"You gotta sell that house!" Uncle Harry adds. "The man's got a college fund to build." Uncle Harry has apparently picked a side.

And now, not so discreetly, his nose.

Eleven-year-old Hannah, who'd gone to the kitchen for a refill of cranberry sauce, pokes her head around the door frame. "Mom, can I let Cricket out of his crate? He won't stop crying."

Clint grunts. "That filthy animal is staying exactly where he is."

"But he's lonely!"

"That's what you get when you shit on the living room rug."

"He won't do it again," Hannah pleads. "I'll take him outside first, just in case."

Joy shakes her head. "Hannah, sweetie, dogs are not people. They don't belong at the table."

"I'm not asking for him to sit at the table," Hannah mutters, trudging back toward the pantry.

"The dog's whining, my daughter's whining, my sister's whining, everybody's fucking whining," my brother says, more to himself than anyone else. He saws viciously at a hunk of dark meat.

Joy frowns and says, "Clint, language," before returning her attention to me. "I understand, Jaime, I do. It's painful to lose a loved one. I know. You have to remember that everything happens for a reason. Claire is in a much better place now."

I imagine Mom sitting across from me, rolling her eyes, pretending to shovel a small pile of invisible bullshit. The truth is that I envy Joy's steady, reliable faith. I wish I could believe Mom was anywhere but buried in a jar at Peaceful Valley Cemetery.

Joy continues, "Sometimes God blesses us in mysterious ways. For example, you haven't been blessed with children, but you simply can't look at it that way. You need to have a little perspective, look at it differently. God has a plan for you. You have to be patient."

And here it is. The rest of the conversation she tried to start two years ago when she asked when Erik and I would have children and "become a real family."

My right eye begins to twitch. I try to laugh, but it comes out defensive and creepy. "Can we please talk about something else?"

Joy gives me a look of pity. "Jaime, it's not a bad thing to process these feelings. It's actually very healthy. And often, you don't recognize a blessing until you—"

"Joy, please stop. Stop talking. If you don't stop, my head is going to explode. It really will. I'm not even kidding you." My face is hot with grief and anger.

Clint gives me an even stare. "Maybe *you* should stop talking. We invite you to our home, feed you, and this is what you bring to the table."

"Well, I actually brought the—"

Clint cuts me off. "I don't know about the rest of you, but I was raised *not* to insult my host."

"Guys, let's take a deep breath, relax a little," Erik says, but it's too late. The entire table falls silent. The clock ticks in the foyer. Cricket begins to whine again from his crate in the back hall. Everyone is waiting for something terrible and exciting to happen.

Earlier in the day, before football and turkey and insults, Erik and I nearly reconsidered our attendance at Thanksgiving dinner, because family get-togethers had grown progressively less bearable over the past few years. Getting out of the car with a glass tub of green bean casserole in an insulated carrier now felt like preparing for battle. "Why do we do this to ourselves?" Erik sometimes asked, and for a shining moment we might consider the brilliant, freeing possibility of simply getting back into the car, driving home, and peaceably tucking right into the casserole in front of the TV. But then, reality would reassert itself. I'd summon my courage and say my usual line: "Because of Hannah," and we'd reluctantly schlepp to the house. This line used to be, "Because of Mom." But now that she's gone, my niece has assumed the mantle admirably. Without even knowing it, she's become the Family

Glue. Now we endure the insults and indignities because maybe one day Hannah might want to escape the angry, rigid cocoon her parents have built for her and seek refuge with her cool aunt and uncle (that's us), who distribute full-size candy bars at Halloween and have Show-time and hemp area rugs.

Also, we endure my brother because once upon a time, he didn't call homeless people "speed bumps." Once upon a time he defended me from a boy who'd bullied me at school. Once upon a time he didn't show open contempt for the homely, the poor, the overweight. He'd been considerate, loyal, even quite funny. I still smile when I remember how he used to make us all laugh when he was younger, doing a keenly accurate impression of the Channel Five weatherman, Skip Hastings, who was once caught on camera sniffing his own index finger after a good root around his left ear. So I cling to these memories in the hopes that one day, Clint's heart will start beating again, pumping freshly oxygenated blood to his brain.

Things hadn't always been this way. Years ago, when Clint first started dating Joy, I'd entertained the notion of being friends with my future sister-in-law. We exchanged small birthday gifts and recipes, met for fitness classes, forwarded adorable e-mails to one another: vid-eos of upended puppies unable to right themselves, kittens sleeping in cereal bowls, that sort of thing. Over time, our shopping trips and yoga classes grew more infrequent. Now I'm lucky to get a preachy opinion in answer to any sort of invitation: writing *X-mas* in your cards instead of *Christmas* was like poking Jesus in the eye, babies must learn to self-soothe by *crying it out*, and so on. That last one particularly bothered me. I kept picturing Hannah in a Romanian orphanage, rocking herself to sleep in a lonely, barren room, developing scurvy and rickets, flies clustered around her eyes.

Sadly, our holiday options are similarly stunted on Erik's side. He's an only child and his mother is also dead. She drove into a tree after six too many Old Fashioneds, and we're always amazed that it took so long to happen, and that no one else was maimed or killed in the process. Erik's father, his mind slowly being erased by Alzheimer's disease, constantly confuses his son with Michael Buble. He (my father-in-law, not Michael Buble) lives in the Pheasant Ridge Assisted Living Community an hour's drive from us, though he has to be reminded of this fact on a daily basis. But it wasn't rosy even when Erik's mother was alive. Once we spent a week visiting his parents for Christmas, only to be billed for our stay—down to the toilet paper and hot water used—in a prorated, itemized, and neatly typewritten list.

All of it is tragic and frustrating and sometimes tragically and frustratingly hilarious any way you slice it, but we cheerfully soldier on, determined that optimism and good cheer would prevail in the end. Until this Thanksgiving.

The bowl of mashed potatoes sits near my plate. I calmly scoop a generous spoonful and suspend it in the air, considering its fate. I feel the hard stone of long-suppressed rage turn over inside me, growing larger and more limber, stretching out, looking around the joint, making itself comfortable. The spoonful of potatoes: my plate, or Clint's face? I blink, and the next thing I know a thick glop of potatoes is flying across the table. At the last second, Clint ducks and the potatoes land with a soft "thwack" on Hannah's chest. She'd picked the worst possible moment to come out of the kitchen.

Everyone holds their breath: me, Erik, Joy, Clint, and the handful of far-flung aunts, uncles, and cousins we see once or twice a year, waiting for Hannah's response.

She stands in the doorway, potatoes clinging to her sweater, her face growing redder and redder, her expression of shock giving way to pain. Tears well in her eyes. Finally, she explodes: "Why do you have to do this?"

"Oh, Hannah," I stammer, "I'm so sorry!" But it's too late; Hannah runs from the room, crying.

"Awesome," Clint says. "Lovely. Best Thanksgiving ever."

Joy clears her throat. "Maybe we should wrap things up early."

Clint glares at me. "Best idea I heard all day."

I return his gaze, tears rimming my eyes, causing him to double in the candlelight. "Who are you? I don't even know you anymore!"

"I don't *want* to know you anymore," he says, with such venom that it nearly takes my breath away.

"It's exhausting trying to like you, Clint," I nearly whisper.

"So don't like me. I don't give a shit. I don't like you, either. Get out of my house."

The tears don't spill from my eyes; instead, they simply evaporate. Dry-eyed, I stand and push my chair back. I'm wobbly with heartache and shock. I feel like some kind of response is in order, but I can't find my voice. Besides, there is nothing constructive to be said. What do you say when you're severing your relationship with your only brother, the boy who once read books with you by flashlight under yards of blanket forts, whose epic April Fool's pranks helped shape your own sense of humor? How do you publicly disown a sibling? By the time I run through and mentally reject the possibilities ("We are done here, brother" ... "Don't call me until you learn to play well with others" ... "I estrange thee!"), it's too late to say anything. I nearly turn back at the door when I remember my contribution to the dinner and consider saying, "Just keep the Pyrex," or maybe "You can stuff my Pyrex up your ass," but in the end, Erik and I simply gather our coats and walk silently into the cold, dark night.

Chapter 2
"A quiet, peaceful life."

Erik drives quietly while I stare out the window at cozy houses tucked into the hillside, some of them already festooned with Christmas lights, some of their driveways bursting with enough parked cars to fill a decent used auto lot. Warm houses filled with happier people roasting marshmallows around the fireplace, laughing at inside jokes, watching old home movies. Maybe they're even singing together around an upright piano, each house a blissful, living rerun of *The Waltons*. "Let's pull into that driveway," I say, pointing at an achingly cheerful, well-lit farmhouse. "See if they'll adopt us."

Erik gives me a look of pity. "Honey, this will all blow over before you know it."

Tears fill my eyes, and I shake my head.

"I'm sorry your brother's such an asshole." He hands me a travel-sized package of tissues just as the tears begin to fall.

"Thanks." When other people insult your blood relatives, you tend to bristle. I used to, like Mom did, because we know the rumors were once true: a softer, gentler Clint *had* existed. You say things like, "Hey, watch it. I know he's a jerk, but he's my brother, and *I'm* the only one who gets to call him a prick!" There's something almost romantic about familial devotion, defending even the biggest yahoo in your clan because you share DNA. Blood is thicker than water and all that. Unfortunately, in these last few years Clint's kinder moments have become about as rare and real as Yeti sightings, and the cumulative hurts have eroded my loyalty. A thousand paper cuts to my psyche later, and he's finally opened an artery. I blow my nose once more and let my damp, crumpled tissue fall to the floor mat. I press my face into my hands. "I can't believe I threw mashed potatoes at Hannah."

"And now you're throwing garbage on the floor." Erik reprimands me as if I'm a child.

I absently reach down to retrieve my tissue and stuff it in my purse.

"I don't mean to change the subject, but we have to get back to the realtor about the showing request," he adds.

Right. Selling my mother's house so Clint can finally go on that canned hunt in Africa or buy his weight in gold bullion. I don't even want my share after the sale. Maybe I'll give it to charity. I'll write *Blood money* in the memo.

"I don't want to show the house anymore. Can we not do it? What happens?"

"Your brother forcibly evicts us, I guess. That would be fun."

Realtors have been touring strangers through my mother's home since August, when we first put it on the market. Open house after open house, showing after showing. You get tired of washing windows and hiding clutter in the oven, figuring out where to go with the cat for an hour. It feels a bit like getting ready for a series of disappointing blind dates, bracing yourself for the inevitable reasons why things aren't going to work out. However, I am glad we've depersonalized the house. No framed photos of my family from happier times to trip me up and hold my emotions hostage for the day.

Now Erik reaches across the console to hold my hand. "Let's get it over with. Move on with our lives."

I used to admire Erik's ability to plow through life's unpleasant situations without getting bogged down in the emotional quicksand that comes along with them. He's very can-do, very goal-oriented, and it was one of the reasons I fell in love with him. Now it's another one of the reasons I feel hollow. I passive-aggressively let my hand go limp in his, and he squeezes tighter.

Later that evening while getting ready for bed, I ask Erik, "How long do you think it'll be before Clint talks to us again?"

Erik is flossing his teeth on his side of our dual vanity. He contemplates this for a moment, puts down the floss, and exhales wearily. "Not long enough."

I dry my face and study my pores in the mirror. I imagine slicing Clint from my life for good, and I immediately feel lighter but also emptier. Orphaned. I feel like a plastic bag swirling around a parking lot. I think of the time when we were kids and he intentionally shot a bottle rocket at my head, rupturing my eardrum and singeing my hair. I still have a scar on that earlobe. I think about how we rode our bikes to see *The Karate Kid* at the theater the week it opened, and how Clint made me laugh when he ordered our tickets: "Two for flinching, please." I think about how difficult it has become now to even make eye contact with him, how spineless and cowed I feel around him. I remember the time Clint helped me bake crushed laxatives into a batch of cookie dough so I could find out who was stealing my lunch from my locker every day.

I remember the hateful glint in Clint's eyes when he said, *Get out of my house*, and something turns over in me.

I crawl into bed and close my eyes. "Do other people have brothers like Clint?"

"Yes. But wait, there is another," Erik says in his best Yoda voice. Erik does impressions when he's trying to lighten my mood. This is another quirk I used to enjoy about him. He's referring to my older sister Gwen. Her name suggests softness, kindness, basic humanity; it's really too bad Mom didn't name her Borg #452. We last saw one another at Mom's funeral, and I hadn't seen her for two years prior to that. To say there is some distance between us, both literal and figurative, is like saying there is some filler in cafeteria meatloaf.

After our parents divorced, the three of us—Gwen, Clint, and I—became parodies of ourselves, perhaps elves in an animated feature: Frosty, Angry, and Grieve-y. Gwen, an icy overachiever to start, became even more driven. At age twelve, Gwen treated life like a competition, and she was going to win top prize even if it meant sacrificing her health, normal childhood interests and behaviors, perhaps a litter of newborn puppies along the way. After Dad moved out, I became a soft, sad lump on the couch, self-medicating with Nutty Buddies and *Little House* reruns while Clint took to Megadeth and ant-burning on the sidewalk. Gwen? Gwen chiseled every negative emotion into a sharp and ambitious laser point. Student body president four years running? Check. Valedictorian with a full scholarship to the university of her choice? Check. College GPA of 4.05 and a shiny, new career as a litigator already lined up at Waxman, Roth, and Keyes, LLP, the most aggressive and successful law firm in Atlanta? Check. You'd think watching a sibling march up the ladder of success would trigger your own competitive urge to win the game at hand, hitting some primal nerve center concerned with survival of the fittest, but it had the opposite effect on me. It made me want to take a nap, hang out with kids who smoked pot, recede into the wallpaper and watch the scenery: "Who, Gwen? Yeah, she's got this. If you need me I'll be at the swim-up bar making fun of that guy with the melting spray tan."

Once I said to her, "I'd hate to see what you would have done to survive the Holocaust." She gave me a cold, considering look and said, "Probably kill you and steal the potato you hid in your shoe." I don't think she was joking.

I suspect Gwen still has the eating disorder that kept her thin as a skewer through her teen years, and I suspect she may be a sociopath. Not a sociopath with a windowless van and a crawlspace, but one who reached her lifetime quota of empathy by the age of three. Growing up, at least Clint treated me like a typical, red-blooded American big brother, with an endless supply of abrasive noogies and a talent for scaring the crap out of me by hiding beneath the basement steps. In Gwen's eyes, I was little more than an irritating insect buzzing around. Something to be ignored, shooed, or verbally squashed, depending on her mood. At least that's how I remember it.

"Gwen?" I roll my eyes, startled at the anger simply saying her name inspires in me. "You know us. We're like peanut butter and jelly. Art and Garfunkel."

"Okay, sorry I said anything. Let's just go to bed. I'm tired."

"Oprah and Gayle," I continue. "Phineas and Ferb. Masters and Johnson. Hall and—"

Erik yawns vigorously. "Okay, you've made your point. Tomorrow is a new day. You'll feel better in the morning." He kisses my cheek and turns over, settling into his usual side sleeping position.

I turn off the lamp and punch my pillow down. My first Christmas without my mother, and now, likely my first Christmas with no family at all. "Who will we spend Christmas with?" I whisper.

"Hopefully nobody," Erik mumbles. Minutes later he's snoring softly.

Call your father, a little voice says, and I immediately duct-tape that little voice's mouth shut.

I am suddenly reminded of my cousin Sandra, whose first reaction after her father's suicide was, "Who will walk me down the aisle when I get married?" and then I feel like an asshole. Children are being sex-trafficked in India and my big concern is who I'm spending the holidays with?

"*Grow up*," I mouth to myself.

I stare at the ceiling, my eyes adjusting to the darkness. Despite Erik's body radiating heat next to me beneath our down comforter, I'm freezing. I can barely feel my toes. Our tabby Nancy jumps onto the nightstand next to me, curls her tail around her haunches, and glares at me: *What's it to you, Bub?*

Chapter 3

"The cheese stands alone."

They're waiting in my driveway by four-thirty in the morning with a Thermos full of booze. Frankie, Liz, and Amy. Our roles have evolved over the years—partners in crime, drinking buddies, instigators, therapists, confidants, consciences—and now we seem to serve mainly as reminders to one another of the carefree people we used to be before adult responsibilities stacked bricks on our shoulders. Before our faces began to betray the various punches life threw at us. Or in Frankie's case, years of baking in a tanning bed. As we did last year and the year before that, we are hitting the stores at an ungodly early hour for the post-Thanksgiving consumer frenzy known as Black Friday.

Erik thinks this is insane. I tried not to wake him, but while I applied makeup in our adjoining bathroom, he rolled over, tangled in the sheets, to frown at me. "That light is blinding me," he crabbed, squinting and throwing a pillow over his forehead.

"Sorry, I'm almost finished."

"Why do you get up so early to do this?"

"It's a tradition."

"So is genital mutilation."

"So is your summer golf outing with the guys."

"We don't get up at three a.m. for that, risking injuries to save twenty bucks on a sweater." He pushed up onto his elbows, yawned, and gave me a cagey smile. "I can't believe you didn't acknowledge my comment about genital mutilation."

"I don't want to encourage you."

He flipped the bedspread open, patted the bed, and gave me a come-hither look. "Come on. Show me your genitals."

I smiled despite myself. He was charming in his own, goofy way, and even with disheveled hair and morning breath, damn if he still didn't look good in a white t-shirt. "Just so you know, this is not foreplay. You're actually kind of grossing me out." I returned to my mascara. Erik pulled the blankets up to his chin, closed his eyes and smiled, pleased at his pre-dawn Jon Lajoie reference.

This is how I like Erik best: sleep-silly, tow-headed, cozily tucked under the duvet. By the time I kissed his forehead goodbye he'd already fallen back to sleep.

The morning sky is a purple bruise over the frosted rooftops and naked tree limbs, the November air sharp in my lungs. After I climb into the backseat of Amy's minivan, Frankie wordlessly passes me a warm Thermos.

"What's in it?" I ask.

"Irish coffee," Liz says.

I unscrew the cap, take a sniff, and recoil. "If I drink that, I'll be passed out by noon."

"That's the idea!" Frankie says. "Get your shopping done with a nice crowd buffer on, something to smooth the edges, come home, take a nap."

"Or get drunk, start a fight over a pair of socks, and get arrested." I have a momentary flashback to Clint's angry mask and take a long slug from the Thermos, wincing as the hot whiskey blazes a trail into my stomach. I shudder, suddenly remembering that I haven't eaten yet this morning. "Probably not wise to drink on an empty stomach."

"I have goldfish crackers." Eyes still on the road, Amy reaches in her purse and withdraws a baggie of smashed orange crumbs. "Want some?"

"As delicious as they look and sound, I think I'll pass."

Amy is the mother in our circle of friends, to us as well as to her own brood of three. She's the designated driver this year because she owns the only vehicle among us large enough to transport four grown women and their half-ton of Black Friday loot. She's also nearly four months' pregnant with her fourth and final child, whom we've taken to calling Baby Surprise. I say Baby Surprise is the last of the Kimmel clan because Amy tells anyone within earshot that her husband Paul is "getting snipped, like, yesterday." Amy has always reminded me of a well-loved doll owned by an enthusiastic four-year-old. She may be a bit disheveled, she may cut her own hair, but she never stops smiling and her nose is so perky it could co-host a morning talk show.

"I'll have some," Frankie says, dumping the orange dust straight into her mouth. She chases this with more Irish Coffee. Frankie is the only single one of us, though she's been living with her boyfriend Ed for two years. Years of inhaling secondhand smoke and shouting to be heard over forgettable bar bands have given her voice a sexy, raspy quality. She's a runner, a rock-climber, a drinker, and a biker (think Harley, not Schwinn), constantly wrestling to make her long, straight hair cooperate with her lifestyle. Frankie once infamously let me borrow her lip balm only to inform me as I applied it that it "has SPF—oh wait, I put that on my nipples before I went tanning this morning!"

Liz rides quietly in the front seat. I can't tell if she's silent because she's not yet fully awake or if she and her husband Steve have had another fight. Liz has twin boys—Luke and Liam, age three—little anchors that keep her tethered to a marriage in which the affection has long since left the building. Every time I see her she looks on the verge of narcolepsy, tears, or both. Perpetually exhausted by life. She's a far cry from the carefree, vivacious dancing queen we knew in college, who could have a bar full of grizzled hunters and ice fishermen shimmying their hips along with her to ABBA by the second chorus.

Now that I've laid things out like that, I have to wonder how my friends would describe me. *"Jaime's been married to Erik for seven years, and the proverbial itch has not only appeared right on schedule, but seems to grow more irritating by the day. She thinks a baby could fill the void in her life now that her mother's gone, but she also realizes that's probably not a good reason to have a baby. Judging by the classic movies in her Netflix queue as well as her latest thrift-store clothing finds, she's nostalgic for an era before her birth. Jaime would like to point out that her clothing is 'vintage,' not 'thrifty,' which implies mothballs and untreatable stains. Like her hair and Nancy Reagan, her patience has grown thinner over the years. She had her first panic attack last month. She's afraid she's disappearing."*

Frankie passes the Thermos back to me and I take another hit, grimacing at the delicious burn. "So what's the plan, ladies?"

Liz clears her throat. "I'm thinking Kohl's first, then Macy's, and on to Burlington Coat Factory for the early bird specials. I also want to hit Target because it's the only place that sells the cleaning stuff I like, and then we can head to the mall at large."

"'*The mall at large*,'" I snicker. "You're too cute."

"Thank God you didn't say Walmart," Frankie says.

Liz laughs. "Frankie's just afraid she'll end up on that *People of Walmart* site."

"They should be so lucky," she replies airily, modeling the leather motorcycle jacket she wears nearly year-round.

Burlington Coat Factory. Even though I once found a cheap, adorable pea coat there, I would rather develop a permanent facial tic than go to Burlington Coat Factory. They never have the cute shoes in my size, the jewelry department makes as much sense as a David Lynch film, and I once saw an old man furtively dry-humping a pair of jeans on a rack. "You do realize," I say, "that if we go to Burlington Coat Factory you're buying me lunch after you change into your new gold sneakers and pink and black checkered pants."

"What's wrong with BCF?"

"First, the fact that you're calling it 'BCF.' Second, the fact that the clothes are straight out of a Kid 'n' Play video from 1991."

Liz rolls her eyes. "Well, there isn't a store called 'Beige, Black, and Boring,' so deal with it."

"Uh, yes there is," Frankie chimes in. "You call it L.L. Bean. You shop there all the time."

"Ladies, we have arrived," Amy announces, pulling into a parking lot already humming with early shoppers. Miraculously, we find a parking space close to the main entrance at Kohl's. We each take a long, bracing swig from the Thermos (except for Amy), and head toward the store. I realize as the crowd swallows us that I've forgotten my shopping list.

But now that I think about it, my list has grown considerably shorter this year. Erik and Hannah and ... a few items for the Toys for Tots bin at Shopko? A box of candy for the mailman, some Secret Santa fluff to bring to work?

If I wasn't listless before, I surely am now.

***

By the fifth department store and the third Muzak version of "White Christmas," I'm ready to head back to the car. My feet ache, I have sensory overload, and I've only purchased three things—a sweater for myself, a shirt for Erik, and a mildly ugly pair of slippers for Hannah that I'm already considering returning. This is the third year we've shopped the post-Thanksgiving sales together, and this is the first year I'm purely going through the motions. Last year, we reveled in the hunt, helping one another track down deals and cross names off shopping lists. Tag-team shopping, with hot pretzels and a hip flask. Amy, Liz, and Frankie appear to be having fun, but I feel as if I'm an actor being paid to walk next to them, feigning pleasure at the feel of a cashmere sweater, saying the lines that might be expected of me.

I see things everywhere that my mother would have liked: a dragonfly-themed birdbath, a whiz-bang garlic press, a tube of hand cream that smells of jasmine and strawberries. Last year it was becoming clear how sick she really was, so her presents revolved around personal comfort. We spoiled each other and plied the family with an obscene number of gifts. It took six hours to open everything. We knew it would be our last Christmas together, so we tried to distract ourselves from the obvious with "stuff." *Oooh, look at the shiny! Nobody's dying here, who could be dying with all this purty, new stuff?*

I study the faces of the other shoppers, but it's hard to read them. Most people seem steamrolled by the day, wearing expressions of grim determination or exhaustion. A few annoyed-looking husbands stand watch outside changing rooms, arms loaded with purses and shopping bags. I used to love the twinkling lights, the decorative pine boughs wrapped in ribbon, the oversized, glassy ornaments, but today I am keenly aware that they are all merely props. Feel-good staging intended to boost bottom lines. I imagine them in July, packed in a dusty garage. I imagine myself more cheerful, less cynical. Not in a shopping mall.

"Oh crap," Amy suddenly says, studying her list. "I forgot something. Would you guys mind if we hit Walmart?" We groan. She clasps her hands together, pleading. "Pretty please?"

"All right, but this calls for some more buffer," Frankie says, pulling a silver flask of rum from her purse. She pours a shot of rum into her Diet Coke, takes a sip, and offers it to us. "Anyone?"

Don't mind if I do!

Appearances to the contrary, we're not really alcoholics. Because we all live at least an hour away from one another, we see each other once, maybe twice a year. So when we do get together, we overcompensate. This usually entails drinking as if we were still in college, lowering our inhibitions and creating the perfect environment for something wild and hilarious and memorable to happen. A liquid time machine back to our college years, when we were sassy enough to extend a tiny, fake hand in greeting to a total stranger, ballsy enough to do an enthusiastic Running Man in front of the hottest guy in the bar. Anything for a laugh.

That's the idea, anyway.

Lately too much booze only makes us sleepy.

I love my friends. I miss my friends. Sure I have other colleagues and acquaintances I'm friendly with here in Madison, but they aren't people I call in a crisis. They're people to gossip with about local politics and horrible students over two-for-one appetizers. We keep things on the surface. Easy. Clean and professional. They aren't really people to call for support when your mother dies and your surviving family implodes. They don't know that I had severe scoliosis as a child. We never mooned our ethics professor together. They've never seen me cry. In fact, I wouldn't want them to. They don't know my darkest secrets, and I don't know theirs. It's the deal we silently made when we assumed whatever roles we decided to play for one another.

As the years pass, the distance between Liz, Amy, Frankie and me is becoming not just physical. Every new child, every new job, every new restaurant tried or vacation taken with other people is one less shared experience. I feel a small nibble of jealousy when any of them mention other friends they now go to yoga or lunch or the beach with. But all of this is normal, and it's to be expected. We're growing up, growing apart, but the bond we forged in college is still there beneath it all—a dusty but miraculously strong adhesive.

At Walmart, I steady myself near a display of Shake Weights. The whirling press of shoppers is making me dizzy. Or maybe it's the whiskey. I catch the eye of a woman pushing a cart loaded with packages. A child with a runny nose rides in the cart, and her older brother tugs on his mother's coat with one hand, holding the massive, shiny box for a dinosaur that transforms into a monster truck in the other: "Mom! Mom! Mom! Can I have this? This is what I want! Mom! Mom! Mom!" She looks like she'd rather be anywhere but here. Perhaps welding sewer pipes in August. As I attempt to smile sympathetically at her, a grizzled man comes crashing into view. "Fucking bitch!"

I recoil. Despite the 25-degree outside temperature, he's wearing cut-off gray sweatpants. But at least he's got shoes on: filthy untied sneakers, laces trailing behind to form an admirable trip hazard. His calves are black and blue with a network of tattoos. One of them appears to be a pirate giving me the finger.

"Cunt in the service department," he announces to the woman. "*You need high performance tires, or you void the warranty,*" he mimics in falsetto. "I about punched her in the fucking face. I'm not putting fucking high-end tires on that goddamn motherfucking piece of shit car."

The toddler in the cart blinks reflexively with every syllable. The woman attempts to calm him, but he pushes her away and continues the rant. Frankie is also watching the exchange. "Pardon me, sir?" she says, approaching him. She's holding a wicker basket containing a jumbo package of paper towels, looking about as threatening as a baby otter.

He stops and stares at her. I notice he's got a teardrop tattooed beneath his right eye. Great. So he's already killed someone. "Are you talking to me?" He says it with much less gravity than De Niro in *Taxi Driver*, though it must be noted that he hasn't had time to practice.

"Yes. Sir, there are young children nearby, so maybe you should watch what you're saying."

Frankie, you are my favorite stupid hero.

He narrows his eyes at her. "Why don't you mind your own business."

"Sorry, I can't. I was recently diagnosed with cancer and I made a promise to myself. I would never be silent again. I will speak up when I see"—she searches for the right word— "*wrongdoings* happening." She lowers her voice. "Setting a nice example for your kid. Way to go."

Well, if we'd been waiting for the tipsy envelope-pushing, here it was.

Finally, the woman behind the cart finds her voice. "Excuse me? This ain't none of your business!"

All of us—Mr. Swear Jar, his female companion, me, Frankie, even Liz—are nearly sizzling with adrenaline when Amy jumps in, putting a hand on Frankie's back to steer her away. "All right, point made. Let's get out of here."

"Fuck off, bitch," he adds, while his wife or girlfriend shepherds him in the other direction.

"Okay, that's enough, thank you," Amy says calmly, and the show's over.

I grin. "*Thank you?*"

She sighs wearily. "I have toddlers. What do you want?"

"He'd be a really great Little League coach, don't you think?"

Liz gives Frankie a playful shove. "You do not have cancer!"

"Well, I haven't been to the doctor in years. Anything's possible."

"I think we've had enough excitement for one day," Amy says. "Let's get some lunch."

***

This is where it gets tricky. With one vegetarian, one person who's avoiding gluten, another on the Paleo diet and the fourth so lactose-intolerant she gets gas just watching a Dairy Queen commercial, agreeing on a place to eat is always a challenge. Though we all nearly break ourselves in half trying to appease one another when it comes to the restaurant choice, we ultimately settle on the food court at the mall. Something for everyone, although the hi-test dining experience comes close to a Hieronymus Bosch vision of hell, with strung-out shoppers stacked on top of one another, children vomiting beneath the tables, the air rank with the mingled smells of sweat, clogged grease traps, and badly burned chicken wings.

We break to make our individual orders at various vendors and reconvene at a table that probably hasn't been washed since the Cuban Missile Crisis.

"What'd you order?" Frankie asks me with her mouth full of burrito. The first to receive her food, she grabbed our table as soon as the previous occupants stood to leave. The plastic chairs are still warm.

I look down at my disappointing tray. "Some kind of stir-fry. There's probably enough sodium in here to mummify my digestive tract."

Liz is the last to join us, tray in hand, irritated. "They spilled soda all over my pizza and had to re-do it. There were like, fifty people in line behind me, glaring at me like it was my fault." After she sits, she wrinkles her nose. "Gross, these seats are hot!"

"I used to get lunch at Sbarro all the time when I worked at KB Toys in high school," I say.

"Didn't they go out of business?"

"Yeah," I say. "Who'd pay fifty dollars for a Diddle Me Elmo when you can get the same thing at Walmart for half the price?"

"People who don't like leaving stores with a bad case of the itchies," Frankie says.

Amy turns to me. "Didn't you smash some toy on the floor when you were working once the day after Thanksgiving because it was the last one and three people were fighting over it?"

"Yeah," I say, smiling at the memory. "I had to pay for it, but it was so worth it."

"Sbarro filed for bankruptcy, too," Liz says. "I'm getting my fill before they're gone."

"I just read an article about Sbarro," I say. "The author called it 'America's Least Essential Restaurant.'"

"Yeah, like Orange Julius is critical to life on earth."

"Hey, it's all part of the food court ecosystem. You pull one thread, the whole thing falls apart."

Amy cuts her sub in half. "I can't believe I'm eating so soon again after yesterday. Thank God for pants with elastic waistbands."

"Speaking of, how was everyone's Thanksgiving?"

"Mom went all out," Amy says. "She's amazing. The turkey, the stuffing, the sweet potatoes, the beans, the gravy, the cranberries, the pies."

I feel something wounded roll over in my gut at the mention of her mother. Or maybe it's something I ate.

"Ed's kids were with us, and we fried a turkey in the driveway," Frankie says. "It was fabulous! Other than Ed nearly setting the garage on fire, I have to say it was a pretty decent Thanksgiving."

"Is fried turkey part of your cancer treatment plan?" I ask, and Frankie flicks her wadded-up straw wrapper at me.

Liz finishes blotting the grease from her pizza. "Ours was pretty quiet. The kids are behaving now that they know Santa is officially watching." She chuckles.

"You're not doing that creepy 'Elf on the Shelf' thing, are you?" Frankie asks. "That gave me nightmares as a kid."

"No, but Steve and I are doing an Advent Calendar. You know, the ones where you open the little door each day and find a bit of candy? It all feels a little like organized bribery, but bedtime has gotten so much smoother."

Steve and I. Not *I*, not even the more ambiguous *we*. From this I infer that things must be better between them lately.

We're silent for a bit, chewing, until I realize that everyone is looking at me. "And how was Turkey Day at Casa de Stewart?" Frankie asks, tearing open a packet of hot sauce with her teeth.

"Oh, my Thanksgiving? Not bad. Other than my brother kicking me out and saying he doesn't want to speak to me anymore, it was great!" And ... I'm openly weeping in the West Towne Mall food court.

Alarmed, Amy rushes to hug me. "Oh, sweetie! What happened?"

Frankie folds her arms, presses her lips into a tight line, and gives me her patented look: *Well, color me surprised.* She's never liked my brother.

"You two will get over it," Liz says. "You'll be talking again next week."

"I'm not so sure. It was really ugly. I told him it was exhausting trying to like him. I also tried to throw mashed potatoes at him and hit Hannah instead."

Amy gasps. "You didn't!"

I nod, cringing at the mental replay.

Liz laughs brightly. "Oh my God!"

Soon we're all laughing. Well, they're laughing, and I'm kind of grimacing while I wait it out. My mother's response in these kinds of situations used to be a gentle, "One day you'll laugh about this." She was always right. Unfortunately, the body's still too warm for me to find much humor in this yet.

After the laughter runs its course, Frankie says, "Whooo! I needed that." She leans back in her chair and rubs her stomach. "Well, he had it coming. Too bad you missed, though."

"If it was anything like before my folks split up, I totally sympathize," Liz adds

I push a carrot across my plate. "God, I can hardly wait for Christmas."

Amy shrugs. "Well, the holidays are complex. All those childhood memories and expectations ... they're stressful times."

"And especially hard for people who recently lost someone," Liz says sympathetically.

"I'd invite you to our holiday spread, but Ed and I are driving to Duluth to spend Christmas with his folks," Frankie says.

Amy snaps her fingers into an inspired, friendly gun pointed at me. "Hey, why don't you celebrate Christmas with us? It's a full house, but the more the merrier!"

I can't quite put into words why I don't want to be the eighteenth wheel at any of my friends' holiday gatherings. Especially Amy's, since her extended family makes the Cosbys look like the Lohans. They spend nearly every weekend together, bowling or playing croquet or hosting their own Iron Chef challenges. At family reunions, nobody gets drunk and belligerent. Instead, they run three-legged races, and no one balks at the idea, and the losing couples never blame their teammates. Amy has a Hallmark family. You want to hate them, but you know that her mother, who chairs the Human Concerns Committee at church, also owns a sizable black dildo. Amy and I found it in her mother's closet while looking for a costume to wear to a seventies theme party. So you figure, hey! Maybe somebody has a secret gambling problem, too! Because otherwise, they just don't seem real.

"Thanks," I say, "but it might just make me sort of sad." I know that watching Amy interact with her loving family would only reinforce my feeling of being an outsider. I'm not one of them. I don't know the secret tribal handshake. I feel like a parent who initially balks at adoption...it's a primal need for something of your own, I guess. Objectively, rationally, I know there's no reason for it, but I'm feeling neither objective nor rational right now.

"I'd invite you to spend it with us, but even I don't want to go," Liz says wryly.

I sip my iced tea. "The cheese stands alone."

"I found Ed online," Frankie says. "You know, there should be a dating site for families."

"There might be in Kentucky," Liz says.

Frankie, whose family moved here from Kentucky when she was in high school, scowls. "Why does everybody always pick on Kentucky?"

"Because it's the lazy joke," I say, coming to her defense.

"Anyway," Frankie continues, "what I mean is, you could go online and find a sweet little old lady who needs someone to help her run errands, and you can adopt her as your new grandma. Or you can find a niece or nephew, or maybe some new cousins."

Amy smiles. "Or a new brother."

"Or a child," Liz says. "My sister found her baby online. Well, the birth mother found her. But you get the picture."

A smile spreads on Frankie's face. "My dear, if you can find a husband online, and kids or adoptive parents, why not a whole new family? Get your ass on Craigslist! I'll help you write the ad!"

"Come on." I'm frowning again, though I do find the concept amusing.

"I'd love to find a few new family members," Liz says wistfully. "My sister-in-law is a malicious, back-stabbing witch."

"Craigslist is kind of creepy," Amy says. "Craigslist Killer, anyone?"

I press my hands together like I'm about to pray. "Thank you."

"Well, I use Craigslist all the time," Liz says, shrugging primly.

Frankie repositions herself, hands extended to frame the picture she's trying to paint. "Think of it as a cathartic yet interactive experience. Writing the ad alone will be like seeing a therapist, and just think of the fun you'll have going through the responses!"

"Well, if it's not really serious. Maybe." I'm indulging to throw them off the chase. It's a crazy idea, though I do recognize its entertainment potential. I change the subject. "I wish you all lived closer."

"Me too!" they say in unison.

But I'm left oddly empty, and wondering. Even if they did, would it change things? Would we really see one another more? A host nation could organize the summer Olympics with less coordination and schedule juggling than today's trip required. And after all, they have their families, and I have … had mine.

Chapter 4
"Yay, Mom's funeral!"

They say more people die in winter, though I've never confirmed it as fact. Something about the rhythm of the seasons. There's a time to be born (spring) and a time to die (winter). My mother, unfortunately, died on the Vernal Equinox—June 21, as spring bloomed into summer. It's not right to die on the first day of summer, just as nature enters its prime. The perennials in her garden were bursting with gorgeous peak color, robins were training their fledglings to hunt worms in the front yard, and the Early Girl tomatoes I'd planted for her the week before Memorial Day were ripening on the vines. She wouldn't live to see the next county fair, enjoy that summer's crop of sweet corn, or watch the most beautiful sunsets of the year from her back deck, fireflies telegraphing their electric love letters to one another in the field behind her property line.

Then again, Mom's always had bad timing. She went into labor with me on a Greyhound bus trip to see Grandma Ellis, she remembered hair appointments a day late ... hell, she *died* mere hours after I'd left her side for the first time in months, holding Clint's hand instead of mine. She was also one of those people with a knack for grandly interrupting anything you were concentrating on. **Me:** sweating as I laboriously, meticulously tried to withdraw the Adam's Apple with my tweezers without tripping the buzzer for the fourth time in *Operation*. (Yes, I was playing alone, practicing in fact, because I was 'that' kid.) **Mom:** sprinting through the room to the front door, throwing it open, wailing on the front steps: "Oh my God, Mr. TeeTee just got hit by a car! Oh, Mr. TeeTee, oh poor kitty. No ... wait! It only nicked him. He's okay!"

BUUZZZZZZZZZZZZZZZZZ!!!!!!!!!!!!!!

Her funeral was held on a quintessential summer day—clear, temps in the mid-seventies, enough breeze to lift the clean, slippery scent of daylilies into the air. Butterflies flit through the cemetery behind the church, reminding me of a text my mother had once sent me (*two monarchs doing it in backyard!!*). I was stoned on coffee, anguish, and cognitive dissonance. Also, two of Mom's pain pills, just to get through the day. How could the phlox bloom without my mother? How could she not be feeling this gorgeous, brilliant sunlight on her face? I'd bought her favorite brand of frozen pizza at the grocery store last week. It was still in the freezer! I felt what the next few months would hold in my bones, in the loopy, desolate syrup in which my brain was suspended: she would still be receiving mail for months—years even, and I would call her voicemail nearly every day just to hear her outgoing message, hanging up every time, until service is eventually suspended. *Oh crap, she's still on Facebook . . . how do I deal with that?*

My body knew even then that grief and I had only smiled at one another, and would become much more intimately acquainted before I could even make a sandwich without thinking of her. Memories paraded through my mind like a marching band, calling their friends, triggering more memories, making it a real grief party: *Mom used to make wheat germ and peanut butter sandwiches. She never bought white bread. Remember the time she broke down and bought you Strawberry Shortcake cereal? Remember when you hid a Barbie in the oven and she turned it on, melting all that flesh-colored plastic over the racks? Remember the time you refused to eat your sweet and sour pork and had to sit at the table, pouting, for three hours? Remember how your mother will never again make bread pudding, resting it on the trivet you painted for her in your ninth-grade ceramics class because SHE'S DEAD?*

She'd had a meager will but couldn't decide on a burial directive, so Gwen, Clint, and I were left to read tea leaves and argue about what Mom would have wanted. In her final weeks, she told me often that she wanted her ashes to be divided in two parts: the first to be buried near her own mother, the second near her twin sister Lori, who'd died of leukemia as a child. Clint was convinced that our mother didn't want to be cremated, and that she'd have wanted a traditional wake with open-casket viewing followed by placement in the vault. Gwen kept reiterating that Mom would have wanted "a celebration, not a typical funeral." Ironically, Gwen's constant insistence on the funeral being a "celebration of life" brought Clint and me briefly closer, rolling our eyes and calling it "the celebration" whenever we discussed arrangements. "Yay, Mom's funeral!" Clint would say in falsetto, doing jazz hands, making me smile and tear up at the same time.

We also shared a moment when we wondered together if Dad would show up, concluding that we had a better chance of surviving a direct hit by a hydrogen bomb. Our relationship with our father is so distorted and thin that most of the time, Clint refers to him simply as "Mom's Ex" or "The sperm donor." I haven't seen him in ten years, since an awkward lunch my younger, traveling self arranged when I was in Portland visiting a friend from high school. Since then, there's been the rare late-night phone call, the even rarer birthday card, but not much more, and I've spent most of my life coming to terms with this.

In the end, we managed to compromise. Mom would be cremated after the service, buried in her own plot near her sister, and we'd set up photo easels with "fun" pictures from her younger years, inviting visitors to share fond "celebratory" memories.

We underestimated the number of mourners, who arrived by the carload: Mom's friends and colleagues from work, church, water aerobics, her garden club, the neighborhood, even old high school classmates (Madison East, Class of '67). The last man she dated came to pay his respects, his new girlfriend on his arm, and we welcomed them both with hugs and smiles. (Mom broke it off with him because he peed sitting down and she once walked in on him doing Denise Austin's *Shrink your Female Fat Zones* workout on DVD.)

"Thank you for coming. I know. She was one in a million. We appreciate your coming. Thank you. Thank you for coming." The line stretched out of the church, and the condolences rolled in. We thanked everyone, shook hands, accepted hugs, laughed politely at anecdotes. We became robots of gratitude, and after awhile, we were grateful for that, too.

Liz, Amy, and Frankie had come, too. "Oh sweetie, we're so sorry," Amy said, giving me a tight hug. Liz had to leave for a nephew's birthday party, but Frankie and Amy stayed for the service, sitting somewhere in the overflow area at the back of the church. I could breathe a bit easier just knowing they were in the same building.

During the service, something about Father Scanlon's high, reedy vibrato juxtaposed against Erik's deep baritone in the pew next to me struck me as particularly funny. My mother's cold, waxy body lay in repose at the altar, and there I was, stifling the hot, insane urge to laugh my head off in the first row. I suppressed most of it by holding my breath and trying to remind myself of where I was and why, but one stream of low, crazy giggles escaped me. I clapped a hand over my mouth, shocked enough by my own hysterical behavior to shift instantly back to despondency. Clint shot me a look that could have sliced a can in half. Ginsu Clint. I imagined Clint dressed in a kimono, flipping shrimp into customers' open mouths at a hibachi-style restaurant, and nearly lost it again. But I could almost feel Mom sitting behind me, leaning in to whisper, "Oh, don't mind him. Father Scanlon *does* have a funny voice. Can you believe Fran Phillips showed up? I can't get over all these people! And great job on the photo display. Except my arms look so fat in that picture with Gwen by the lake."

Speaking of Gwen, she joined me in weeping through the eulogy. I can't remember seeing her cry since Dad accidentally backed over her foot with the station wagon when we were kids, so it was a relief to see that she actually responded to loss with the appropriate human emotion. She hadn't hugged me when she first arrived, but then, Gwen was never a hugger. She tended to lock up when touched, which made watching Aunt Carol greet her with a bear hug that much more entertaining. "Uh-oh, I think Carol's going to break one of Skeletor's ribs," Erik whispered to me, and I hip-checked him. My sibling, my snark.

One of Mom's closest friends, Alice Baxter, came with her elderly mother, who was so old she could have predated the postage stamp. I met her while we stood in the receiving line. The senior Mrs. Baxter extended a shaking, liver-spotted hand to me, and

I clasped it. "Thank you so much for coming!" she said brightly, "I'm truly glad you could make it." Erik, standing to my right, stopped rocking on his heels and stood perfectly still.

"I wouldn't miss it for the world," I replied in a rare moment of quick thinking. I could feel the church giggles I'd struggled with earlier poke their sleepy heads up and look around: *are we on again?*

Her daughter blanched and laughed self-consciously. "Mom, I think you have that backwards." She turned to me. "I'm so sorry," she said, her cheeks flooding with red. She leaned in to whisper, "She's not altogether here these days."

"It's okay," I said. "Neither am I." I was on autopilot, just trying to look normal.

Later, mom's friend Penny offered me a joint behind the vestibule, and I took a small hit. "Wow. So, Mrs. Baxter. Senile, drunk, or having a flashback to her daughter's wedding?" Penny asked, trying to hold the smoke in.

I exhaled deeply and coughed. My lungs were scorched. "All of the above."

I'll never get to see my mother grow senile, I thought. Strange, the things you think you'll miss when you lose someone too soon.

***

There was a luncheon in the musty church basement after the service. By the time Erik and I arrived, nearly ten other relatives and well-wishers were already eating with plastic cutlery, chatting and chuckling in low voices. Pangs of loss pulsed through me. Mom had prepared fried chicken and massive tubs of green beans down here for the famous Sacred Heart chicken dinner fundraisers. Gwen was already there, sitting at a long, shiny table next to our cousin Scott, who was also a lawyer. They were whispering intimately in a way that gave me the creeps. About a dozen people quietly shifted down the buffet, loading their paper plates with potato salad and ham sandwiches and pickles and orange gelatin embedded with chunks of canned pear. Erik and I filled our plates and sat in the quietest place we could find, near an old piano in the corner, at the end of Gwen's table.

As I chewed, I read the felt wall banners that had been decorated by the kids in catechism: *Holy spririt, rain down!* (whoever made the banner spelled "spirit" wrong, the letters pasted around a blue watering can sprinkling three pink daisies) ... *He's alive!* (above two white doves that looked like sick chickens).

"*Blame the holy spririt ... on the rain,*" Erik sang softly, loosely paraphrasing Milli Vanilli.

Clint, Joy, and Hannah entered the basement a few minutes later. He made a sour face and greeted the dining room with, "It smells like a fart in here."

I took a listless bite of celery and added under my breath, "Stay classy, Clint."

I could feel Erik's silent annoyance next to me, radiating from his body at Clint.

I glanced down the table at Gwen and wasn't surprised to see she only had a few raw carrots and red peppers on her paper plate, no dip. Clint leaned over her shoulder to viciously whisper, "Eat a goddamn sandwich, will you?"

Joy's brow darkened. "Language, Clint!"

Clint chuckled to indicate he'd only been "teasing."

Joy was the only woman Clint ever deferred to, and I had no idea how she came to wield any kind of power over him. She wasn't witty or brilliant or gorgeous, she had no obvious feminine charms with which to subtly manipulate. Look at her in that impassive maroon pantsuit, her hair severely gathered at the nape of her neck, her only jewelry a pair of nearly microscopic pearl earrings. You could easily picture her as head of a woman's prison in some dystopian future, a small, electroshock stun gun in her front pocket. Maybe Clint was afraid of her. I leaned over and whispered to Erik, "Do you think Joy beats Clint with a small whip when he's bad?"

"Yes. Her tongue."

I wrinkled my nose. "Your breath smells like summer sausage."

Erik shrugged and said, "It should," before taking another bite of his sandwich.

Gwen folded her arms and looked coldly at Clint. "I've lost my appetite." He grunted in response and settled down to tuck into his meal. Moments later, Gwen stood, smoothed her linen skirt, and locked eyes with me. I struggled to interpret this look: *I hate you? Do you agree that Clint is an asshole? How could we have come from the same womb?*

I finished chewing my potato salad and swallowed. "What?"

Gwen ignored me and walked over to Hannah. "Be good, sweetheart," she said to our niece, resting a hand on her shoulder.

Hannah blushed and looked up from her plate, confused. "Okay?"

Without a word to the rest of us, Gwen headed back upstairs, and presumably, back to her motel, the angry clack of her heels echoing behind her. She left the next morning without saying goodbye, leaving Clint and me alone to open the mountain of sympathy cards. It occurred to me later that perhaps she was waiting for me to stick up for her, and I spent the better part of a morning feeling guilty about it. However, when I remembered her leaving without a word, my guilt quickly transitioned into defensive anger. Who leaves her mother's funeral without saying goodbye? Who goes months without calling, and when she does call, you hang up feeling incapable of doing anything right? A hapless blight on humanity?

Rumor has it the death of a parent can bring brothers and sisters together. It must make some people so glad to have siblings with whom to endure the ordeal. They are your clan. You share memories that keep that lost parent alive. You help define one another. You hold each other up, cry on one another's shoulders. I know that losing someone you love can make you a little crazy, dig up old resentments. And we do hurt those we are closest to. We take them for granted, screaming at them before answering the phone all sweetness and light, Hyde back to Jekyll in less than two seconds. But what happened here? How did my brother and sister and I fall so far away from one another? If Clint or Gwen even noticed our distance, if they mourned our lost connection even a little, I failed to see it.

Chapter 5
"Happy little trees."

I return to work the Monday after Thanksgiving. While my students take a standardized test, I furtively text Erik beneath my desk: *I'm starting to forget what Mom looked like.* Instead of hitting 'Send,' I delete it and pick up a freshly sharpened pencil. I begin to make a list:

1) *It's okay if you have strong political opinions, but please keep them to yourself. Unless we all clearly agree.*

2) *Same goes for religion. There will be no preaching the good news. Chances are, we've all heard it by now.*

3) *I'm not interested in any pyramid schemes or buying a bottle of fish oil from the case of vitamins you store in the trunk of your car. Don't try to sell us anything.*

4) *One of us might be gay, one of us might be divorced, one of us might have had an abortion, one of us might not believe in God. Note that I capitalized 'God,' so that's not specific to me. These are only examples. If you have a problem with any of them, you may want to move along.*

5) *Please have a good heart and be a thoughtful, polite person. No sociopaths, no arrest warrants, no pedophiles, no thieves, no fans of the Kardashians. They've done nothing to merit your interest or admiration. Have empathy.*

6) *Please don't be judgmental, arrogant, or boring. Have something engaging to say or a useful skill to contribute. If you have little more than a nodding acquaintance with a topic, please don't pretend you're the expert. The most interesting people don't say everything they think.*

7)   *Please be funny. Don't take yourself seriously, but remember that self-awareness goes a long way. If we keep laughing, you're welcome to keep talking.*

8)   *Please don't watch golf on television.*

9)   *Please don't hit on anyone. Nobody is looking for a date.*

I grin when I realize that I'd just made a list of my criteria for ideal relatives. Almost as if I'm writing an ad. A picky and neurotic ad, to be sure, but it's better to err on the side of specificity. My family planning is interrupted by one of my students, Tanner Vandenberg. "Mrs. Collins? Can I go to the bathroom?" The rest of the students are still hunched over their exams, furiously filling in circles.

"What's the process, Tanner?"

"Raise your hand, don't speak until called on."

"Let's try it again."

Tanner raises his hand. I smile. "Tanner?"

"Can I please go to the bathroom?"

I keep smiling. "I don't know, can you?"

Tanner sighs deeply. "May I?"

"Ding ding ding!" Right as he's about to leap from his desk, I lower the boom. "You can go when you hear that sound. That's the bell ringing in ten minutes."

"Aw, Miss Collins!"

"Are you finished with your test?"

He nods vigorously.

"And you can't wait ten minutes?"

He nods some more, adding a pained expression to his face.

I shake my head and extend the laminated hall pass. "I'm such a pushover."

"No, you're the best teacher in the world!" Tanner grabs the pass and heads for the hall.

·"Don't make me regret this," I call after him.

I have a soft spot for Tanner because his parents are unreliable hillbillies barely capable of parenting a piece of paper. Despite their chronic dysfunction (his father's probation was just revoked, his mother was recently fired from her hostessing job at The Golden Corral), Tanner's a good kid. He turns his work in on time, and right now he's earning a solid C.

The rest of my students are a mixed academic bag, though they all carry the label that landed them in my classroom: emotionally disturbed. Three of them are technically homeless, living on relatives' couches. Most live with single parents. And none enjoy the security of household incomes over $50,000. I keep a cabinet in the back of the room stocked with school supplies and healthy lunches (instant oatmeal, apples, carrot sticks). I've paid for field trip admissions, bus tokens, new shoes, even utility bills, anonymously. You get more involved with a class like mine because you have to.

The rest of the week passes uneventfully. Friday after work I have a drink with Linda Hernandez, who teaches Spanish. Linda is one of my favorite coworkers. Her husband, who has lime-green eyes and the oddly dirty appeal of Benicio Del Toro, owns a construction firm. I can honestly say that after visiting her three-story house, sharing a bottle of Château La Fluer Pétrus with her in her hot tub, seeing her shoe collection, and eating bruschetta made by her whip-smart, hilarious, and remarkably level-headed teenagers, the only thing that stops me from calling her the luckiest woman alive is the fact that her husband has a micro-penis. This she confided in me last spring, adding, "And he has the clichéd hobbies and vehicles that go along with that kind of thing, but he compensates in other ways." I didn't ask what those other ways were; her arched eyebrows and crafty smile pretty much outlined them in detail.

Usually a mob of us meet for Happy Hour if we don't have too much homework to grade, but tonight only Linda and I had the time and inclination to decompress. I order a margarita on the rocks and a basket of fried cheese curds, then tell her that because my living family members treat me like something stuck to the bottom of their shoe, my friends suggested I post an ad for a new family online.

"Oh God, I wish I could!" she says, delighted by the concept. "You have to do it. Just to see who answers. Have I ever told you about my sister?"

"Maybe." My margarita arrives, and the bartender extracts a ten-dollar bill from the cash we've placed on the bar. From the corner of my eye, I catch a group of men in the corner scoping Linda with interest. One of them is wearing a light blue shirt, red tie, and suspenders. He looks like a cross between Gordon Gekko and a circus clown. "Today I made a list of my criteria."

"Here's one." She sips her mojito. "Please don't give me any sweater vests embroidered with apples and alphabet letters for Christmas just because I'm a teacher."

I laugh. "No, not the embroidered sweater vest!"

"Speaking of clothing, where'd you get that dress?"

I'm wearing a vintage blue frock that I bought because it looked like something Joan might wear on *Mad Men*, and the darted bodice and nipped-in waist actually give me a figure. "Online," I say. "You like?"

"Stop fishing for compliments, you look fabulous in it! You found it on ModCloth, didn't you?"

At that moment, two of the guys from the corner materialize behind me. "Buy you ladies a drink?" Gordon Gekko the Clown asks. He's tall, and really not bad looking, though his slick confidence and potent cologne suggest he's on a first-name basis with the girls at Starz Cabaret—no tops, no bottoms.

Linda is staring at his expensive-looking leather loafers. "Fratelli Rossetti?"

He looks gobsmacked. "I think I love you!"

She continues to thoughtfully appraise them. "Size thirteen?"

"The lady is correct!"

Linda looks up and smiles demurely. "You know what they say about men with big feet."

"They wear big shoes!" I interject, downing my margarita. The ice cubes rattle around the bottom.

Linda boldly picks up his massive hand and measures her own tiny one against his, her manicured fingers twinkling in the dim bar lights. "My, what big hands you have!" she says mischievously, Little Red Riding Hood on late-night Cinemax.

He jumps right in with, "The better to meet you with, my dear!" Cue gregarious chuckles all around. I roll my eyes while he shakes Linda's hand and introduces himself. "Call me Tex. This is Dave."

I groan. "Call you Tex?"

"Hi, Tex," Linda says, delighted.

"Hi," Dave says to me. Looks like I'm stuck talking to Dave. Dave has freckles. Lots of them. He's also got to be at least ten years younger than me. While we make small talk (I made the mistake of asking what he does, and it turned out to be something completely dreadful—he's an "associate" at a collection agency), I watch Linda banter with Tex. He's also wearing a wedding ring. More specifically, he's wearing a tan line where his wedding ring *should* be. She's practically glowing from the attention (from a man with a penis that's at least average-sized), the mojito, the chance to look fabulous in public. Linda loves her husband, but if flirting were an extreme sport, she could medal at the X-Games. She pushes things right to the line, walks it precisely like a high wire act, but as far as I know, hasn't crossed it yet.

I hold up a hand to interrupt Dave's droning. "I really do want to hear about your divorce, but can I ask what year you graduated from high school?"

"Uh, 2004. No, 2005."

"Well, which is it? Did you even graduate?"

"Yeah, I graduated!" He blushes scarlet. He's more than a little drunk and having trouble focusing on my eyes.

"But you probably shouldn't serve on the class reunion committee." I know I'm being rude, but I wasted much of my twenties pretending to be interested in things wingmen had to say after too many Heinekens. And I miss Erik. I want to leave so I can hug him before he heads off to play poker with the guys. "I know we haven't gotten to the part where you show us your tattoos," I say, hopping down from my barstool and shouldering my purse, "but I've got to go."

Linda is visibly disappointed. "I guess I should go, too. It's getting late."

"Are you sure I can't talk you into staying?" Tex asks, stroking her forearm, and I suppress the strong urge to kick him square in the taint, which would go far toward wiping that seductive smile from his face.

"Nice shootin' Tex, but we have to go home to our HUSBANDS," I say, pulling Linda toward the front doors.

On the way out, we link arms and sing: "The stars at night, are big and bright ... (clap-clap-clap-clap) deep in the heart of Texas!"

The house is dark and chilly when I get home. I wrinkle my nose at the smell of old coffee grounds and rotting melon rinds. The note I'd written to myself yesterday is still stuck to the fridge with a magnet: TAKE GARBAGE OUT. Nancy is meowing loudly, pacing by her empty food bowl. Erik named her. She was originally part of a pair— Sid and Nancy, brother and sister, toilet paper-shredding partners in crime. Unfortunately, Sid escaped through an open door two years ago, and we haven't seen his orange and white face since. It troubles me to imagine how he may have met his fate, but I like to pretend he was found by a precocious seven-year-old and adopted by a loving, rambling family that live in a much nicer house in a better part of town.

There's a scribbled note on the counter: *Left early for poker night. Be home around one. Love you!* I turn the thermostat up a few degrees, pop a bean burrito in the microwave, pour myself a glass of wine, and— emboldened by the alcohol already coursing through my body—call Clint.

I don't know why, really. Perhaps to see if he still hates me. He doesn't answer, and after six rings, my call goes to voicemail. I hang up. Nancy is staring at me, patiently waiting for me to feed her. She follows me to the pantry, meowing desperately, nearly scarfing the food in mid-air as I pour it into her ceramic bowl.

I crouch to pet her, and she arches her back to meet my hand. "I wouldn't forget you, Nancy." I'm stalling, waiting for enough time to pass so I can try Clint again without looking like a complete weirdo. Still no answer. So I call Hannah on her cell.

"Hello?" she asks warily.

"Hi honey, it's your Aunt Jaime. How are you?" My palms are sweaty.

"I'm okay."

"What are you up to?"

"Reading."

"Hey, I'm trying to get a hold of your Dad. Is he home? Can you put him on?"

At this point I realize that I don't even know what I'm going to say. I scramble for a narrative. Do I simply say I'm calling to see if he's still mad at me?

There's a long pause. I hear muffled voices, then Hannah's *"But Dad!"* She returns to the phone. "He doesn't want to talk to you." I hear the pain in her voice when she says it. Clint bellows something in the background, and Hannah relays the latest to me. "He says he only wants to hear from you if someone makes an offer on the house."

"I miss you, Hannah."

I hear Clint yelling something that sounds like, *Get off the phone!* followed by Hannah's response: *"I am!"* Then she whispers to me, "I miss you, too."

"Can we go to a movie together soon? Maybe shopping?"

"Yeah, sure," Hannah says, noncommittal.

"I love you, sweetie."

"Love you, too."

We hang up, and I feel a lump forming in my throat. *Snap out of it*, I tell myself. I need a distraction from Clint, from the first-floor bedroom my mother died in, so I call Frankie. I shake my head to clear it while I wait for her to answer, do a few chamber kicks in the kitchen, scaring Nancy, who zips into the dining room. I greet Frankie with, "Is it normal to be afraid of your siblings?"

"Wait. Are they pointing a gun at me or not?"

"An emotional gun."

"Does it shoot metaphysical bullets?"

"Maybe," I say, growing tired of the game already. "So what are you guys up to?"

"It's just me tonight. Ed's working late."

"I'm alone, too. Just me and Nancy." I tell Frankie about Linda's flirtation ("Wait, is that the woman whose husband has a micropenis?"), and we laugh together at a story Frankie tells about Ed's mother, in whose world a treadmill is pronounced "threadmill," and when you go to a salon, you get your "hairs" cut.

"So I started writing my Craigslist ad today," I announce, pouring myself more wine.

"You did! What did you write?"

"Hang on. I'll read it to you." I rummage through my briefcase, find my notes, clear my throat and begin to read.

"You know, that's not bad."

"Any suggestions?"

"Make it like an invitation. And then sit back and wait for the freak show!"

"I'm not really doing this, am I? Inviting strangers over for Christmas dinner."

There's a pause. "I don't know," she finally says, using the same voice that used to dare me to do another shot of tequila. "Are you?"

"I'd vet them carefully, of course," I say, all business.

"Of course."

I realize I'd completely forgotten about my burrito, which is now cold. I dump it in the overflowing trash, tie the bag shut, and heave it onto the back steps. "Holy hell, it's cold out," I say, feeling more alcohol than blood cells doing the backstroke through my arteries. I'll have a headache in the morning, but I don't care.

"What are you doing?"

"Throwing the garbage out."

"Get your ass back inside and let's write that thing."

We spend the next forty minutes drinking more wine and writing the rest of my ad, occasionally getting sidetracked by sad ASPCA commercials or "weird noises coming from the basement."

"I don't know what category to post under. It's not really a personal."

"Hmmm. Try community groups," Frankie suggests. "Oh my God, some of these personals are *hilarious!*" She reads quietly while I type, occasionally interjecting: "Oh, I hope this guy from the Missed Connections finds the redhead" ... "Yeah right, this guy just wants to cuddle and watch a movie" ... "Learn to spell, people!"

I hit Enter, and sit back. "Okay, it's up."

"Excellent."

"You are a terrible influence on me."

"The worst," she says gleefully.

The ad contains a slightly condensed version of the list I'd written in class, plus a brief introductory bit that reads:

I'll be Home for Christmas

Are you an orphan?

Do you feel disowned or estranged from your family of origin? Or is your family so distant or dysfunctional that spending quality time is out of the question this year?

We know the feeling!

Look, I know it's crazy to post an ad for a new family to share holidays and milestones with, but we miss stress-free family holiday get-togethers, and we are wondering if there are others out there who might feel the same.

If this is going to work, upfront honesty is key. Please don't be crazy or have ill intentions. This is not some weird sexual thing. Religion and politics don't matter, but if you feel exceptionally strongly about either, we don't want to hear it. We won't push our beliefs on you if you return the favor.

We're not weirdos, I promise. I'm a teacher, and my husband is in city planning. I love old Steve Martin movies, new Steve Martin banjo tunes, Indian food, and reruns of Bob Ross painting happy little trees on PBS. So if you're looking for a new family with whom to share Christmas dinner and board games this year, drop us a line. It could be fun!

"Oh, that's perfect," Frankie says. "Bob Ross is a nice touch. He's dead, right?"

"I think so. Happy little trees."

"Hey, why don't you paint any more?"

"Because I'm horrible." This is true. I dabbled in acrylics in junior high, but gave up when it became obvious that I could only paint clouds and pine trees. I once did an acrylic of two Amish kids on a beach, facing the water. I buried their toes in the sand because I couldn't make their feet look like anything but catcher's mitts.

"You should paint again."

"I'd rather take up gardening. What if someone I know answers the ad?"

"Then it's kismet."

"What does kismet mean? Who even uses that word anymore?"

"I love that word. It sounds romantic, doesn't it?"

"It sounds like a trendy kids' name. You wait—in twenty years, I'll have two Kismets in class." I pause and add, "Oh God."

"What?"

"I just realized I'll still be teaching in twenty years. *Thirty* years, even!"

Later, long after we've stopped making sense, we hang up. Still wearing my dress with the darted bodice and nipped-in waist, I kick off my shoes, curl up on the couch, and channel surf. I finally settle on a rerun of *I Love Lucy*, which I used to watch with my mom. I relax for the first time all week and close my eyes, comforted by Lucy and Ethel's foibles, smiling at a memory of my mother helping me frost cupcakes to bring to school for my birthday. I fall asleep to a laugh track, and I dream in black and white.

***

I wake up late Saturday morning. My head feels like a hotel room trashed by Keith Moon, and the parched, foul climate of my mouth makes me wonder if Nancy's been using it for a litter box. Erik is up, making coffee and balancing our checkbook online. He beams at me when I shamble into the kitchen. "There's the party girl!"

"Aspirin. Water. Coffee. Please." I slide into the breakfast nook, cross my arms on the table, and put my head down. I open my palm, onto which he shakes two aspirin. "Thank you. You're a nice man. Are you single?"

"I accept payment in blowjobs."

He presses his crotch against my ear, and I groan and push him away. "You can leave now." After I drink half a glass of water I remember that I've posted an ad on Craigslist for a new family, inviting them to Christmas dinner. Uh-oh. "Shit," I mumble.

"What?"

"Nothing. I feel like shit," I say, my synapses stumbling into the briefing room for marching orders. I won't tell him, I decide. Nothing will even come of this.

Chapter 6
"You must really like celibacy."

After my hangover dissipates somewhat, I check my e-mail, not expecting much. I'm shocked to find twenty-six replies. In less than twelve hours, more than two dozen lonely people have responded to my ad. I hunker down and begin to feverishly read. I immediately delete ten because they invite me to engage in various acts of perversion that would violate the sanctity of my marriage as well as most laws of state and physics. I delete twelve more because they are badly misspelled jokes, they are boring, their authors sound like serial killers, and/or they try to sell me Viagra or Jesus. But the remaining four have piqued my interest:

Hello, my name is Evelyn Richards, and I live here in Madison. I'm a 74-year-old widow, and I enjoy knitting, swimming, and welding. I'm a metal artist (primarily garden sculptures), but don't worry, I won't try to sell you any. I was just thinking of doing something different for the holidays this year, and I read your ad. What sort of Christmas get-together are you planning? I'm interested in learning more. Thank you in advance!

***

TESTING, TESTING, ONE TWO THREE! PLEASE COUNT ME IN ON THE X-MAS SHINDIG, WHAT A GREAT IDEA!!!!!! I AM ALSO BOYCUTTING MY FAMILY THIS YEAR, SO I THINK WE ARE ON THE SAME PAGE. I AM ALERGIC TO PEANUTS. ALSO, I HAVE TWO RECUE DOGS I CAN'T LEAVE HOME ALONE SO CAN I SUGGEST WE EAT AT TWO DOG CAFÉ? THAT WAY I CAN

BRING MY DACHSHUNDS. ALSO, I KNOW THE OWNERS, THEY ARE GREAT AND MAKE A MEAN REUBEN–A REAL SERIEUS SANDWICH. SORY FOR THE ALL-CAPS AND BAD SPELLING, MY KEYBOARD IS GOOFY. MY NAME IS PAUL BY THE WAY. PAUL STANLEY. LIKE THE ULTRA-TALENTED GUITARIST IN KISS, BUT I DON'T LOOK ANYTHING LIKE HIM.

***

Wow, I can't believe I'm answering this…I guess I really don't want to spend Christmas alone. This is the first time I've even used Craigslist (I always associated it with oddballs—sorry!), but something about your ad compelled me to answer. (You are serious, right?) I'm a grad student here in the molecular biology program, and my schedule won't allow me to make the trip back to Fargo to see my family this year. My friends are all traveling or with their own families, and I just lost someone dear to me, so here I am, with that horrible power ballad "All by myself" stuck in my head. I am definitely not a fan of the Kardashians but I do like Bob Ross.

Sincerely, Alyssa P.
PS: Sorry if I got that song stuck in your head now, too.

***

Oh my dear, can I just tell you how happy I was to see your strange, wonderful, unconventional, refreshingly honest, perfectly timed invitation? So let's see, I should tell you who I am. My name is Chris. My family disowned me after they learned I was transgender. Possibly perpetually pre-op, unless I win the lottery. And honestly, perhaps I had clues that coming out to them would go badly (what, tell your extended relatives who believe the earth is less than 6,000 years old that you're a woman trapped in a man's body and you wear more mascara and perfume on the weekends than your sisters do? What could go wrong? I mean, seriously!) I sing at various clubs on the weekends, and I am a well-camouflaged office drone during the week. I typically share the holidays with friends, but I'm fresh out of a long-term relationship, and unfortunately, he stole most of them in the split. And to be quite honest, I need a small break from the rest of them. So it's time to make some new ones! I love, love, LOVE to cook, and I would be happy to bring a dish to pass. Are we doing potluck? Looking forward to meeting you and the other lost souls!

***

I'm so engrossed in my reading that I jump when I hear Erik holler up the stairwell: "What are you doing up there?"

"Nothing!" I frantically log out of my e-mail account and minimize the window as Erik ascends the stairs.

He enters the office and peers over my shoulder. I've switched to the local radar, which fills the screen with an animated loop of rainbow-hued reflectivity ticking toward the city. "And what are you up to, Little Miss Secretive?"

"Checking the weather. I heard it's supposed to snow later." I realize I'm compulsively jiggling my right leg and force myself to stop. "Hey, want to go to brunch at Man's Breakfast?" Man's Breakfast is not normally a place I'd suggest, but I'm trying to change the subject. With Erik, slabs of hickory-smoked bacon usually do the trick. Bare breasts also work, but I don't feel like flashing him right now.

I turn around and see his eyes light up. "Now you're talking!" But just as quickly, he's suspicious again. "Wait a minute, you never suggest Man's Breakfast."

"Would you prefer the Marigold?"

Erik hates the Marigold, with its epic waits followed by chaotic, nearly violent dashes to claim opening tables. Not to mention the fact that he finds the menu prissy, though I enjoy it. ("This menu shrinks balls," he loudly declared the last time we ate there.) He's immediately sunny again, rubbing his hands together, already crib-shopping for the impending food baby. "Man's Breakfast it is!"

***

Man's Breakfast is a theme restaurant. The theme being imminent quadruple bypass surgery. It's located in an old gas station. Two years ago it was called The Pump House, but the bland, typical menu wasn't a big enough draw to overcome its inconvenient location. Thus, the thematic renovation and grand re-opening. We slide into a sticky, vinyl-covered booth near the front window, and a waitress with black streaks in her angular bob stops by to run a gray dishrag over the table. "Water?" she asks in a hateful monotone. We nod, and she returns to the clattering kitchen.

"Wow," Erik mutters, "Someone run over her dog this morning?"

"Thank you for not suggesting that she has her period."

"You're welcome."

I pluck a greasy, laminated menu from the condiment rack and study it. "What do they say about restaurants that have photos of the food on the menu?"

"That they're awesome," Erik says firmly, case closed.

"It smells like fried lard in here."

"As it should." Erik smiles. "Hey, you wanted to come here! Now suffer the consequences." He adds a quiet, measured laugh like The Count from *Sesame Street*, and I can feel my libido hang up the *Sorry, we're closed* sign for the foreseeable future.

"Will you still be quoting Muppets when we're in our seventies?"

"Maybe by then it'll be robot Muppets." He does The Count with a digital voice box: *"I'll have three ... three ... three sides of ham. Ah—ah-aaaah."*

"You must really like celibacy."

"Why?"

"Because the more you do that the less I want to have sex with you."

"And that's different from now in what way?" Erik says, and I smack him with my menu. It's all very playful, but it hides a sad fact. Nobody tells you when you're giddy with new love, pushing all imaginable sexual boundaries with the person who consumes your every thought, that there will come a day when you choose sleep over sex, when you have to psyche yourself up to participate. There will come a day when the idea of having sex feels like going to the gym—you know you should do it even when you don't feel like it, because you're usually glad you did afterwards.

Our waitress returns with two glasses of water, slaps them on the table, pulls out her pad and pencil, and glares at Erik. I'm getting the feeling she might want to kill us. Erik requests a meat-stuffed egg atrocity, and I go with the blueberry pancakes. "Side?" the waitress asks, stabbing me with her eyes. I add a side of grapefruit, even though I would prefer something salty to balance the sweet. But I remember from experience that the hash browns aren't so much "hashed" as they are mangled into charred potato hunks ranging in size from a peanut to a stability ball.

While we wait for our food, I glance around the diner. It's filled with families who appear to be making some kind of concession to the man in their mix. They hunch over steaming plates heaped with bacon and hash browns and eggs—a mountain of food on every plate, each man an intrepid culinary explorer bent on conquest. Occasionally they look up, remembering to breathe, and I hear a few groans of blissful determination. Eating here is an event. The wives wear expressions of stoic sacrifice, grimly perusing the menu or blotting spilled chocolate milk with a stack of napkins, trying desperately to flag down a waitress. The kids don't seem to give a rip where they are, as long as there are crayons and paper placemats on the table, chicken fingers on the menu, and strangers in the next booth to belch the alphabet at.

I can't help but wonder if anyone who answered my ad is here. Maybe the chunky, bearded man reading the paper in the corner is Paul Stanley. Then again, he doesn't go anywhere without his dogs, so probably not. I feel my anxiety begin to accelerate when I consider how to close the can of worms I've opened. These people believe my offer is real. They're invested, at least partially, in the idea of spending Christmas with some fresh faces. I suppose I could still back out, but … I'm invested in the idea, too. I feel like people are depending on me, and I don't want to let them down. And I *want* to take this crazy leap, while it's still possible. It's possible because I'm still raw from losing my mother, and when your wounds have yet to scab over, life is more malleable, full of new potential. People don't wake up one day and decide to climb Mount Kilimanjaro or sell everything they own and give the profits to a leper colony in Bangladesh. No, they do it because their late father always wanted to, or because they've been diagnosed with cancer and have eight months to live, or they found their husband in bed with his best friend Gary, or their beloved mother dies and their brother reveals his true identity as Beelzebub. For those of us in a rut so deep we need a periscope to see over the top, it takes a painful push from life to get us up and out.

Now that I think about it, that's also the beginning of every movie I've ever seen.

"You're awfully quiet," Erik says.

"Just thinking." I'm suddenly reminded of a line my Grandpa Harold used to say: *"This is another fine Tony's Pizza you've gotten yourself into."* I grin at the memory.

"What?"

"I'm thinking about my Grandpa Harold. He'd have loved this place."

"He was a great guy," Erik says, sincerely. Our food arrives, and we dig in. There are pebbles of baking soda studded throughout my pancake, but the grapefruit looks and tastes as it should, plump and astringent, with the classic half-maraschino cherry topper.

Things were nice when my grandparents were still alive, before my father left. Clint, Gwen, and I were still kids, couldn't even fathom paying a cable bill or applying for a job or drinking black coffee with our dessert. We'd play auto bingo in the back seat of the station wagon on the way to family reunions, where we'd watch our aunts, uncles, and older cousins play volleyball and drink Hamm's (the beer refreshing). My Aunt Carol would be pregnant again, and she'd always tell me she was so big because she'd swallowed a watermelon seed. My Uncle Harry would sneak up behind me and pretend to cut my hair, my cousins and I would huddle behind a dumpster in the parking lot and dare one another to eat a Gainesburger pilfered from the dog, and Clint would inevitably ruin an article of clothing or give someone a bloody nose, sometimes accidentally, sometimes on purpose. Grandma Ellis would chain smoke and tell stories with her sisters Betty and Ruth while they played Sheepshead. We were deliciously horrified to learn they never had toilet paper growing up, so they had to wipe themselves with pages torn from the Sears catalog in the outhouse. Great-aunt Ruth would always add the story about sharing the same bath water with her five brothers and sisters, which grew progressively funkier with each use, because they didn't get indoor plumbing until she was—

"You're smiling again," Erik is saying. He spears a chunk of sausage and pops it in his mouth.

"I am?" Now I can feel the smile on my lips.

"Yeah, goofball," he says affectionately.

"Still thinking about Grandpa Harold and the good old days."

Erik sits back and sighs heavily. "I think I feel the meat sweats coming on."

"Then maybe you should stop eating."

"It's never this good after you reheat it." He takes a deep breath and digs back in.

After Dad left, we drifted a bit; Mom took a second job to pay the bills and keep the refrigerator stocked, and we saw our relatives less and less. The years passed and we lost our older relatives, one by one. Puberty turned us into surly, pimply adolescents who knew everything and listened to bands whose names contained two consonants where one was warranted (Ratt, Tuff, Enuff Z'Nuff) , and eventually our aunts and uncles lost interest and wandered away.

Now we're all adults who hold real or imagined grudges and barely know one another. Who struggle to make small talk at weddings and funerals.

I wonder if any of them have eaten at Man's Breakfast. I wonder if any of them eat pancakes and miss those days like I do.

Chapter 7

"We're not normal people."

The next day I read my ad's responses to Frankie over the phone. "When are you telling Erik?"

I look at the goosebumps that have suddenly appeared on my forearms. "I'm not. This isn't going to happen."

"Okay," she says, not really believing me.

"It's not! The whole thing was just for fun."

"Okay," she repeats.

"It was!"

"Uh-huh."

"Frankie, come on."

"Yep."

***

I'm nervous through dinner, pushing my peas around my plate, wondering how to broach the subject. *"Hey honey, guess what? We're spending Christmas with total strangers who might have criminal records!"*

I don't go with that one.

Erik interrupts my reverie with, "Organizing a parade?"

I look up, confused.

"Your peas. You have them all lined up like they're in a parade."

I laugh half-heartedly. "Oh, sure. The pea parade."

"Okay. You've been acting weird for two days now. What's going on?"

"I did something."

He looks nervous. "What."

I sigh and pull the printed responses from the pocket of my cardigan. I unfold them, pressing them neatly open, and pass them across the table to Erik. I feel a bead of sweat trickle down my side.

"What are these," he asks flatly.

"I posted an ad for a new family on Craigslist? To spend Christmas with? And these are the responses I like?"

Oh my God. Hearing it out loud like that sounds as sensible as blowing my life savings on beachfront property in the Maldives. Still, I double down on my case, which has become the pattern in our arguments.

I watch a frown take root on his face as he reads them. "You can't be serious."

I fumble for a moment before replying, "Well, hear me out. I'll do background checks on them, and—"

"Jaime, come on."

"It'll be fun!" I try to sound like Jocular, Fun Jaime! Always pulling the wacky stunts, having the best time!

"No. We are not doing this."

"Well, I want to."

He softens. "I know things are ..." he struggles to find the right words, "out of sorts right now, but why can't we just take a vacation over the holidays?"

I sit back in my chair and cross my arms. "I don't want to spend Christmas in some hotel."

"Hotels have Christmas decorations."

"Yeah, depressing Christmas decorations. Also, we're broke."

"We have credit cards."

"No. Absolutely not. If I have to go into debt to take a vacation, I won't be able to enjoy it. We have to start looking for apartments, and money's tight, and—" I can feel my throat closing, giving my voice a shrill edge. I take a deep breath and lower my voice. "Erik, I want to do this. Please, can't you try to understand?"

"Let's skip it this year. Skip Christmas altogether."

"Too difficult to escape," I counter, as if Christmas were an Iranian prison. I had considered the possibility, but festive reminders were hidden everywhere, little red and green mines that could explode at any time: a holiday commercial, the glow of lights from the neighbor's over-decorated yard, the tinsel covering every square inch at school. The main office alone looked like the Tin Man had wandered in with radiation sickness, shedding strands of silvery hair and puking his shiny, happy guts out.

"Why can't we volunteer at a soup kitchen like normal people?"

"We're not normal people," I say, somewhat irrationally. Actually, the idea isn't bad, and I'm surprised it didn't occur to me earlier. Regardless, it still doesn't get at what I want and need: to actually form my very own new family of kindred spirits, everyone just as wounded and lonely yet hopeful as me but taller, better-looking, and more interesting.

"No! This is crazy. I don't want to spend Christmas with total strangers."

"I do."

"I don't."

"These people are spending the holiday alone, too."

"But you're not alone! You have me!"

At that moment I finally see the shadow of something much bigger, much more ominous, circling below our boat. I realize I don't *want* to spend Christmas with only Erik. But I can't deal with that unpleasant reality right now, so I ignore it, paddling faster. "I need family, Erik."

"I'm your family!"

"No, you're NOT!"

He stares at me, and I can nearly see the bruise my words have left on his heart. Once it's out, I know I can't take it back. I try to soften the blow and explain myself by shakily paraphrasing Joy. "We can't be a family because we don't have any children." But it's too late. The words fall from my lips and drop to the floor, dead. I can nearly hear my mother's disappointed *Oh, honey.*

Erik wipes his mouth with his napkin, pushes back from the table and stands. "You're wrong," he quietly says before leaving me alone with my parade of peas.

***

After dinner I eavesdrop on Erik. He's on the phone in the den, his face illuminated only by the green-shaded banker's lamp on the desk. It takes me a few seconds to figure out that he's called the nursing home where his father lives.

"Dad? Hi Dad, it's Erik. Your son. Yep, hi Dad. How are you? Oh, you did? That's great. No, this is Erik. Your son." There's a long pause, and I can hear the emotion in Erik's voice. "Yes, but I'm all grown up now." There's another pause, and Erik's voice cracks when he repeats himself. "No, Dad. It's your son. Erik. Yes, that's right. I love you. Okay. Bye, Dad."

Later in bed, before we fall asleep, I reach for Erik and silently curl my body around his. He finds my hand and pulls me close, and we cling to one another in the dark, our breath rising and falling together as it has for the past seven years. "I'm sorry," I whisper. *For pushing you away because I'm afraid you'll leave. For blaming you for things that aren't even your fault. For sometimes hating you despite sometimes loving you so much it scares me.*

Erik is quiet for a moment before saying, "I still don't understand this. But I love you, and if this helps you get through whatever it is you're going through, I guess I'll support it."

"It's silly of me. We don't have to do it." I feel ashamed of myself. Contrite. Ridiculous even.

"No, I think we should. You clearly want to. And who knows, it might be fun. Crazy, but fun."

"You're a good man, Charlie Brown," I murmur into his shoulder blades. I love him so much right now I want to cry. A wave of self-loathing washes over me.

"But we have to meet these whack-jobs in a public place."

"Okay."

We're quiet again, and then Erik says, apropos of nothing, "Dude's a tranny." He sounds both bemused and concerned.

"So there's no risk of him borrowing your clothes without asking. And don't call him that, by the way." I feel strangely hopeful for the first time in months. Right before I drift off I add, "It's going to be great."

Chapter 8
"So you're having Christmas dinner with these people?"

Erik and I tried for two years to have a baby before my mom got sick. After eleven grueling months without luck, coordinating our intimacy with my fertility chart until we'd successfully transformed our once-enjoyable and spontaneous sex life into just another mechanical routine on the chore wheel, we asked Dr. Nelson to run the usual tests. My reproductive system checked out all right, though with "low ovarian reserve," ovulation would be growing more "sketchy" as I got older, Dr. Nelson emphasized, as if my ovaries were drinking forties and shaking dice on street corners. We also discovered that some of Erik's sperm were misshapen. They were shaped like little cubes, actually. Small squares.

My poor little potentials, doomed as nerds before they entered the race. Total L-7s.

I didn't even realize one could have sperm shaped like squares. Wow, I thought, if this were possible, there must also be little octagons ... trapezoids ... miniscule Stars of David paddling strangely around in men's testicles! And what on earth could twist sperm into tiny, little pieces you could use in a tiny, little game of Perfection? Too much hot-tubbing? Too many spin classes washed down by too many sports drinks high in Red Dye #40?

So we cashed in our savings on one round of in-vitro fertilization. More specifically, we completed IVF plus a process called "intracytoplasmic sperm injection," or ICSI, which is a real couple's jamboree. ICSI is pronounced "icksee," and yes, it is. Unfortunately, the pregnancy didn't take, and we became a statistic. Soaring highs met searing lows.

Before we could figure out how to pay for more rounds of treatment or investigate other options that might have been available to us, Mom was diagnosed with ovarian cancer. Some people would take the opportunity to kick the conception quest into high gear ... one life ends, another begins and all that. Discouraged on every front, I took my ball and went home. Living with and caring for your dying mother is stressful and emotionally devastating enough. I simply didn't have it in me to cycle through any more feelings of excitement, hope, anger, or despair. I didn't want to take any more drugs or medications, drive to any more clinics for any reason at all.

I'm getting older now. I'll be thirty-eight this year, and I'm afraid the window to traditional parenthood has been shut. It's not nailed shut, boarded over, and sprayed with graffiti like my uterus is some kind of abandoned insane asylum, but it would take an impressive bit of muscle to open it again.

And Erik never was much of a weightlifter.

***

Dear Evelyn, it was great hearing from you! Thank you for responding to my invitation. I know how odd it must have seemed—sharing Christmas dinner with total strangers? But I'm so happy you were curious enough about the experiment to answer.
I'd love to learn more about your art—it sounds amazing! At this point, it looks like there will be six of us sharing Christmas dinner at Two Dog Café. I'm told they make a fantastic reuben sandwich. Is there a particular time that works best for you? I'll wait to hear from everyone before making the reservation. Thanks again!

***

Dear Paul, thank you for writing! I would love to meet you and your dogs. Two Dog Café sounds wonderful—great suggestion. I'll call to make a reservation. I think there will be six of us. Are you a big fan of KISS?

***

Hi Alyssa, I'm so glad you wrote. I know it was a really weird thing to do (who posts an ad for a new family to share Christmas dinner with?), but I guess it was born of frustration, disappointment, and a little too much wine on Friday night!

Here I hesitate, deleting the line only to re-type it.

I recently lost my mother, and she'd been the anchor holding our family in place...without her, we're all sort of floating away. Plus, my brother is king of the assholes and my sister is queen of the bitches.

I delete this, adding instead:

I recently lost my mother, and it's been difficult. And I'm sorry to hear you've lost someone close to you as well. So I'm looking forward to meeting you all, sharing Christmas dinner, and making some new friends! Oh, there will be six of us, meeting at the Two Dog Café for dinner. Have you ever been? Will 7 p.m. on the 25th work for you? I hear they make a great reuben.

***

Dear Chris, I love what you wrote. Thank you so much for your refreshing honesty, and for the laugh. You're quite a funny writer. There will be six of us, meeting at Two Dog Café. I hope you aren't allergic to dogs! Thank you as well for your kind offer to bring a dish to pass—we'll definitely take you up on that next time. I'll be making a reservation for seven o'clock on Christmas night, will let you know if anything changes.

***

I sign them all, "Take care, Jaime" before sending them on their merry, digital way. Then, I delete my ad.

***

Dear Jaime, I am so looking forward to meeting you and the rest of our Christmas collective. I've been to Two Dog Café—excellent choice! The last time I was there I fell hard for a young Norfolk Terrier. Alas, he was there with someone else. Have a great week, and don't forget that *A Charlie Brown Christmas* is on next Tuesday! It's just not Christmas until you hear Linus lisping about the "Angel of the Lord." And I don't know about you, but I'm convinced that Linus? Is totally gay. The oral fixation? The lisping? The aversion to Sally? It adds up. All my best, Chris King

***

Hi Jaime, thanks again for organizing this! It'll be fun. I don't want to be a bother, but I am allergic to dogs. But PLEASE don't change the plans, because it sounds like this works best for everyone. I'll take a Benadryl and be fine. And I'm sure they have good ventilation, which helps. It's a shame, because I adore animals. There's a stray cat in my neighborhood that decided to make my deck his winter residence, and I started feeding him dry cat food—until the raccoons discovered the free buffet, that is. A few of them took up residence in my garage and I had to call a wildlife person to get them out. Such adventures in my own backyard—who needs a travel agent?

At any rate, I'm very much looking forward to meeting you all. This will be such a nice change of pace! I am also getting a jump-start on my New Year's Resolution: get out of my comfort zone and meet new people from all walks of life.

Sincerely, Evelyn

***

JAIME, THIS WILL BE GREAT. YOUR GOING TO LOVE TWO DOG CAFÉ. I SOMETIMES WONDER IF THEY NAMED IT AFTER THE IMPRESSIVE ROCK BAND "THREE DOG NIGHT," OR MAYBE THE DOG TREAT MANUFACTRER, "THREE DOG BAKERY," BUT PROBABLY IT'S BECUASE THE OWNERS HAVE TWO DOGS, AND IT'S A CAFÉ. I CAN'T WAIT FOR YOU TO MEET MY DACHSHUNDS. SORRY MY KEYBOARD IS STILL BROKEN, PAUL

PS: HAVE YOU EVER HEARD OF THE KISS ARMY? YOU COULD SAY I'M A CHARTER MEMBER. THANKS FOR ASKING. I'LL BRING A CENTERPEICE FOR OUR TABLE

***

Hi Jaime, thanks for writing. I'm so glad you're serious, and normal! It's been a rough fall for me ... my boyfriend Ryan was killed in a car accident at the beginning of the semester, and I don't need another night alone in the lab with bad take-out—especially on Christmas. I'm pretty close to my family, and it breaks my heart that I won't be seeing them this year. So, here we are. Though I did meet Ryan online, I never imagined

I'd make friends that way. It's definitely unconventional and even a little scary for me, but you never learn to fly if you don't take the leap, right?

Thanks, Alyssa Peters

***

Dear Alyssa, I'm so, so sorry to hear about your boy-friend. I know how hard it is to lose someone you love—everybody asking, 'Is there anything I can do?' and you just want to tell them, "I don't need anymore casseroles or weird, lingering hugs or stories about how you just lost your dog." I don't think you ever get over it. You adjust to the new hole in your life and you never stop missing them, because there are remind-ers around nearly every corner. It's been six months for me. I was Mom's caregiver for the last year of her life. Even though it was hard to see her growing sicker and weaker, it's time I'm grateful I had with her. She was amazing, my best friend, and I think of her every day. I knew this first Christmas without her would be hard—and after an argument with my brother, I posted the ad. It was the spontaneous kind of thing I always used to do, so it's good to know I still have the ability to surprise myself.
Please don't be afraid to email any time you feel yourself slipping. From personal experience, I know it can help to talk to people who've been there.
xo, Jaime

***

I hit "Enter" and sit back, swallowing hard. Frankie was right. This is already more cathartic than I imagined it would be.

***

The following week during a prep period I drop in to chat with our school mentoring program coordinator, Emily Garrison. "Hey, Em, got a minute?"

She looks up from her computer, tiny white screens reflected in the lenses of her glasses. "Yep, let me quick finish this e-mail."

I take a seat in the chair facing her desk and listen to the clattering of her keyboard. There are three framed photos of Dalmatians amidst the drifts of clutter ready to spill like an avalanche from the desk. Emily's funny. She's very particular about words. She recently told me that she despises the word "moist." She hates it so much it almost makes her puke, and now I find myself self-consciously censoring the use of this word around her all the time: during a coworker's birthday party ("This cake is so moi- *rich!*"), during a particularly humid August inservice ("Ugh, it's so mois—*thick* in here!"). I had no idea how often I was using the word "moist," which I too have come to despise. Since I've known her, Emily has also invited me to six home business-based "parties" peddling products from brands you can't find in stores: jewelry, clothing, kitchenware, natural foods, organic makeup, knockoff purses. I'm running out of excuses, and we're about due for another party. I wonder what it will be next time—wrinkle cream infused with peptides, pomegranate, and the tears of a clown? Vibrating slacks that shake away the cellulite?

Emily finishes typing and flashes a professional smile. "What's up?"

"You do background checks on the mentors for the after-school program, right?"

She nods.

"Can you run these names?" I hand her the names of everyone on my dinner party list. I am the worst hostess ever. Mrs. Suspicious.

"Sure." She looks at me, puzzled, expecting some kind of explanation.

"A grief group I met online," I say, feeling heat bloom in my cheeks. "We're spending Christmas dinner together." I feel only mild guilt at flashing my bereavement card again, which usually gets me out of anything I want to avoid, from chaperoning a school dance to household chores to sex that requires my full attention.

"Oh!" She lowers her voice. "I can still give you the name of that psychic I talked to. If you want."

Last year Emily's older sister died of a brain aneurysm. She was two months' pregnant, shopping for paint for the baby's room, and she dropped dead at Sherwin-Williams, just like that. It was one of those horrible, unexpected deaths that make you nervous for weeks, glancing over your shoulder and hugging your husband two beats longer before leaving for work in the morning. Emily's handled it fairly well, mostly because she's been paying a woman to tell her things like, *Your sister is in the room with us—with a fabulous new haircut, by the way! She says not to worry, she's always with you. In fact, she rode with you on your commute to work every day this week.*

"Thanks," I say. "I'm still thinking about it."

I'm not thinking about it at all.

"Anyway, everyone on that list? I'm not too worried about the women, but you never know with guys."

"Gotcha." Emily gives me a knowing look. "Hey," she says, switching gears, "you up for margaritas at Salsa Jim's tonight? Two for one 'til six o'clock!"

"Not tonight. I'm a little tired, and I think I feel a cold coming on. But thanks for looking that up for me."

***

The next few weeks are hectic, my students antsy for Christmas break. I watch *A Charlie Brown Christmas*, *Miracle on 34th Street*, and the Reginald Owen version of *A Christmas Carol*. I bake almond cookies, peppermint pinwheels, and my mother's homemade caramels, cut into small squares and tucked in twists of wax paper. I wrap gifts, though that process doesn't take nearly as long as it did last year. We buy and decorate a real Christmas tree while sipping hot toddies and listening to Bing Crosby and Burl Ives, and Erik and I even go ice-skating one Friday night. We prep for Christmas like it's an exam. And beneath it all runs a current of nervous excitement about Christmas dinner, tempered always by the omnipotent absence of my mother. It's so sharp at times I have to steady myself.

Growing up, we wore hand-me-down corduroys, drove an ancient station wagon with blooms of rust on the doors, and ate the generic macaroni and cheese. Still, Mom always found a way to put something we desperately wanted for Christmas on layaway. If that didn't work, we got a reasonable facsimile of what we wanted, wrapped in the special paper and signed, *Love, Santa*. When I was seven, I wanted a horse more than anything in the world; I begged, I bargained, I made hundreds of crayon drawings of the horses grazing in the paddock my bus passed on the way to school each morning. Instead of a real horse in a giant red bow under the tree that year, she arranged occasional rides for me on the back of a tired pony belonging to a coworker and got me subscriptions to *Young Rider*, *Horse Illustrated*, and *Dressage Today*. I enjoyed *Young Rider* and *Horse Illustrated*, swooning over the photos of sleek, long-lashed quarter horses stretched out in mid-gallop, but I'll tell you: nothing slaps the horse lust out of a first-grader more quickly than a magazine called *Dressage Today*.

She was always paying attention, always trying, and I wish I'd appreciated it sooner.

Emily stops by my office while I'm grading papers one Thursday after school. I'd just given Tanner his first F of the semester, and I'm troubled by this when I look up to find her about to knock on my door. "Am I interrupting?"

"No, come on in."

"Well, you were right. The girls checked out mostly fine—Alyssa had an underage drinking ticket a few years ago, but who didn't? A few more things came up on the guys. There are three Christopher Kings and two Paul Stanleys in the Madison area, so without addresses, I can't say for sure which record applies to whom. One of the Christophers is about to be foreclosed on by the bank and hasn't paid his water bill in over nine months. Another has two speeding tickets, though both have been paid, and it looks like an ex-girlfriend took a restraining order out on him a few months ago." She squints at the printout in her hand. "One of the Pauls has citations for disorderly conduct, animal and noise violations, vandalism, and trespassing. There's also an old shoplifting incident. The other was nabbed for drunk driving three years ago."

"The one with the restraining order is probably not my Chris, since mine is gay," I say defensively, as if gay people are immune to restraining orders. Look at me, all possessive of my new friends already. Well, this whole exercise was about as useful as a sixth toe.

"So you're having Christmas dinner with these people?" Em asks. She's trying hard to sound open-minded.

"We're going to Two Dog Café. Have you ever been?"

"They have the best reuben!"

"So I hear." I smile and thank her again before returning to my grading. I wonder how Gwen will be spending the holidays. We stopped sending cards and calling years ago, for no particular reason I can think of other than distance and mutual resentment. We've entered a silent standoff. Our own little Cold Shoulder War. Or maybe Gwen just doesn't care. Maybe Gwen doesn't even celebrate Christmas anymore. Maybe she's bringing a bottle of wine and a spinach salad to a Winter Solstice party, and there will be that one cynical guy there, stridently bitching about how the Christmas tree was a pagan symbol that was co-opted by the Church.

I wonder what Clint has planned for Christmas. I wonder if the aunts and uncles will come over for dinner, and everyone will joke about keeping the mashed potatoes grounded.

I haven't spoken to Clint since Thanksgiving. I suppose we'll eventually have to talk to one another, but right now, it's easy to imagine us never talking again. It's a thought that fills me with an anxious sort of peace, which is actually not that peaceful at all.

Chapter 9
"Beers that end with the letter 'z.'"

On Christmas morning I call Hannah and leave a message on her voicemail: "Hi Hannah, how are you? I miss you! Merry Christmas honey. I hope you have a wonderful holiday, and Santa is good to you. I have a gift for you, um, I was hoping to see you at some point, but I guess I'll have to mail it to you. Say hi to … have a great Christmas, and I miss you so much. I love you, sweetpea. Okay then, bye-bye. Love you." I started out light and upbeat, the affectionate, jet-setting aunt checking in before she bustles off to meet friends for cocktails, but by the end of my message I'd devolved into the lonely aunt who washes and reuses plastic bags and sends ten-dollar checks to animal charities. I hang up and stare at the living room wall. After a few minutes I shake it off and get on with the day.

***

We find Two Dog Café bustling with customers and dogs; it's one of the only businesses on State Street casting friendly squares of light onto the snowdrifts outside. As I pull open the front door, the overhead bell jingles and I'm hit with the sentimental smells of Christmas: cinnamon, pine, vanilla, mistletoe, cloves. I stand there for a second and take them in, tripping on real or imagined memories of sledding, hot cocoa, even roasting chestnuts on an open fire, which I know never happened because we didn't have a fireplace and my family was more a nut cracking kind of clan. So to speak.

A guitarist is sitting on a barstool in the corner, strumming "Greensleeves." Framed black and white photos of dogs nearly cover the exposed brick walls, and a chalkboard easel near the front window explains the special holiday menu in round, girlish letters: lobster salad in endive, apricot-glazed ham, pumpkin gnocchi with caramelized onions or parsnip mash, garlic-roasted green beans, figgy pudding for dessert. Around half the diners appear to have brought their dogs, which range in size from Malamute to Chihuahua. Most lie quietly and loyally at their owner's feet. A Yorkie sees me and begins wagging his tiny tail, ears flattened in submission. A perky young hostess dressed in black greets us. "Hi! Do you have a reservation?"

"Table for six under Jaime?"

"So this is Two Dog Café," Erik says, admiring the punched-tin ceiling and stained-glass sconces. "This place is busier than I figured it would be on Christmas."

I make eye contact with a young man in honey-colored dreadlocks eating potato soup in a plush chair and feel myself blush when he smiles: *caught you looking.* A mottled Australian Shepherd sleeps at his feet. The hostess leads us to our table, which has already been set for six. The silverware gleams in the candlelight. "Looks like we're the first ones," I say, claiming a chair.

"Good. Then we can bolt if we don't like the looks of anyone."

"Thank you for doing this. You'll be nice, right?"

"No, I plan on being a complete douche," Erik says, grinning at our hostess as she delivers ice water adorned with slivers of lemon and cucumber to the table. She smiles neutrally.

An older woman with cropped gray hair enters the restaurant. The door jingles behind her as she stomps snow from her boots and unwinds the longest scarf I've ever seen. She surveys the restaurant and slowly unsnaps her puffy down coat, hanging it on the coat rack near the door.

I tentatively wave. "Evelyn?"

She smiles in relief when she spots me and heads directly over. "You must be Jaime."

Erik stands and extends a hand, which Evelyn shakes. "I'm the loyal husband, Erik."

"It's a pleasure to meet you both!"

"Did you have any trouble finding the restaurant?"

"Only a parking space. I had no idea it was supposed to snow earlier! You forget how to drive in the stuff."

Our waitress arrives and introduces herself. "Hi! I'm Carly. I see you're still waiting for a few members of your party, but can I get you three drinks while you wait?"

"No, but you can get me one," Erik says. "I'll have a Newcastle."

"I'll just have water for now …"

Evelyn adds, "Yes, water is fine for now."

The "for now" implies we're going to wine it up later, I suppose. A bit of social lubricant sounds fantastic, but I feel funny ordering before the rest of the group arrives.

Chris arrives next, and he's hard to miss in an elegant turtle-neck sweater dress, black, knee-high boots, meticulously applied full makeup, and curly wig the color of molasses.

"Buckle up, Evelyn," Erik says. Evelyn smiles like she's expecting one hell of a punch line.

I wave, and Chris makes his way toward us. He air-kisses my cheeks, and introductions are made. "I love your boots," Evelyn says.

"Oh, thank you! It was so hard to find a pair I liked in my size."

Poor Chris. For him, every store must be like Burlington Coat Factory. Before we can even sit down again, Paul arrives with more door-jangling and foot-stomping. I know it's him because even though he looks nothing like I pictured, he's got a toy Dachshund tucked under each arm. Somehow, he also manages to hold an obnoxious silver and red holiday centerpiece bursting with sprigs of pine, dogwood and holly. I'd imagined him pimply and tall, in a worn black concert T-shirt, but he's short, maybe thirty-something, with full mutton chop sideburns leading to an impressive, fluffy beard that fans over his chest like a bib. Paul and his dogs are wearing matching chunky blue sweaters that look hand-knit. Paul's is stretched taut over his round belly, the white snowflakes straining, nearly horizontal. Without hesitation, he shuffles directly toward us—a regal walrus and his pocket-sized pets.

"Oh, let me take that for you," I say, reaching for the centerpiece. "It's beautiful!"

"I thought it would make our table a bit more festive," Paul explains. "Get us in the holiday mood."

"I like your sweaters," Evelyn says, and I can tell she genuinely means it.

"Thank you. My sister knit them for us. She also knits little sweaters for her chickens. She sews tiny bells on so they don't get lost in the yard." The dog tucked under his left armpit starts to wiggle. "This is Auschie," he tips his head to the left, "and this is Abe," he adds, tipping his head to the right.

"Abe, like Abe Vigoda?" I ask, scratching behind Abe's ears.

"No, Abe Froman, the Sausage King of Chicago."

I smile. "Such a cutie pie. And this one is … Ouchie?"

"Auschie. Short for 'Auschwitz.'"

"Oh dear!" Chris draws a manicured hand to his mouth.

"Wait," Erik says. "You named him after a concentration camp?"

"Look at those ribs! What else do they make you think of?"

Erik tries in vain to turn his laugh into a cough. The dogs just look at me like, *Can you believe this shit?* Paul lowers them to the tile floor and they immediately begin to sniff everything within reach of their leash. One of them lifts a hind leg on the table and Paul instantly corrects him with, "No urinating on table legs. Remember, we talked about this?"

Erik stares at me with giant eyes. He clearly thinks Paul has a formal diagnosis in a manila folder in some doctor's office, and perhaps the medication to accompany it. This is going to be fantastic.

As I finish introducing Paul to the others, Alyssa slides in, brushing snow from her hair and stomping her feet on the front mat. She nervously pans the room, looking for us. I raise a hand and smile, waving her back. "You must be Alyssa!"

"I'm sorry I'm late. I had a hard time finding a place to park."

Everything about her is gentle, almost vulnerable, from the way she walks to her wide, questioning eyes. She's tall and thin, a paper crane of a girl. A gentle breeze could break a limb. Even her outfit—a silk tunic embroidered with delicate beads and flowers over black leggings—is fragile.

Paul extends a hand to her. "You remind me of an Indonesian Wayang Golek puppet, and I mean that in a very complimentary way."

Alyssa shakes it and smiles crookedly. "Thanks, I think."

Evelyn's eyes brighten. "Oh, have you been to Indonesia? Last year a troupe of puppeteers brought a Wayang show to the Orpheum. Such marvelous folk art, I'm happy to know it's still thriving." She turns to Alyssa and warmly greets her. "I'm Evelyn. It's a pleasure to meet you."

"No, I haven't been there," Paul says, "but I know someone who collects the puppets. He is also arguably the best castanet player in the Midwest."

"Sounds like a fascinating person."

"Oh, he is."

I try to rein things in again. "Alyssa, it's so nice to meet you. I'm Jaime, this is my husband Erik, and this is Chris." She greets us all and takes the last seat.

Our server appears again, as if on cue. Chris asks for and is immediately handed a small drink menu.

"Buy you a beer, Paul?" Erik asks. He's using his gruff, male-bonding voice.

"No, thanks. I only drink Blatz. Sometimes Schlitz. "

"A man who knows what he likes," Erik says. "Beers that end with the letter 'z.'"

I pinch his thigh below the table. "That's interesting! Any particular reason?"

"Not really."

"I'll have a glass of the house chardonnay," Evelyn says.

Chris hands the drink menu back to the waitress and smiles elegantly. "I'll have the Mendota Martini, extra dirty."

I order a glass of the house cabernet, and Alyssa orders the same. "No, wait. Let's get a bottle," she corrects herself. "Is that okay?" she asks me, brows nervously knit together. "If we get a bottle to share?"

I shrug. "I guess so."

At this point Paul stands and withdraws a folded piece of paper from his front pocket. "To commemorate today, I wrote a brief haiku, which I would like to read for you now." He clears his throat while we wait expectantly. Things have taken an even more interesting turn. "Six strangers, Christmas. Meeting, sharing, laughing. A bond built today."

"Yaay!" I say, like a small girl. We all clap.

"Aren't haikus supposed to have five, seven, and then five syllables?" Erik asks, still clapping.

"Yes."

"That middle line had six syllables."

I sigh and pinch the bridge of my nose.

"No, it didn't," Paul says defiantly.

"Yes, it did." Erik repeats the line verbatim, tapping the syllables out.

Paul looks temporarily stunned, then quickly adds, "No, it had seven. *'They're meeting, sharing, laughing.'*"

"You didn't say 'they're.'"

"Yes, I did."

"No, you didn't."

"Okay!" I say brightly. "It was a great poem nonetheless."

"Haiku," Paul corrects.

"Wow, everything looks divine!" Chris says grandly, opening his menu with a flourish. With one raised eyebrow, he catches my eye. Chris gets it, and I adore him already. "Paul, what would you recommend?"

"The reuben. I'm not sure if it's the dressing, the sauerkraut, or the corned beef, but I've never been able to replicate it at home."

"Maybe it's the rye," Erik says. "Bread is the foundation of any good sandwich." Erik is messing with Paul, but only I know it.

"You're right!" Paul concedes, nodding seriously.

Half an hour later, after we've collectively polished off three bottles of wine and four appetizers, I realize what a coup I've pulled in bringing such a motley band of people together. Maybe it's the wine, maybe it's the relaxed atmosphere, but we're laughing, enjoying one another's company, telling stories. None of us discuss why we've chosen to spend Christmas together, preferring the bunny hill of conversation to the more treacherous black diamond slopes. Chris regales us about a recent trip to Thailand, and I can almost hear the din of Bangkok traffic, taste the mango and sticky rice, smell the night-blooming jasmine on his hotel balcony. Evelyn—despite the onset of allergic sneezing and watery eyes—has us captivated with stories about her youthful indiscretions in Europe. "One day I'll have to tell you about the time I had drinks with Mario Bava in Italy."

"I don't know who Mario Bava is, but he sounds fabulous," Chris says. "Is he a chef?"

"He directed *Planet of the Vampires*," Paul explains. "I streamed it at my Halloween party this year." He leans under the table to feed bits of lobster to Abe and Auschie. I think if asked, Paul could give me the exact speed of light in a vacuum as well as Ace Frehley's preferred style of underwear.

"It's interesting how we don't watch movies anymore ... now we stream them," Evelyn observes, amused.

"Or, if they're romantic comedies, we painfully endure them," Erik says.

"I find romantic comedies to be neither romantic nor comedic," Paul adds, and Erik nods his approval.

At this point I offer my first test of the evening. Or maybe it's not really a test, but a chance to use one of my favorite clichéd sayings. "It's been said that great people talk about ideas, average people talk about things, and small people talk about other people." Everyone is quietly looking at me for an explanation. I clear my throat and add, "So it's nice to be among great minds!"

"That is so true," Alyssa says, boozy and emotional. I wonder if it's time to worry about Alyssa yet; I have no idea what her proclivities and patterns are when it comes to alcohol.

"I thought small people talked about wine?" Evelyn says.

"I think small people talk on tiny telephones about their fear of raindrops," Paul says.

Erik turns to stare at me again, one direct, sustained look that manages to convey both glee and horror, and Chris laughs with delight. "Oh Jaime, this is so much better than being berated by my family. Thank you!"

Paul brings Abe and Auschie up to his lap for a visit, and Chris and I fawn over them. He tells us about their lineage, his "dog-parenting philosophy," and some of the recipes he uses to make their meals. "It's called the BARF diet, which stands for 'bones and raw food.' It took awhile, but I've actually come to enjoy the smell of unbleached tripe."

Evelyn nods, not put off in the least. "I know what you mean! I'm one of those people who doesn't mind the smell of gasoline."

"I like the way skunks smell," I announce loudly, happy to contribute. A bespectacled man sitting at the table next to us raises an eyebrow at me. His dog, a glossy Irish Setter relaxing at his feet, smiles at me, panting. I smile back.

Alyssa flags down our waitress. "Can we please have another bottle of wine?" Her cheeks glow a vibrant sunset pink. She's been holding an intense, quiet side conversation with Chris, who looks troubled.

Our waitress returns with a fresh bottle of syrah and an entourage of servers bearing our dinners. Each plate is a three-dimensional work of art, decked with sprigs of rosemary or basil, drizzled with vinegar reductions, fruit coulis, or herb-infused oils. Paul snaps a photo of his reuben before taking a bite. He chews, and nods slowly. "It's definitely the rye." My gnocchi tastes as good as it looks: tiny pillows of rich, sweet dough crisped on the outside from a few buttery rolls around a blazing pan.

"Oh my God," Chris moans, fork in hand. "This is a life-changing ham. This is a pageant-winning, porcine masterpiece."

The conversation encounters its first lull as we lose ourselves in our meals. Evelyn continues to sneeze, and Alyssa seems to be playing her own personal drinking game: two swallows per bite, three when anyone within earshot laughs. She's quiet, occasionally glancing around the table with watery, emotional eyes. Now I am worried. Did I really think I could bring a random group of strangers together for a major holiday meal without something strange or disastrous happening? "Are you feeling all right, Alyssa?" I gently ask.

She nods, a drunken wobble with fluttery eyelids. "Fine. I just need to use the bathroom." Her chair squawks as she pushes back, and the ears of every dog in the dining room perk up.

"Poor girl," Chris says after she's gone. "To lose a boyfriend like that."

"What happened?" Evelyn asks, worried, and Chris and I fill in the gaps.

"Tragedy strikes," Paul simply says, as if he's suggesting a headline for the news story.

We proceed more slowly with our meal and begin to reveal some of the death-related reasons that brought us here. I imagine myself pacing before a massive stone fireplace, a creepy portrait with eyes that seem to follow you hung on the mantle: "I'm sure you're all wondering why I've called you here today."

We cover the usual logistical questions (*When did your husband die, Evelyn? How long was your mother ill? Did your friend leave a note?*), and the mood darkens from devil-may-care to one-day-we'll-all-be-dead.

"She's been in there a long time," Erik says, frowning.

"I'm sure she'll be fine," I say. It wasn't long ago that I was also stumbling off to privately weep in bathrooms, particularly after too much wine. I crane my neck to look toward the restroom. There's a woman waiting in line, arms crossed. "I'll be right back," I tell the table.

When I reach the bathroom I apologize to the woman who is waiting her turn. Her hair, thick and gathered in a messy chignon, is the color of mushrooms. "I'm sorry, excuse me, but my friend is in there, I need to make sure she's all right." I knock on the door. "Alyssa? You okay in there?"

There's no response, so I knock harder. "Alyssa?"

I wait, but again ... silence. I knock once more.

"Do we need to get a manager?" the woman asks me. She's holding her purse so tightly the knuckles of her left hand are white. "Is your friend sick?"

"She had too much to drink," I say. Maybe she dozed off on the toilet. Wouldn't that be embarrassing! A great anecdote to share at Christmas parties years from now, after she's found the humor in it. I jiggle the handle, but of course it's locked. I knock again. "Alyssa?"

Another woman joins us in line. She's holding the hand of a little girl who is maybe four-years-old, and the lady with the mushroom-colored hair explains the situation. "Her friend is passed out on the toilet."

"We don't know that yet," I snipe.

"Mom, I really have to go!" the young girl says, hopping anxiously on her toes. Her mother glances at the men's room, considering Plan B. The guitarist is playing "Carol of the Bells," a song I normally love but the frantic escalation of which is not helping the situation.

"Okay," I say, taking a breath. "I'm going to get a manager."

I tell a bartender, who relays the information to a manager, who joins me with a ring of jangly, official keys. "All right, let's get to the bottom of this."

More knocking ensues, plus anxious yet firm inquiries: "Miss? Everything alright?"

"Mommy, I'm going to pee!"

The manager extracts the bathroom key from those on his ring, unlocks the door, and slowly pushes it open, only to be stopped by a pair of outstretched legs. Alyssa is lying sprawled on the cold tile floor. "Oh my God!" someone says. It may have been me. A dog starts barking. The manager rushes in, crouches at her side. She starts to gag, legs twitching. "Call an ambulance," he yells.

Chapter 10

"Either way, Merry Christmas!"

Sometimes it feels like Death is that guy you keep running into anytime you're out and about. Have to mail a package at the post office? There he is, and you know it's him because his eyes bug out ever so slightly due to thyroid issues and his collarbone is sharp and wide like he's swallowed a kite. Planning to swing by the store on the way home from work because you're out of milk? There Death is again, standing in lane four with a box of Hamburger Helper and a tub of Metamucil. The store is so busy that you have to join the same line, so there you are with Death, and he's trying to engage you in awkward small talk like, "Think it'll rain later?" or "Do the unbleached coffee filters really make a difference?" or "Eighty-two, peacefully in your sleep, but completely and utterly alone."

I met the man I wanted as Mom's hospice volunteer in line for coffee two weeks before she died. He was standing in front of me when he suddenly turned around to smile broadly and ask, "How are you going to enjoy your youth today?" I was taken aback and even a bit annoyed, but as we talked further, I understood what he meant. He told me that in his work with hospice he sometimes asked the dying what they would do just one more time if they could do it all over again. "One elderly man I cared for said he would cut the grass one more time."

It was so simple, yet so true and perfect. He paused to let what he'd said sink in. My eyes welled up, my heart melted, and I'm getting choked up again just thinking about it.

When I told Erik about this later he said, "Guy can come over and mow our lawn if he wants," which irritated me because he intentionally missed the point.

I scowled. "When you're on your deathbed I'm reading you everything Nicholas Sparks ever wrote."

"And I will muster up exactly enough strength to smother myself with my pillow."

Last summer, as my mother was dying, I taught a few remedial classes both for the distraction and the extra money. Tanner enrolled in my math course. One morning he came in sweaty and wild-eyed, greeting me with, "Last night a kid got smoked trying to run across the Beltline!" In his voice was a mixture of voyeuristic excitement and relief—this horrible, stupid thing happened to someone else. Someone who drank too much and tempted fate on a dare. I didn't tell Erik about it, because I knew if I wondered aloud why on earth a kid would run across a busy highway like that, he'd make some stupid joke like, "Isn't it obvious? To find out why the chicken crossed the road." But the message wasn't lost on me: sometimes you quite literally run into Death. The fortunate among us have the luxury of preparing. Brushing our hair and picking the nib of broccoli from our teeth before we answer the knock at the door.

And now here we are again. Death, rarely invited to the party (he's a bit of a downer), this time with an engraved invitation. Alyssa had finished an entire bottle of wine along with nearly half a bottle of Vicodin. If she wasn't actively trying to shut down her nervous system, "It was a cry for help if I've ever seen one," as Paul said while we ran out of Two Dog Café. Chris, Erik, Evelyn, Paul and I followed the ambulance to the Alliant Medical Center, where the five of us now sit on stiff vinyl chairs in the emergency room waiting area, which despite being decked in shiny holiday garland, still looks and feels cheerless. Paul's contraband dogs are tucked in a black KISS tote bag; one of them occasionally peeks over the edge to sniff the strange hospital odors, which to my untrained nose, consist mainly of latex, rubbing alcohol, and panic.

Or maybe my nose is well-trained. Though we tried our best to spend as much of our fading time together in happier places, even if that happier place was only the kitchen table poring over old photo albums, my mother and I spent far too many of her final hours in offices and exam rooms that smelled exactly like this.

There are four other people in the waiting area—a man wearing a makeshift sling sitting next to a woman who looks as if she only smiles by accident, and a worried-looking father holding a little girl in a red velvet holiday dress. He holds her close and rubs her back, whispering reassurances in her ear. She's trying desperately to be brave.

"Maybe I should check again, see how she's doing," Evelyn says. She's been knitting a long, soft, multicolored scarf.

"They said they'd let us know when there's any news," I reply. Already, I can tell Evelyn is a good woman to have on your team. She will hail the cab in the rain, ask to speak to the manager, and deal with the insurance company when they deny your claim.

"Is anyone else hungry?" Paul asks.

We all look at one another and shrug. I love food, and often after I eat I'm already fantasizing about my next meal. But right now, fasting until Groundhog Day sounds like a great idea. And even if we were hungry, who could eat?

"I feel simply terrible for her," Chris says again, troubled. "The poor thing."

Erik is snoozing next to me, a stinky ball cap he found on the floor of our car pulled down over his eyes. He's made the mistake of assuming that I will wake him when Alyssa's condition improves, or I get up to leave.

"She'll be all right," I say, though I have no way of actually knowing this. It seemed like kind of a bad idea to attempt suicide in a public bathroom during a meal with strangers, so I theorized in the car on the way over that maybe it was an accident.

"That was no accident," Erik said. Snow flew at us through the headlight beams, giving the illusion that we were blasting through space at warp speed.

"Maybe she had too much to drink and wanted only one pill? But, I don't know, she just couldn't stop?"

"What are they, potato chips?"

"Or maybe she didn't really want to die, but she just wanted the pain to end. Someone she loved very much recently died, for crying out loud. She's heartbroken. Totally lonely."

"Either way, Merry Christmas!"

"Remind me to enroll you in an Empathy Development course."

I watch as a nurse guides the father and his brave, small daughter through a set of swinging doors into the labyrinthine hospital hallways beyond. Somewhere a phone is ringing. Or, to be more accurate, warbling. I miss the sound of a real telephone ringing.

"What time is it?" Paul asks.

I check my phone. "Nearly ten."

"I should get going. The dogs are usually in bed by ten-thirty."

Evelyn, Chris, and I stand to say goodbye to Paul. And the dogs.

"Will you let me know how she is?" he asks me.

"Of course."

Evelyn hugs him, so I follow her lead. Up close, his beard smells like a strange combination of peppermint and liverwurst. Chris opens his arms for an embrace, and Paul turns it into an awkward man-hug, complete with two back pounds. Our commotion wakes Erik, who extends a relaxed hand to Paul, like we're at a breezy summer barbecue at which none of the guests tried to kill themselves. "Take care there, buddy. Good to meet you."

After Paul leaves a handsome young doctor in blue scrubs and glasses with black hipster frames approaches to tell us that Alyssa is now stable and resting, but she'll be staying overnight for observation, after which she'll be evaluated for mental and behavioral health services. Depending on the results, there could be a brief inpatient stay for the recommended treatment.

"Could we see her for just a minute?" I ask.

"She's awake," the doctor says, considering our anxious faces. "I suppose it would be okay, but she does need to rest. You have five minutes."

"We'll be brief," Evelyn says, and we follow him back to the ICU. He stops at one of the small triage rooms and pulls the curtain back to reveal Alyssa, clad in a flimsy hospital gown, resting on a partially inclined orthopedic hospital bed with side rails. Her eyes are closed, but she opens them as the clattering curtain rings announce our arrival. She's tethered to an IV drip. Dark half-moons float in the hollows beneath her eyes. She looks like she could sleep for months.

"Hey kiddo," Erik says as we file in, "How are you feeling?" He pulls the curtain closed behind us.

"I've been better." She attempts a smile and smoothes her hair, tucking stray strands behind her ears. "God, I must look horrible."

Chris sits in a plastic chair next to her and pats her forearm. "Honey, it's not possible for you to look horrible. Even in a hospital gown. What is that print, are those daisies?"

"I think so." She manages a shaky smile. "Sorry I ruined your Christmas."

We make gentle noises of protest. "Nonsense," Evelyn says. "You didn't ruin anything."

"They pumped my stomach. That was fun."

"I had my stomach pumped once," Chris says. "I was three. I'd eaten a few fistfuls of Comet cleanser. I'll never forget it. Such a traumatic experience. I think it's actually my first memory."

Suddenly Alyssa begins to cry. We rush to comfort her. "I'm so embarrassed."

Chris pats her hand. "Oh honey, this is nothing to be embarrassed about. Wearing denim on denim, now that's another story."

"You're going to be fine," Evelyn says, stroking her hair. "The priority here is to get you feeling better and smiling again."

Alyssa wipes her eyes and I hand her a tissue. "My mom is coming," she says. "Tomorrow. I guess they might keep me for awhile."

"Well, that's good," Evelyn says. "You need your mom right now." There is a soft tug on my heart, only an echo, and then it's gone.

A nurse in cheerful pink scrubs knocks on the doorframe. "Hi, sorry to interrupt, but—"

Evelyn finishes for her. "Yes, we're just saying good night." She turns to Alyssa. "We'll be back to visit. It's been a long night, so get some sleep." We gently hug Alyssa and say goodbye, then quietly return to the waiting area. A middle-aged man in a tweed newsboy cap is pushing a wheezing elderly woman in a wheelchair through the sliding glass doors. He notices Chris, whose makeup hasn't smudged a bit despite the drama, and stares, pushing the woman into a potted ficus. One more Christmas visit to the emergency room, one more woman trapped in a man's body than he's probably seen in his life. We stand together near the entrance, collectively steamrolled by the night's events.

"When I got up this morning I never imagined I'd end up here by the end of the day," Chris says, clucking and shaking his head. "Poor thing."

"I think she'll be all right," I say. "But yeah, it was quite the surreal evening. Thanks for sharing it with me." It feels like a strange thing to say, but I'm at a loss. Emily Post never outlined the rules of etiquette when a guest attempts suicide at your dinner party, did she? I suspect if she had, flowers would be involved. Something cheerful yet elegant. Tulips, maybe?

"Our pleasure, honey," Chris says, patting my back the way my grandmother used to do.

Evelyn adjusts her purse. "Would anyone like to have coffee in the cafeteria?"

I can sense Erik balking.

"I would," I enthusiastically declare.

Erik sighs. "Hon, I'm tired," he says, a rind of irritation lining his voice. "I'd like to head out, get a good night's sleep."

"That's okay Erik, one of us can give Jaime a ride home," Chris says, and it's the most amazing thing, but I'm one hundred percent convinced I won't be robbed, beaten with a tire iron, and left for dead in a drainage ditch.

"Are you sure?" Erik asks.

"Of course," Evelyn adds. "It's no trouble at all."

Erik kisses my forehead and leaves me alone with two members of my brand-new surrogate family. I was surprised he left me so easily, with two virtual strangers, but then, it's been a night full of surprises.

When it's just the three of us—Chris, Evelyn, and me—we share a brief, self-conscious moment. We are completely aware that we are embarking on a strange, grand experiment. We are making it up as we go along. We are rafting Niagara Gorge without life vests, rock climbing without harnesses, eating pork that's still pink in the middle. All of which, strangely enough, feels the farthest from Death I've been in a long time.

Chapter 11
"I can see how it might be a little complex."

The hospital cafeteria is closed, though there is a vending area stocked with snacks and beverages, even a bulky machine that dispenses hot coffee, like a relic from the seventies. It's flanked by a cart containing cups, plastic stir-sticks, napkins, and packets of sugar and creamer. Evelyn, Chris, and I select Styrofoam cups and take our turns at the machine. I watch Chris patiently filling his cup. In his dress, wig, and tasteful makeup and modest jewelry, he's not outrageously fabulous like a drag queen; he looks classical, even conservative. You can tell he's a man, but when you absorb the quieter details—the demure way he carries himself, the way he truly listens to what you're saying—the overall effect isn't shocking. Without your glasses, you could mistake him for your cousin Jen, who actually played junior varsity football in high school and now repairs helicopters in Afghanistan. When we're stocked with our coffees and condiments, we sit at an empty table near a fake Christmas tree decked with silver and gold balls.

"I have to ask," I say, "Have either of you used Craigslist much?"

"I sold a desk on there once, but that's about it," Chris says.

"Me too," Evelyn adds. "I sold some furniture when I moved. No Missed Connections, none of that funny business." She tears open a tiny tub of hazelnut-flavored creamer and pours it into her coffee. "You? What inspired you to post that ad?"

I boil it down to the basics. "My mom died," I say, "my father left years ago, and I had a fight with my brother, my sister is just, I don't know, we don't talk ... and I just ... I needed ..." I struggle to say what is really a simple, desperate truth: *I wanted a family. A kind, warm, loving family of my own. The kind I never had, the kind I know is possible.*

Chris pats my forearm. "Say no more. I know exactly why you posted the ad."

Evelyn gives me a sympathetic look. "Well, I'm glad you found us, and I'm glad we found you," she says, still stirring her coffee.

"Me too," I say.

She blows gently on her steaming Styrofoam cup and takes a sip. "Feels kind of funny to decompress with a stimulant."

"An addictive one at that," Chris adds. His earrings jingle as he shakes a hard, caked packet of sugar to break up the crystals. "My goodness, this sugar has to be older than the pope."

"Are you Catholic, Chris?" I ask.

"I was raised Catholic, but I haven't been to church in years." He offers a wry smile. "I can't imagine *why.*"

I smile. "Same here." Mom had been a plucky, guitar-mass Catholic, less an embracer of all things fetal and more a *Social and Environmental Justice for Those Who Get Consistently Screwed by the Man* kind of gal. Myself, I'd been a *Fine, I'll Go to Church So You Don't Guilt Trip Me and I Can Have the Car Next Weekend* kind of person.

"Oh, will you look at us," Evelyn interjects. "Three lapsed Catholics. See how they run."

"You too, Evelyn?" Chris asks.

She shakes her head slowly, frowning. "I consistently gave up masturbation for Lent all through the seventies. What I wouldn't give to get those three hundred odd days back."

"Amen!" Chris says. I try to swallow my mouthful of coffee before I start laughing, but most of it ends up on my sleeve. I'm still laughing and coughing while Evelyn passes me a stack of napkins and Chris pats me on the back.

"Chris, forgive me for being so ignorant and frank," Evelyn begins, "but I'm fuzzy on the difference between 'transvestite,' 'transsexual,' and 'transgender.'" I'm glad she asked, because I'm a bit fuzzy on the details, too.

"Oh, it's fine. I get asked this all the time. At the most basic level, a transvestite is a man who dresses in women's clothing. Technically, a man can be a transvestite attracted to women. 'Transgender' is a much broader term used to describe a person whose gender identity differs from their birth sex. You could probably use 'transgender' and 'transsexual' interchangeably. I was born a man, yet I identify as a heterosexual woman. Though because I'm still in transition for a variety of reasons, the people I work with would probably consider me a gay man. But in my ex-boyfriend's eyes, I was all woman."

Evelyn is nodding her head slowly, squinting as if everything he said is written on an eye chart a mile away.

Chris smiles. "I can see how it might be a little complex."

Evelyn clucks her tongue. "Well, there you have it. My late Uncle Nelson suddenly makes so much more sense." She clears her throat. "So. Our dear girl Alyssa. It sounds like they'll admit her for treatment—"

"I certainly hope so," Chris says, wide-eyed.

"—and when they do," Evelyn continues, "I plan to come visit her. She needs to know there are people nearby who care what happens to her."

"I'll come, too," I say, feeling noble and altruistic and terrified of what I'm committing to all at once.

"Absolutely." Chris nods, like it was no question. We're quiet for a moment after the PA system interrupts us with a page for Dr. Franklin. "I tried to kill myself when I was younger," Chris adds.

I don't say, "So did I," because technically all I did was press a pink Gillette Daisy disposable razor to my wrist whenever the needle on the pressure-cooker of puberty swung into the red zone. I'd let my self-pity build and swirl into an impressive thunderhead of teen angst, a pathetic fit of woe-is-me, bang-your-head-on-the-piano, slide-onto-the-floor-and-lay-there despair that nearly completely dissipated when I got my driver's license and could see beyond the horizon of high school. Today they'd call me a cutter, prescribe a mood regulator or two, and set me up for regular chats with a therapist in pantsuits and a perm. Now I look back and think, what was all the fuss about? *I'll show them! I'll—I'll* SHAVE MY WRISTS!

"I'm so sorry, Chris," Evelyn says.

"I was fifteen, struggling with who I was, my gender, my sexuality, my urge to wear a dress to prom instead of a tux, the whole nine yards. I mean, you're basically just a kid, and you know something's wrong with you, you know you're different ... but no matter how hard you try to fit in, Jeff Simpson will always punch your head against your locker when he walks past, because he somehow also knows you will always prefer heels to loafers." He takes a sip of coffee, contemplative. "I swallowed pills too, like Alyssa. My mom found me.

"And you know," he continues, his voice rich and angry, "it didn't get easier. It's hard enough to finally be honest with yourself, and then you have to do the same with the people who think they know you best, whose personal happiness seems to depend on your own life remaining static. My father won't speak to me. My mother ..." here he trails off, lost in thought, ending abruptly with, "Enough. This is getting depressing. Evelyn? Tell us your tale of woe." It was good timing, because I was developing the urge to find a disposable razor.

"Well, it's not so bad, really." She tells us about her beloved husband Tom, who died two years ago, and their three children, all of whom seem incredibly self-involved. There's Bradley, a surgeon in Minneapolis; Kimberly, currently backpacking through South America; and Nick, who just moved to Idaho with her only grandchild—Chloe, age eight.

"Why Idaho?" I ask, genuinely curious.

"He had an opportunity to help a friend expand a big-game hunting outfit. I don't go for all that hunting nonsense, but he lives and breathes it. And now my Chloe is so far away."

"Poor kid's going to get so many potato jokes when she goes off to college," Chris frets.

"You say potato—"

"And I still say Idaho is too far away," Evelyn sighs. "Skype is no substitute for a real hug."

"Well," I say, "We're here with you tonight." I raise my coffee for a toast. "To family," I say. "Of origin, of choice, of the Holy Ghost." Evelyn and Chris raise their cups to mine.

"If fences make good neighbors, what makes a good family?" Evelyn muses.

"Lobotomies," Chris says.

"State lines and boxed wine," I say.

"Hospital coffee," Evelyn says, smiling. "With cream and sugar."

***

The next day Erik and I visit his father, Frank. The Pheasant Ridge Assisted Living Facility is built like a Viking Hall, with soaring ceilings above the communal living and dining areas. An easel displaying a Dry-Erase board greets us at the front door, announcing the day's schedule and menu: *Breakfast (pancakes, eggs, sausage, cling peaches) from 7 to 8:30, Arts & Crafts from 9 to 11, Lunch (meatloaf, mashed potatoes, corn, pudding) at 11:30, Tuba Dan at 1 pm, followed by Bingo at 2, Dinner (roast chicken, green beans, baked potato, and brownie) at 4:30.* "Seems like a lot of dessert in one day," I say to Erik. "A lot of sugar for people with Type II diabetes and whatnot." As much as my coworker Emily despises the word "moist," I despise the word "whatnot." But once in awhile it sneaks in. It's a crafty, multipurpose bastard.

The Christmas tree in the corner is decorated with paper chain garland and mismatched ornaments. It's nearly lunchtime, and you can still smell the pancakes and sausage served at breakfast. Every so often I also catch a whiff of that enzymatic spray you use when pets piddle on the rug. Most of the residents are in their private rooms, but a few are gathered in the common area, napping in their wheelchairs or staring at a show about wildlife in Africa. The announcer intones, "The regal Tendaji is nearly eighteen—a remarkable age for a lion in the wild. Unfortunately, this will likely be his last rainy season. Zuberi looks for any sign of weakness, waiting for his opening, beginning to challenge

Tendaji for his place as king of the pride. The vultures are already circling overhead."

"Wow," Erik dismally comments. "Was the euthanasia channel not coming in?" We pass one of the nursing assistants on our way to Frank's room. Erik smiles at her and asks brightly, "Hey, when will Tuba Dan be here?"

The girl, who can't be more than seventeen, clarifies. "Oh, Tuba Dan doesn't actually come here. We just tune into his show on the radio. The residents love him."

Erik laughs, incredulous. "You're kidding. They listen to Tuba Dan on the radio?"

She shrugs and smiles. "Sorry."

When she's out of earshot, he whispers, "That is so fucking depressing. And what's with the uniforms? Everyone who works here looks like they're at a slumber party."

"Would you prefer the staff don formalwear before helping the elderly to the toilet?" I ask. But now that he mentions it, it appears that at least the dozing residents parked in the common room *are* at a slumber party, right down to the *Light as a feather, stiff as a board.*

Erik is surly because he doesn't like coming here, of course. The last time we visited, Frank furtively showed me a large jar of pennies he pulled from the depths of his closet and said, "I'm hiding this for safekeeping. Don't let anyone know where it is. They all try to steal from me." There is now a mysterious and mildly malicious "they" or "them" in Frank's world, trying to steal his pennies, his keepsakes, or his long-gone wife, who Frank recently informed us "whored it up with every man in town." Erik's late mother never wore makeup and frowned at even a suggestion of recreational sex on television, so her "whoring it up" back in the day is fairly unlikely.

Erik's father is in his early seventies. He and his wife married later in life, with barely enough time to have Erik before gearing up for retirement. After Erik's mother died, Frank began to dissolve. "I'm rudderless," he'd forlornly say when calling to thank us for the casserole we'd brought him, sometimes holding back tears over a dead sparrow he'd found on his front porch or the new planned subdivision he read about in the paper, the one that would raze the field he'd hunted rabbits in decades earlier. When he started pouring birdseed in the water softener and forgetting to take his medication, once even waving a knife and threatening to kill Erik when he came over to fix a leaky faucet, we knew it was time to make the arrangements that most people don't have to make for their parents until they're much older.

After a full two minutes of knocking, Frank finally shuffles to his door with his walker. "Hi, Dad," Erik says, steeling himself. "Merry Christmas! How are you?"

"It's Christmas?" Frank runs a hand through his thin hair, confused. He's freshly shaved and dressed in clean beige slacks and a plaid button-down shirt, all positive signs.

"It was Christmas yesterday. We're here to take you to lunch."

"Where are we going?"

"The Viking Hall," Erik says, referring to the cavernous Pheasant Ridge dining room. Frank smiles and adjusts one of his hearing aids; it's a joke he does seem to remember. We're always overly solicitous with my father-in-law, speaking too slowly, enunciating too loudly the way the goofy sitcom character does when speaking to foreigners or the disabled.

The dining area is already half-filled with wrinkled residents by the time we make it down the hall, and we claim a table near the cafeteria pass-thru. "They're trying to kill me," Frank whispers as we sit down.

Erik sighs. "Who's trying to kill you, Dad?"

Frank narrows his eyes at his neighbors: at their tufts of white hair, their shoulders hunched with osteoporosis. "All of them."

"Well, that would be truly creepy if they were all trying to kill you, but I think you're safe."

"For now."

One of the kitchen staff pushes a cart loaded with trays of food to our table. A shiny laminated badge dangles from a lanyard around her neck. "I hope you're hungry, Frank! We're having one of your favorites today. Sara's special meatloaf!"

She sets a tray before him, but he only stares at it. "Are you two having lunch as well?" she asks us.

"Yes, thank you," I say, and we're also given trays of bland, institutional food.

"Mmmm!" Erik says theatrically, rubbing his hands together and grinning at the wad of instant mashed potatoes centering his plate. I laugh.

After our server moves on to the next table, Frank leans over to his son and says, "There's a darkie. That colored gal." He points at the woman pushing the cart. "She's a darkie, all right."

"Jesus Christ, Dad." Erik turns red and pushes Frank's bony finger down. A feeling of horrified excitement rises in me. "You can't say that."

Frank smiles and begins picking at his meatloaf. "I can so."

"Promise me you won't call her that again? People don't say that anymore. It's racist."

"Fine, fine, go on, leave me be." Frank scowls, but takes a few bites of meatloaf. His hands are all gnarled, spotted knuckle. Hardworking hands that once knew how to change a spark plug, swing an axe, mince a shallot for an omelet. He suddenly looks up from his plate, startled, the last thirty minutes wiped clean from his memory. He has no idea who we are again. "Who are you?"

"I'm your son, Erik. You're my father. Eat your carrots."

I put on a happy face, attempt to lighten the mood with some dark humor. "Whooooo are you? Who-who, who-who?" I sing softly, channeling Roger Daltrey. I can get away with this because we've been asked this question so many times. The first few times left us stunned, broken, scrambling for a response. Now we've come around to meeting it head-on with simple facts and twisted jokes. *Fuck you, Alzheimer's Disease.* Frank resumes eating, albeit at a snail's pace, and we join in.

"I told you I'm planning to visit Alyssa in the hospital on Tuesday, right? With Evelyn, Chris, and Paul." I butter half a roll. "Do you want to come?"

Erik lowers his fork and rolls his eyes. "Jaime, for real? You're really going to keep up with this?"

"What do you mean, 'Keep up with this?'"

"You can't make a new family out of total strangers."

I look around at the residents clustered together at tables, widows and widowers sharing another daily meal together and discussing the new pain in their hip, critiquing the pudding, perhaps sharing their excitement about the Tuba Dan show. I wonder how often their children and grandchildren visit. Sure, there may be the lucky few who get weekly visits, but my money's on "yearly at best" and "utterly obligatory" for most of them. "People do it all the time," I say. "*The Golden Girls* did it."

"They were also menopausal characters on a TV show," Erik says.

At this point Frank suddenly attempts to tell us a story, but he has trouble remembering so many words that we have no idea what he's trying to tell us. It seems to involve a man of Polish origin and a wheel of cheese, but it could just as easily have been about an Orthodox Jew with a talent for juggling. Erik tries to fill in the gaps ("They ran the store, Dad? Oh, it was an Oldsmobile?"), but eventually his father gives up, frustrated, scanning the room with his cloudy, distant eyes, searching for an exit. Occasionally during these visits I feel a surprising sense of relief that Frank isn't altogether there upstairs, because if one were completely aware of these surroundings at all times, one would feel a strong urge to steer one's Hoveround into oncoming traffic. If Frank were more lucid, he'd probably answer every polite inquiry about his well-being with, "Just waiting to die, thanks." I can see it in some of the residents' eyes: *perhaps the Eskimos were onto something with that whole ice floe business. Also, will you please get me the hell out of here?*

Sometimes on the drive home after these visits Erik darkly says, "When I'm old and senile and have to wear a diaper, promise you'll take me in the backyard and shoot me. Just dig a hole and toss me in."

"Okay," I always say, though we don't own a gun and I doubt I'll have the strength to dig a hole of his size when I'm in my eighties.

***

Erik and I both know that he loves me a little bit more than I love him. I can say this because once he even told me, after a late night out with friends. "I know I love you more than you love me, but that's okay." The vulnerable, unpleasant honesty of his statement made my cheeks burn.

"That's not true," I lied, and we fell asleep. I knew he was fishing for reassurance. I did love him, and I wanted to go to sleep, so I stretched the truth enough to cover both bases. In the middle of the night, after you've both been drinking, you must never tell your spouse that you love him slightly less than he loves you. Or that the sight of him shirtless, once thrilling, now reminds you of your first training bra. Until recently, our arrangement has felt like an insurance policy. I was pretty sure he would never suddenly pack his Volkswagen and disappear in the middle of the night or return from a business trip with gonorrhea, though lately I've started to secretly wish he would develop something of a wandering eye. Well, maybe not that exactly. Not long ago we went to see a friend's band play at Flannigan's Pub. They invited Erik onstage to sing a few old favorites they'd played in high school, back when Erik was still in the band and they practiced in his parents' garage. And even though they were guys in their mid to late thirties who worked day jobs at insurance companies and office supply stores, even though some of them were already taking medication to lower their cholesterol, even though they were covering Foreigner and Rush (badly), women in the crowd locked eyes with them over their drinks, wagged their hips, smiled and flirted! With my husband! After the show we had sex in the car, still parked behind the bar. It was the first truly hot sex we'd had in years, though Erik was afraid we'd be caught and kept glancing nervously around the parking lot.

Another time while Erik was lying on the couch watching TV I snuck up and slapped him on the cheek, just hard enough. "Ow!

What'd you do that for?" Shocked and angry, he drew a hand to his face and scowled at me.

"To see what you'd do," I simply said, surprised and ashamed at my own restless audacity. I tried to turn it into a playful wrestling match, but I'd actually pissed him off. The truth is, I was trying to provoke him from his happy complacency. Why was he so content? So secure? I wanted in on the deal. Whenever something like this happened, the little routines of our life together would eventually scour away my sharp edges, and I'd remember that our marriage, with him as the rock, kept me from floating off into space entirely.

Trouble is rocks can also crush you, if they're big enough. If you're not careful. If they love you a little bit more than you love them.

***

When we prepare to leave after lunch, Frank tearfully stands with the support of his walker. He reaches out to touch Erik's sleeve with a shaking, bony hand. "Take me with you. I want to go with you. Please."

Erik's face crumples. "Sorry, Dad. I can't. You have to stay here. But we'll come see you again soon, I promise."

"No! I want to leave. I need to go with you!" His voice echoes in the dining hall.

The young nurse's aide approaches, worried. "Frank? Can I help you back to your room?"

He swats her away. "No. I don't live here. I'm going home."

She firmly takes his elbow to guide him back to his room. "Mr. Collins, you do live here. Your son will be back to see you very soon."

Frank looks down at his comfortable, orthopedic shoes. When he looks up, we are strangers again. "Who are you?"

Erik takes a deep, brave breath. He extends a hand, which his father hesitantly shakes. "Erik Collins. It was so nice having lunch with you."

We overhear Frank talking to the aide as we walk away. "What a nice young couple."

And in this way, we are able to leave.

Chapter 12
"I called him 'The Rapist.'"

By the kind of miracle that usually only applies to Olympic hockey teams or crippled children from Lourdes, I convince Erik to not only come with me to visit Alyssa in the hospital, but to also give Paul a ride, since his van is in the shop. Unfortunately, we get lost trying to find his house, circling the one-way streets around the well-lit Capitol dome and wasting ten minutes after a wrong turn on John Nolan Drive.

It's been said that Madison is the Berkeley of the Midwest. Twenty square miles surrounded by reality. It's not so easy to see why in winter, when the hippies are all discussing Howard Zinn indoors, warmed by a fleet of burning incense, but it's much easier in the summer. Particularly during the Farmers' Market on The Square every Saturday. Last summer, while buying some of my favorite cheddar at the market (well-aged, white, from pastured cows, speckled with the ammonia-scented salt crystals Erik and I blissfully call "crunchies"... as in, "Oooh, get the cheese with crunchies!"), I watched a man dressed like Benjamin Franklin approach a group of protestors on the lawn of the Capitol. He handed them a piece of paper and shouted, "In case you missed the memo, the sixties are over!" We all booed him. If he wanted well-behaved citizens in polo shirts and flag pins, he could move to Waukesha. Somebody shouted back, "Go fly a kite in a lightning storm!"

Madison has not one, but *two* Nepalese restaurants on State Street—the only two in the entire state. If you asked anyone living north of Madison if they've ever had Nepalese, they'd probably reply, "I think so. But I took some antibiotics and it cleared right up."

There's a formula somewhere: once you hit X number of tattooed, pierced street performers accompanied by adorable dogs, once someone dressed as a dragon, werewolf, or giant mushroom has been observed chasing teenagers down the main drag at least X number of times, your city must adopt the tourism slogan, "Keep (City in Question) Weird!" Madison should have tripped that trigger by now, with the accompanying bumper stickers and t-shirts for sale at venues around the city. Even the *squirrels*, inbred from years of street-locked living on the grounds around the Capitol, are weird. I can't look at them without thinking of banjos and crutches.

By the time we find Paul's house, we're twenty minutes late and Erik is ready to "turn the car around and go home." Paul lives in a house that appears to have been designed by Mike Brady: a quad-level straight from 1978, with a magnificent outdoor swag chandelier suspended by chain rope over the front door. I hope the kitchen is decorated in shades of harvest gold and avocado. I'll be disappointed if the living room carpet is anything other than orange shag. Unfortunately, we won't get to see the interior design tonight, because Paul is outside in adult-sized snow pants and a parka, arguing with an older neighbor in a tasseled knit cap. After Erik parks in the driveway, Paul waddles over to greet us. "Thanks for picking me up. I'll be right with you." And then he returns to his property line to resume the heated discussion with his neighbor, who is shouting and gesturing wildly. If the neighbor were holding an axe instead of a snow shovel, we'd probably be witnesses to a brutal murder.

Erik frowns in confusion. "What the hell is this?" He puts a hand on the horn, ready to honk, but before he can do so, Paul returns and heaves himself into the backseat.

"Sorry about that."

"Everything okay?"

"Oh, sure!" Paul says blithely, unzipping his parka. "That's my neighbor. He's a really great guy." He doesn't elaborate further, and Erik gives me The Wary Face: one eyebrow raised, lips pursed crookedly. Paul suddenly sits forward and asks, "Hey, you guys? Do you mind if we hit the drive-thru at Taco Bell? I could really use a run for the border."

Erik surprises me with his genial, accommodating response: "No problem." Actually, I'm not that surprised, because there's something about Paul that lulls you into a gleeful, anticipatory calm. You settle down a little, distracted from the current crop of anxieties humming through your mind, because here is a person that is unpredictable, nuttier than your Uncle Pete, and entertaining as hell. You can't help but sit back, relax, have a Coke and a smile. You can't wait to see what he'll say or do next.

In the winter, the city actually glows orange at night from the sodium-vapor street lights reflecting off the snow, bringing to mind John Boehner's face, or a pack of dancing Oompa Loompas if you're less politically inclined. We find some relief from the alien hue with a brief foray onto the beltline, from which Erik exits near the first Taco Bell we see. In the drive-thru, Erik rolls down the window and Paul leans forward to shout into the microphone: "I'll have a chicken-chock-tock ... a chickatock-sock ... a chockasoft ... fuck it, I'll have a bean burrito. And a cheese quesadilla. And some hot sauce." He sits back, but then quickly leans forward again. "And fifteen napkins!"

Erik clears his throat and adds, "and I'll have a Beef Chalupa Supreme and a Cheesy Gordita Crunch." He turns to me and asks if I want anything. When I say no, he asks if I can drive while he eats.

I sigh dramatically as Erik pulls ahead to the window. "Fine."

"Jeez, I'm not asking you to donate a kidney here," he says while we do a quick Chinese fire drill to switch seats. Paul chuckles heartily, which will only encourage Erik to be more of a pain in the ass. I roll my eyes while I hand them their jalapeno- and desperation-scented bags. I just wanted to visit someone in the hospital, clean and simple, and now I'm driving the parade float for the Standard American Diet, Taco Tuesday edition.

I hate when Erik eats fast food. I also hate when he sneaks cigarettes, drinks too much, fails to eat anything of plant origin in a forty-eight-hour period, and exercises so infrequently that opening a tough jar leaves his shoulder tender the following morning. Maybe I'm expecting too much, but when you're a grown man who won't eat fruit unless your wife cuts it up for you, it could indicate a problem.

I wasn't such a stickler for healthy habits until three things happened: Erik turned forty, his father's brain began to dissolve through the horrible alchemy of Alzheimer's, and my mother was diagnosed with Stage IIIc ovarian cancer. There's nothing like watching a loved one eaten alive by disease to remind you that we're all loaded guns, just walking around, oblivious to the imminent blast. Genetics filled the chamber, and our environment and daily choices are the itchy fingers conspiring to pull the trigger. I can't do a thing about my genes at this point, but the daily choices? Those I can work on. I know I sometimes drink too much, and I'm not exactly the poster child for Pilates and juicing, but I do pack salads for lunch. I take the stairs, I say no to the Cheesy Gordita Crunch when I'd rather say yes. I know I can't cheat death, but maybe I can avoid carting around a wheeled canister of oxygen in my golden years. Pushing my husband around in a wheelchair, however ... that outcome is up to him. Sometimes I think of our marriage like this: Erik and I are in a rowboat, but I'm the only one paddling, so we go nowhere. We turn in circles. Constipated Erik and his nagging wife, round and round they go. And then I remind myself that without Erik, my computer would be completely hobbled by viruses, the floor would still be squishy in my mother's guest bathroom, and I'd be dead or comatose after a massive car accident because I was driving at night with both headlights burned out. "She didn't know ... *how to change them*," Frankie would sob in the ICU, one of my only visitors because, as we've covered earlier, Clint and Gwen are assholes.

When we arrive at the hospital, I'm pleased to see that Evelyn and Chris are already there. We hug, as if we're old friends. Chris is wearing a flattering wrap dress checkered in blue and beige with matching high-heeled leather slouch boots—I recognize them as a Rachel Zoe pick, a pricey pair I regretfully clicked past on piperlime.com because my salary and the fact that one day I want to live in my very own house *without* a pink acrylic bathtub or painful memories have perpetually restricted me to the "Girl on a Budget" page. I greet him with, "Chris, I hate you because you're wearing the boots I wanted *and* you look fabulous in them."

"And I love you for saying that!"

I can't wait until Chris and I are comfortable enough to greet each other with things like, "That shade of lipstick really brings out your eyes…what's it called, Burnt Labia?" or "Love the new highlights, you Supercuts Slut!"

In the elevator to the second floor, Evelyn smiles at Paul. "How are the dogs doing?"

"Oh, they're terrific, though Abe's been a little gassy this week. My sister is dog sitting tonight."

"Does she live in Madison, too?"

"No, she lives in Mount Horeb. She used to be the Head Brewmaster at The Grumpy Troll, but she quit to raise heritage breed chickens and start her own mead brewery."

"Mead, huh?" Erik says, nodding approvingly. If he had more ambition and cared less what others think of him, he would attend the annual Bristol Renaissance Faire in a kilt with some of the guys he works with, tearing turkey from a drumstick with his teeth and calling every woman in earshot a wench; instead, he indulges his inner Viking/Scotsman by reading George R.R. Martin, occasionally listening to Norwegian death metal, and now, hitting the Medieval nerd trifecta by revealing an appreciation for mead.

"Hey, I'll hook you up. You haven't had mead until you've had my sister's."

I'm taken aback by how filthy this sounds. "I don't think Erik's ever had mead, actually."

"Yes, I have!" Erik insists. "In college. I had some in college."

I smile patiently.

He whispers, "I've tried mead before, *Dear*. You don't know everything about me."

I know Erik's irritated when he calls me 'Dear.' "Me too," I say. "I had Mead notebooks every year in grade school."

Erik rolls his eyes, and Paul lets out a one-note laugh, like a harsh clap: "HA!" He follows this with, "Would you like some cheese with your crackers?" He looks back and forth at us, waiting for the Big Laughs, and his excitement slides into disappointment as he realizes he mucked up the punch line. "No. Wait. I mean, crackers with your cheese?" He smiles again and nods, pleased to have righted the ship.

Evelyn checks in with the on-duty nurse at the front desk, and we're ushered into the psychiatric unit's common area to wait for Alyssa. Several patients are playing checkers or cards, some are watching *Jeopardy!*, others are chatting with visitors in blue-upholstered chairs and sofas clustered in cozy conversation groupings. Nobody looks particularly crazy or drugged except the on-duty nurse, who has the vacant, traumatized stare of a battle-weary soldier or new parent.

After we sit down, Paul, still stuffed in his adult snow pants (though his coat is open), reaches into his satchel and pulls out a carton of eggs. "Did you guys bring gifts?"

"You're giving her a dozen eggs?" Erik asks, both appalled and oddly delighted by the idea. "What's she going to do with a dozen eggs in the hospital?"

Paul shrugs. "Truly fresh eggs don't require immediate refrigeration."

"Are they from your sister's chickens?" Chris politely asks.

"Yes. I'll probably be getting eggs for the rest of you once we get closer to spring and they begin laying more frequently. But you have to remember to crack them into a separate bowl, because my sister does have a rooster. Once I accidentally added a chicken embryo to a loaf of zucchini bread."

"I sent her some flowers yesterday," I say, feeling cheap because I'd used a coupon and gone with delivery so I wouldn't have to pay inflated gift shop prices.

"Do you think she'll like this?" Evelyn asks, pulling a fluffy, bright purple scarf from her purse.

"Oh, it's beautiful! Did you make that?" I reach over to touch it. "So soft!"

She nods while Chris and I admire her handiwork. "I can teach you how, if you like."

"Thanks, but I don't even have the patience to set the DVR."

"I got her a spa gift card," Chris says.

"Hi guys." Alyssa suddenly enters the day room, smiling broadly, blushing at her wealth of visitors. "I'm so touched you all came."

"Of course we would," Evelyn says, enveloping her in a generous, maternal hug.

We all get a hug, and when we're seated again, Paul presents her with the eggs. "Thank you so much," she says, laughing. "This is awesome! I'll see if there's a fridge I can store them in." Next she admires Evelyn's hand-knit scarf.

Chris gets down to business. "Are you doing okay, honey? How long are they keeping you?"

"I have four more days of inpatient therapy, followed by a few months of outpatient treatment. It's really not so bad here. The food's decent, and my therapist has a good sense of humor."

"I once knew this guy who was a therapist," Paul contributes. "I called him 'The Rapist.'"

We all ignore this. "Did your mother come?" Evelyn asks.

"She'll be here 'til the end of the week." Alyssa murmurs a quick hello to a passing patient before continuing. "I still feel horrible for how everything ... you know. I reached my breaking point, I guess. I have no idea what I was thinking. I wasn't, I guess. But thank you for being so kind. You barely even know me."

It was the human, decent thing to do, though I don't say this. Also, in a strange way, I feel partially responsible. Hadn't I approved that fourth bottle of wine? Then again, if she hadn't been with us on Christmas night, maybe she'd be dead.

"My lab mates haven't visited, but my roommate sent flowers."

"Did you get mine?" I ask, secretly hoping my bouquet was fresher and fuller and feeling like an asshole because this is a concern to me.

"Yes, thank you. They're beautiful. First thing I see when I wake up." Her expression clouds for a moment, and I can't tell if she's remembering that her late boyfriend used to be the first thing she saw when she woke up, or she's alarmed to have come *this close* to never waking up again in the morning, or she actually hates my bouquet because it contains daisies and carnations that have been dyed colors that don't exist in nature.

As we continue to visit, making talk both large and small, something wonderful and strange happens. We forget that we just met, and we forget how we met. While Chris animatedly regales us with amusing and awkward anecdotes only a transsexual can share, he becomes the funny and wise older sister trapped in a man's body I never had. While Evelyn describes the trip she saved five years to take with two friends—a trek to Everest Base Camp South, she is transformed into the strong, spirited great-aunt I never met. While Paul lists his top ten movies of all time plus his detailed rationale for their rankings, he becomes the quirky, endearing younger brother I always wanted. As Alyssa tells us about rescuing her family dog Pooch, she morphs into the tenderhearted, sensitive younger sister I wish I had. And while Erik laughs or simply listens, he becomes the husband I'm glad I married. The husband I extend my hand to on the ride home, the husband I harmonize with to The Beatles' "In My Life," smiling out the window at the velvet night sky so he doesn't mistake the tears in my eyes for tears of sadness.

Chapter 13

"Give my best to Ryan Seacrest."

"I don't think he's after my money."

"Evelyn! The very fact you said that to me makes him suspect." For the last twenty minutes, Evelyn and I have been eating stuffed mushrooms and tiny meatballs from paper plates balanced on our knees, discussing her love life. She's seeing a man ten years her junior. His name is Carl Anderson. Listening to her gush about him, you'd almost believe that dating a partially divorced, unemployed former Eagle Scout with a latex allergy was the romantic equivalent of scoring free, front-row tickets to *The Book of Mormon* on Broadway. If there's a difference between honest optimism and sugarcoated denial, Evelyn doesn't seem to know it. "The fact that you met him at water aerobics also makes him suspect, though for a different reason," I add.

We're at a New Year's Eve party at Paul's house. The party is well-attended by dozens of interesting-looking people I'll be getting to know later, after another martini or two. I define "interesting" in this case as the strong possibility that at least six of them have grown up on communes. We'd also been invited to attend Frankie's annual New Year's Eve bash, but I wasn't feeling up to the drive to Appleton.

Frankie was disappointed. "But you missed it last year, too! Don't you want to stay up 'til 3 a.m. playing Scattergories?"

"Not really." I hadn't told her about the responses to my ad, or the fact that I'd vetted and shared Christmas dinner with four of them, or that one of them attempted suicide mid-meal, or that I'd already committed to spending New Year's Eve at a party hosted by the one in the KISS Army to also celebrate the release of my other new, suicidal friend from inpatient treatment at the Alliant Medical Center.

So I told her.

"Holy crap," she said. If she were the whistling kind, she might have added a long, low whistle. "I can't believe you went through with it!" I made her promise not to tell our other friends until I had a chance to, because I couldn't believe I went through with it, either. "When can I meet them?" she asked, and I told her we'd all go to dinner the next time she was in town, though that could be months from now and who knows what might happen in the interim?

I am pleased to report that not only does Paul's house have orange shag carpeting in the den, harvest gold appliances in the kitchen, and a wood-paneled den stuffed with KISS memorabilia, but the living room has a fully-carpeted ring of built-in seating around the fireplace—his own mini-stadium from which to watch guests roast marshmallows or burst into spontaneous wrestling matches. Erik nodded his approval during the tour. "Nice rape pit you got here."

Paul was unfazed. "You think this is something, wait'll you see the bomb shelter in the back yard." He went on to tell us he suspected the house was haunted because he sometimes heard noises late at night.

"Is it Barry Manilow and the ghostly clinking of keys in a bowl?" I asked, grinning madly at my own joke.

"No," Paul answered ominously, "sometimes I hear a chainsaw, followed by muffled, tortured screaming. It happens probably once a month or so, always at four thirty-two in the morning. It's faint, but really quite off-putting."

At that point, I excused myself to visit the buffet, where I ran into Evelyn. "I love the novelty plates," she said. The plates featured a Western theme with pictures of boots, lassos, and a fringed cowboy hat—a curious choice for a New Year's party.

"Yahoo," I said, plucking a cherry tomato with a pair of tongs.

We wove our way through the crowd, found a place to sit, and began to talk. After Evelyn tells me about Carl, she asks if I want to meet him.

"Sure," I say, though now I'm slightly biased because I've already cast him as the clichéd charismatic younger man with a history of swindling affection and money from lonely older women. "Tell me again ... he's separated from his wife? Have either of them filed divorce papers?"

"Yes," she simply says, and changes the subject. "Is this endive or radicchio?" she asks, lifting a small red leaf stuffed with a dollop of creamy green paste. Abe waddles over and begs before us, his skinny little tail whipping joyfully back and forth. I sneak him a bit of meatball, which he wolfs down.

"Radicchio, I think." I don't pursue my line of questioning, because Evelyn is a smart cookie. I'm sure she's perfectly capable of managing her own private business. "Hey, how are your allergies?"

"I took a few Benadryl earlier," she says. "As long as I don't touch the dogs, I should be okay."

"Oh, I couldn't think of a worse fate!" I say, leaning down to scratch Abe behind the ears. He blissfully leans into my hand. I'm distracted from my thoughts when I suddenly notice—really notice—what the guests are all wearing. "Is this actually a costume party?"

A quick survey of the living room (excuse me—"rape pit") reveals the following clothing items: a denim zippered jumpsuit paired with a mint-green ascot, a tweed jacket with leather elbow patches, what appears to be an authentic Members Only jacket matched with tapered acid-washed jeans, black and white-striped spandex leggings, rainbow suspenders, a floral apron, a baggy sweatshirt with the neckline ripped to strategically bare a shoulder, and an honest-to-God silk caftan, which I should point out is worn by Chris. All we're missing are lederhosen and a billowy pair of Zubaz pants in a zebra print. Altogether, they'd make for a clever scavenger hunt.

As Paul marches past with a roll of paper towels tucked under his arm, I flag him down. "Hey Paul, is this a costume party?"

"Not really. I told people they could come as their favorite TV or movie characters if they wanted." He appraises my dress, which has a pointed Peter Pan collar that had me reaching for my credit card the instant I saw it online. "Peggy Olson?"

I laugh, secretly pleased. "No, Jaime Collins."

He turns to Evelyn. "Meryl Streep in *Prime?*"

"Evelyn Richards in *Whatever Works.*" She sneezes heartily and Paul passes her a sheet of paper towel.

"Huh. I didn't see that one." He zooms off again while Evelyn blows her nose.

"He is such a character," Evelyn muses, smiling.

"Yes, but which one?"

We watch Alyssa chat with one of the partygoers, a man who seems to be emulating a less repulsive, recently deceased zombie from *The Walking Dead*. Or perhaps he's just tired and slovenly.

"How do you think she's doing?" Evelyn asks, apologetically showing Auschie her empty hands after he puts an imploring paw on her knee. "I have no food, puppy. All gone." He's been patiently sitting at our feet for the last ten minutes, watching our every bite.

"See, that's why he's so skinny," I say, stealthily passing him an eraser-sized nib of cheddar, which he delicately takes from my fingers.

"He's got your number."

"Don't let me feed them anymore. I'm going to get in trouble." I return to the question at hand. "Alyssa seems okay. What do you think?"

"It's hard to tell." We study her for a few minutes. I'd wish for more experience with this sort of thing so I knew how best to support a friend in peril, but then I'd have to face big questions about my own ability to set healthy boundaries and make competent decisions.

"We'll have to keep an eye on her," Evelyn says. "I don't know if she has many friends in Madison."

"If she does," I add, "they're not very good ones. I am glad to see she's not drinking tonight."

She sees us looking at her, smiles, and gives a shy, surreptitious wave. Evelyn and I wave back. "Okay, now she knows we're talking about her," I say through clenched teeth and a frozen smile.

Chris minces over on three-inch heels and says, "Did you know this is a costume party? Some guy in a bowler hat and black eye just came up to me and shouted, '*The Crying Game!*'" Pinkie extended, he takes a perturbed sip of his martini.

"Better than *Silence of the Lambs*," I point out.

"I think you're much more Felicity Huffman in *Transamerica*," Evelyn says. "Classy and sweet."

Chris pats her shoulder. "Oh, bless your heart." If Frankie were here with me, she'd build a layer of liquid courage and ask Chris—not rudely, but with sincere, genuine curiosity—what he does with his penis. But she's not here, and the question shall go unasked by me. If I had to guess, I'd venture some sort of discreet folding, a type of genital origami that Erik might describe as "rocking the tuck." It's all a bit much to imagine, but you can't help yourself.

"Hey, has anyone seen Erik?"

"He's been in the bathroom for the last ten minutes. Something about the crab dip not agreeing with him?"

Uh-oh. "How long 'til midnight?"

Evelyn glances at her watch. "Fifteen minutes."

Last year, Erik and I welcomed the New Year with my mother—just the three of us. We rented movies and played Scrabble. Instead of champagne, I made organic smoothies from kale, kiwi, flax, and apple, which we gamely drank in the crystal flutes my mother had received years earlier as a wedding gift. Lulled by the twinkling white lights on the tree, Mom and I fell asleep on the couch by eleven. Erik watched the ball drop on TV by himself while the snow fell in soft clumps outside. Everything felt different when I woke the next morning, still on the couch. I was the first one up. *This is the year I'll lose her,* I remember thinking as I made coffee, which was a sad way to greet such a fresh new day—the first day of a brand new year, the whole world draped in pristine, white snow. A perfect clean slate.

When I was younger, my Aunt Karen threw the New Year's parties, at which Clint, Gwen, and I would surf-sled in the backyard with our cousins and sneak the holiday treats laid out buffet-style for the adults: caviar served with a tiny silver spoon, lye-scented pickled herring, Swedish meatballs skewered on colored toothpicks, and the e.coli delight everyone called "Cannibal Sandwiches"—raw hamburger served on cocktail rye and doused in pepper. At one of these parties I walked in on my mother slow-dancing with the neighbor's husband in Karen's darkened bedroom. I'd been dispatched there to retrieve my Uncle Harry's winter coat when I discovered them, shifting quietly back and forth in the shadows, a scene more intimate and confusing than if I'd found them naked on the coat pile. I retreated quietly, closing the door behind me, and told my uncle that I couldn't find his jacket. If he also walked in on them, he never said. Later we all gathered in the living room to count the final ten seconds until the New Year with Dick Clark. Afterwards we went home like nothing had happened, nothing beyond the flipping of another calendar page. I stopped playing with dolls after that. Adulthood made less and less sense the closer I got to it, and suddenly the dress rehearsals weren't nearly as fun.

I knock on the door to Paul's guest bathroom. "Erik? Are you in there?"

There is a long pause. Then, a pained, "Yeah."

"Are you all right?"

"I don't know." There is another long pause. "Don't eat the crab dip!" Followed by a quieter, observant, "Hey, there are skylights in here."

"It's almost midnight."

"Give my best to Ryan Seacrest."

"Can I get you anything?"

"Yes. You can reverse time so I can go back forty minutes and not eat the crab dip."

"Okay. I'm on it." I scribble my nails on the door. "Love you. Don't fall in."

"Love you, too. Don't leave without me."

I wouldn't, but I will ring in the New Year without him. Alyssa stands next to me as we count down to midnight. We shout the numbers together, *FIVE ... FOUR ... THREE ... TWO*, really getting into it, noisemakers ratcheting as they spin in our fists. We are ready for something amazing to happen. We are ready for our clean slate.

Chapter 14

"Have you considered a restraining order?"

We are entering my least favorite time of year in Wisconsin—that frozen, dreary long night that lasts from January to March from which we will stagger in April, our skin pale, our pupils dilated, our muscles atrophied. But I always get a dose of perspective when I consider, usually while I'm shut-in during a three-day howler piling snowdrifts against the front door, that the Woodland Indians who once called Wisconsin home lived through this shit in wigwams and moccasins, subsisting on nothing but withered parsnips and raccoon jerky.

My least favorite holidays also fall during this stretch of time. Unless I'd planned on buying a mattress during the President's Day sale at WG&R, there is nothing in these months I look forward to more than the end of Daylight Saving Time, when we can set our clocks ahead and actually see the sun on our commutes home from work. It's like the Great Leap Forward, without the mass murder.

My students returned from winter break with attitudes, as if they'd been at Magic Kingdom with their grandparents and came back home to brussels sprouts and grout that needed scrubbing with a toothbrush. Nonetheless, we all hunkered down to tackle the work at hand, really slogging through it, each day a grueling academic triathlon. Reading, writing, and 'rithmetic followed by an orange slice and collapse.

For a break in the monotony and a reminder that it was actually possible for sweat to bead on a person's upper lip, Chris and I made plans to visit the Bolz Conservatory at Olbrich Botanical Gardens two weeks after Paul's party.

"You know the cops came after you and Erik left the party, right?" he asks me, pointing out a family of quail pecking in the underbrush. We are wandering through the tropical dome, delighting in the humidity and the fact that bananas and cacao are growing in Wisconsin in January, right before our very eyes.

"No way! Who called them?"

"I think it was Paul's neighbor. He told me that his neighbor actually sets out baited coyote traps just over the property line, in case Abe and Auschie dig under the fence."

"That's terrible!" I say. "And here Paul told me his neighbor was a great guy."

"If by 'great' he actually meant 'totally sadistic and unreasonable.'" Chris stops to examine an orchid, and a woman frowns at him, steering her gape-mouthed toddler around Chris in a wide berth. "Hi there," he says lightly. The woman ignores him, but her son gives us a toothy smile and waves one chubby fist. I suddenly feel protective of Chris. Do people really think he'd choose to be so different, so out of step with the conventions of society? Do they think he woke up one morning in middle school and said, "What a beautiful day! I think I'll put on my sister's pleated skirt and purposely ostracize myself, because nothing delights me more than hostile stares from complete strangers, cracked ribs, and combing chewed gum from my hair."

I link arms with Chris and we cross the bridge over the koi pond, looking down at the hundreds of pennies gleaming at the bottom of the pool, magnified by the clear water. We pause for a moment to watch the fish swim ponderously by. They're fat and sleek, dappled orange and white like elegant, piscine Dreamsicles. While I watch, mesmerized by the shifting underwater patterns of their shadows, I wonder if I'd eat them if I were hungry enough. Alton Brown pops into my head and says, "Good eats!" I reach in my purse and retrieve two dimes. I hand one to Chris. "Make a wish."

He closes his eyes for a moment, then opens them and tosses his dime. I wonder if he's wearing false eyelashes or uses Latisse. Either way, I'm envious. I make my own wish and toss my coin. Together, they break the skin of the water with soft *plops* and seesaw down, flashing as they catch the light. "What'd you wish for?" I ask.

"I can't tell you, or it won't come true," he says coyly. At that moment his phone rings, to "You Keep me Hanging On," by The Supremes. "It's my ex." He looks at me, eyes pleading, as if asking permission to answer. But I won't grant it. Because earlier, over lunch at The Great Dane, Chris told me all about his recent breakup with his boyfriend of three years, David.

Let's play a word game. You say, "Chris's ex," and I'll throw out the first words I think of. Ready? Okay, my turn. "Abusive, manipulative, cold, arrogant, insensitive, controlling, insecure, cruel, Clint and Gwen."

Sorry, those last two just slipped in there.

Truly though, it was an epic, final breakup from a relationship filled with more dramatic, unpredictable stops and starts than a game of musical chairs played by a gang of sugared-up toddlers. Dishes had been thrown. Cars had been keyed. Locks had been changed. Other peens had been touched. Chris even has a scar from a cigarette burn on his upper thigh, left during an ugly, crying argument. Seriously! A cigarette burn! What is this, a trailer park in 1962? It's horrible, horrible. Chris tried to find the silver lining in his domestic abuse when he said, "Well, at least I didn't have to wear sunglasses for a week that time."

"That time?!" I said, my expression of shock and concern conveying the gravity of the situation to Chris, who sighed heavily and slumped in the booth. "You need to get away from him. It's not healthy. It's dangerous, Chris," I said, using his name to emphasize my point. "Do not talk to him any more."

I dated a boy in high school who was controlling, insecure, manipulative, abusive, the whole nine yards. While walking down the hall between classes one day, he suddenly and without warning punched my upper arm hard enough to leave an angry, violet bruise the size of a peony blossom. "What did you do that for?" I'd asked, tears blurring my vision.

"To see what you'd do," he'd coldly replied. I still remember the squeak of his sneakers on the cool tile floor, the humming fluorescents overhead, the metal clanging of lockers. The bruise lasted for three weeks, yellowing and finally fading, before I woke up from the nightmare and figured it might be a smart idea to end things. But I know the allure of The Bad Boy, particularly if your self-worth at the moment could be described as "minimal at best," for whatever reason. You convince yourself you don't deserve better, a viewpoint also championed by the delightful blob of cells you're being isolated from your friends by (you swear, he passes for a human when it's just the two of you!), until one day reality hits you upside the head along with the calloused, open palm and you say, "Screw this noise," and hit the road. Usually with help and support from your friends, family, and a trained professional or two. In my case, they included my mother, my high school guidance counselor Mrs. Wilcox, and my two best friends from high school, Nora and Kate.

"Do. Not. Talk. To him. Anymore." I repeated. "Have you considered a restraining order?"

"Well, he actually took one out on me when I kicked a hole in his front door."

"Chris!"

"I know! I know. I found out he was cheating on me, and I kind of lost it."

I was smiling inside, remembering my cocky, idiot comment to Emily after she'd presented her background checks to me: "*The one with the restraining order is probably not my Chris, since mine is gay.*" Plots all around me were thickening. Turf wars, suicide attempts, broken hearts, con men, restraining orders ... well, that's Craigslist for you.

"I'm seeing a therapist, which is helping," Chris continued.

"Not *The Rapist*'" I joked, echoing Paul.

"No. Definitely not. I'm pretty sure she doesn't even own a strap-on."

I laughed. "But seriously Chris, this really isn't something to take lightly. Get away from him by any means possible, and never look back. You deserve to be in a healthy, caring relationship."

"I know. I'm learning not to be an adrenaline junkie when it comes to romance. That I do deserve better."

"Good." As we finished our peanut stew, mopping the bowls with hearty beer bread, we talked further about love, about waiting for the phone calls that never came, about the blissful highs and the crushing lows, and about the marathon of marriage, where you have to consciously choose every single morning to love your partner, even if he never cleans a toilet and tells the same stories over and over and farts with abandon after a meal. Because you forget that you too have wandered into the weeds of routine, familiarity, and complacency. You have been peeing with the bathroom door open for years, you no longer shave your legs between November and March, and your voice has developed a nasally, nagging quality when it comes to things like golf outings, missing ATM receipts, and tangles of shoes piled all over the house, as if you live with the seven dwarves and not just one sweet but lazy man who may have a shoe hoarding problem.

I took a long sip of water. "In time, young grasshopper, the ringing phone will not give you such a sick rush. It will simply remind you to ask your kind, handsome boyfriend to pick up a loaf of bread on his way home from work."

He reached for my hand and looked me in the eye. "Thank you." I was surprised to see that he was near tears. "I guess I didn't know how badly I needed a real friend. Someone without any ulterior motives, who liked me for me. Someone who wasn't using me."

"Well, don't get ahead of yourself. I was going to make you pay for lunch," I joked, half-heartedly. I don't know if it was the peanut stew, but a queasy feeling began to take root in my stomach. Because did I really like him for him, or was he playing a role in a game I'd dreamed up—**Your Brand New Family**™ by Hasbro (instructions and DNA connection kit not included). Do we always have motives, ulterior or obvious, when it comes to our interactions with others? What kind of sick experiment was I conducting, anyway? If and when it ends, do I submit a paper to a conference on my findings? *"The Repercussions and Unintended Consequences of Trying to Assemble A Family From Total Strangers (or How Sibling-inspired Tantrums Don't End in Adulthood)," by Jaime Collins.*

My anxieties started to subside on the drive to the botanical gardens, and wandering through the climate-controlled conservatory, touching the leaves of the tropical plants and watching the birds flit from branch to branch above, soon inspired in me a feeling of tranquility I hadn't felt in a long time. It occurred to me that I really should take up gardening.

And then Chris's phone rang, and my bliss was shot all to hell.

"Okay, it went to voicemail," he says. He is silent for a few more seconds, keenly observing his phone. "He didn't leave a message," he finally announces.

"You'll probably get a string of these last-gasp phone calls when he realizes you're really not coming back."

"I'm not," Chris says emphatically. "No way."

"Promise?" I raise my eyebrows.

"Promise. Pinkie swear, even."

We hook pinkies and shake, which makes me smile because I haven't made a pinkie swear since I was eleven.

"Now, I'm afraid we'll have to leave," he says, gingerly patting his curls. "The humidity is frizzing my hair, and my makeup is starting to melt."

Chapter 15

"Yeah, but you're in the hundredth percentile for bad breath."

I receive a text from Hannah while I'm in a meeting after school the following week: *Can u pick me up from Vilas Park? Need a ride home.*

I text back, delighted to hear from her: *What r u doing at Vilas Park?*

Hannah: *Ice sk8ing!*

Me: *Be there in 20 mins. xo*

Madison has half a dozen parks that feature bodies of water large enough to skate on when they freeze over in winter. Vilas Park is my favorite, with a concession stand, ample lighting, a warming house, skate rental, and a hockey rink. We used to come here in high school to watch the boys we had crushes on "slap the puck around," a dirty name for an innocent activity that we said as often as possible, especially in front of authority figures. After I park, I make my way to a bench overlooking the skating area. The snow crunches beneath my winter boots, my breath fogging the air before me. I sit on the bench and pull my knit cap down over my ears. I can't pick her out of the other skaters until she flaps a bright red mitten at me. I wave back, smiling, and watch her glide backwards, legs scissoring gracefully.

"This is called a back swizzle," Hannah shouts. She's bundled in a gray down jacket paired with a red stocking cap and matching scarf. Her light brown hair fans neatly out beneath the hat. She is a Campbell's Soup ad come to life: girl twirling in a skating rink, stars twinkling against a lavender sunset, chubby pine trees in the background, even a stout, one-armed snowman taking the whole scene in.

"Do a flip!" I yell. "A triple sow cow! *Do* it! *Do* it! *Do* it!" I clap along with my chant, purposely trying to embarrass her.

"It's called a salchow, and I can't do those," she yells, matter-of-fact.

Look at that kid. When I was her age, I could barely walk a straight line without tripping on a daydream. Hannah weaves effortlessly between the other skaters and climbs off the ice, marching through the snow as she makes her way over. She plops onto the bench next to me and swings her feet back and forth.

"You're pretty good," I say.

"I take lessons." Her breath condenses into a tiny white cloud when she speaks.

"Did you come here by yourself?"

"No, with my friend Sasha." She points her out on the ice: a skinny freckle-faced kid in a powder blue coat, carefully doing laps with another girl. "Her sisters came to meet her and I was getting too cold to stay."

"Where'd you get those skates? I love them!" Hannah's skates are retro, emblazoned with pink, silver, and white swoops: roller derby skates with blades instead of wheels. We admire them together.

"Grandpa sent them to me."

Grandpa. My father? I am dimly aware that my smile has shifted into a frown. "Grandpa Jim?"

She nods.

I tread carefully. Play it cool. "How often do you talk to Grandpa Jim?" The chorus to "How Long (Has This Been Goin' On?)" flickers to life in my head, with "Baby Come Back" hot on its heels. I must have fallen asleep to a Time-Life music infomercial recently.

"Um, I don't know," Hannah says. "Like maybe once a month."

I'm taken aback. I hear from the same man twice a year at most, on my birthday (sometimes) and Christmas.

"So you guys talk on the phone?" I ask. *I am breezy! I am noncha-lant!* A skater spins in a jerky circle near us, his skates crisply slicing the ice before he gracelessly falls, arms flailing. *Maybe not!*

"Yeah. But e-mail mostly. Sometimes Skype."

"Huh." I am ashamed at how deeply this bothers me. Either he feels guilty for his absence in my life and is therefore avoiding me, or he simply never liked me all that much to begin with.

"You should rent skates and come with me next time," Hannah says.

I manage a smile. "Me and ice skates ... oh, that's a bad combination. I'd probably break an ankle. Embarrass you in front of your friends. Totally ruin your rink cred."

She laughs and rolls her eyes. "Come on. It's not that hard."

"You are talking to a person who was the last in her class to learn how to tie shoelaces. I sprained an ankle filling a birdfeeder." I stand and extend a hand to pull her from the bench. "You didn't get your coordination from your dad's side of the family, that's for sure."

Hannah giggles. "You should see him try to snowboard."

I can't help but smile at the idea of Clint trying to snowboard. "Oh, how I wish I could see that." After Hannah waves goodbye to Sasha, we head to the warming house to fetch her belongings. A swarm of children push into the shelter behind us, laughing and yelling, teetering woodenly on their skates. I feel a bit off-kilter myself, thinking of my father again for the first time in months. While Hannah sits on a bench to unlace her skates and slip them off, I spot the concession stand. Three teenage girls lean on the counter, flirting with the boy working behind it. "Want some hot cocoa for the road? A bucket of nachos? How about a giant sheet of Laffy Taffy?"

"No, thanks. I shouldn't spoil my appetite."

I smile and shake my head. "How'd you get to be such a good kid? I try and try, and I can't corrupt you."

She smiles, plugging each foot into a boot. "I'm not that good." She ties the laces of her skates together in a loopy bow.

"Yes, you are. You're like in the ninety-fifth percentile for good-ness among kids your age."

Hannah laughs, because this is an inside joke we share—about people with new babies who suddenly start dropping the word "per-centile" into conversations like it's going out of style. "I'm in the eighty-fifth percentile for height," Hannah would tell me, measuring herself against my shoulder on her tiptoes.

"Yeah, but you're in the hundredth percentile for bad breath," I'd shoot back, earning a playful smack.

"So speaking of cool skates, I am definitely taking you to see some roller derby one of these days. I think you'd totally love it." One of my colleagues at school—Greta Dalton (stage name "Bust Her Keaton")—used to skate with Madison's Unholy Rollers until she fell and shattered her coccyx. She'd been a month pregnant and hadn't known it, but mother and baby are fine. In fact, baby was born in the ninetieth percentile for length and weight.

Hannah weaves an arm through her backpack and throws her skates over the same shoulder as we head to the car. "Well, my mom probably won't let me."

"Sweetie, let me carry something for you." I extend a hand to help her.

"No, I'm okay." She pulls away, asserting her independence even with me. *It begins.* We head to the parking lot, the blades of her skates clinking softly with her every step.

"So we'll go to a bout when you're older." I pause, and add, "Or maybe we won't tell your mom." Because I am the cool aunt, and this is what we do. Corrupt the Youth of America first with loud, battery-operated toys and later with midnight showings of *The Rocky Horror Pic-ture Show* and roller derby. Besides, roller derby is harmless fun. Unless you're actually skating, in which case you risk life and limb, but being a spectator seems safe enough. Safer than participating in an experimen-tal drug trial, that's for sure.

I was around Hannah's age when my father left—such a fragile time to have to deal with the unexpected loss of a parent. After dolls but before junior high, in that wonderfully self-absorbed tween bubble before puberty barges in and changes everything.

After he moved out, sure, there were a few visits to Portland: a long summer weekend here, even a full spring break there. Gwen never went with me, since she was so much older, but once or twice Clint did. What do I remember about these visits? The lumpy mattress and sour smell in his guest bedroom. Eating frozen pizza nearly every night: "How about a survival disc?" he'd hopefully say, preheating the oven and scattering frozen mozzarella shreds over the counter when he tore the plastic from the pizza. I remember hours spent watching MTV, reading *People* magazine, writing desperate, lonely letters to friends. *"His apartment smells like a divorced guy,"* I wrote to Jenny Thompson, homesick and angry that I had to spend Easter break across the country with a person who had no idea how to interact with a thirteen-year-old girl (though—to be fair—most of humanity falls in that camp). *His apartment smells like a man who made my mother cry.* Those were the days before texting and e-mail, before cell phones, and what I remember most was a feeling of intense loyalty to my mother, of being marooned with a person I barely knew, a stranger who abdicated his role of husband and didn't seem all that interested in the role of father, either.

The visits pretty much ended when I hit tenth grade. When I graduated from high school, he sent a card. He sent another card when I graduated from college. He was on a trip to Australia when Erik and I got married; that time, he sent a check.

The years ticked by, and here we are. Near-total strangers, though he seems to be making much more of an effort to be a grandfather than a father. I wonder when this started—and how closely Clint was involved. An unpleasant combination of jealousy and paranoia takes root in my heart. If I had a child, would he call me more often? Synapses begin to fire, and my brain strikes up the band: *If I had a baby,* to the tune of *"If I Were a Rich Man."* I force myself to stop. Now is not the time for Selfish Fiddler on the Roof.

My car was running less than twenty minutes ago, but it's already freezing inside. Tendrils of frost are beginning to reclaim the back window. I start the car, blast the heat, and sigh heavily. "I hate Wisconsin in the winter."

"That's because you don't ice skate," Hannah says, smirking as she climbs into the passenger seat. She buckles her seat belt without being told.

"If I ice skated, you'd be driving me home, because I'd be in a full-body cast." I glance at her, smiling mischievously. "Say, do you want to drive? Just for a few blocks?"

She breaks into delighted laughter. "No!"

"All right, just let me know if you change your mind. Totally incorruptible." I turn on the radio, settling on a Top Forty station that I think might appeal to her. Z-104—your home for Connie and Curtis in the morning. "Is this what the cool kids are listening to?"

"Not really," she says, still smiling.

The DJ is playing Katy Perry or Kelly Clarkson or that irritating woman with the dollar sign in her name. We drive and listen. Hannah's not exactly a shy kid, though she isn't the chatterbox she once was. At eleven, Hannah is winding down from her jibber-jabber childhood, and I can feel her turning inward as she reaches the cusp between childhood and adulthood. Growing more thoughtful and contemplative as junior high looms ominously on the horizon. Soon, there will be boys. A driver's license. Homecoming dresses.

There is also this: her father and I are not speaking right now, and I'm sure that's done a bit of long division on her loyalties.

I turn the radio down. "So. Can I ask why you didn't call your mom or dad for a ride?" Once again, I keep my voice neutral, betraying no hint of the heartburn the mere thought of her parents can inspire in me.

She tugs at a skein of yarn unraveling from one mitten. After a thoughtful pause she says, "Because I haven't seen you in so long."

"Well, I'm glad you asked. Let the record show that I am happy to be your driver any time."

She pulls out her phone and begins texting someone. She crinkles her brow in displeasure at the response. "Ugh. Mom's making asparagus and a survival disc tonight."

I raise an eyebrow and glance at her. "Did Grandpa Jim tell you that? About the survival discs?"

"No. That's what Dad calls it."

There's that tenacious yet tenuous thread again. I can't even think of a frozen pizza without being reminded of my family. And lost chances and miscommunication and time slipping away.

"Is it a Tony's Pizza?"

"I dunno. My Mom only buys what's on sale."

I sigh. "Hannah, you know you're growing up too fast, right?"

"Oh - kay," she says, stretching her voice out in slow motion. "I'll ... tryyyy ... to ... growww ... up ... sloo ... werrrrr."

I laugh. "You are such a nerd and I absolutely adore you."

"I know you are but what am I?"

Still a wonderful, goofy kid, I think. *For just a little while longer.*

Chapter 16

"...nobody wants to discuss diarrhea at the table,"

From: Joy and Clint jch_3@tdsmetro.com
To: Jaime Collins jbcollins@madison.k12.wi.us
Sent: Monday, February 4, 8:58 AM
Subject: mom's house
Sell the house yet?

From: Jaime Collins jbcollins@madison.k12.wi.us
To: Joy and Clint <jch_3@tdsmetro.com>
Sent: Tuesday, February 5, 4:34 PM
Subject: Re: mom's house
No.

***

Valentine's Day arrived before anyone had time to really prepare, leaving great swaths of the population without an ample supply of drinking water, fully stocked first aid kits, or batteries for emergency lighting. Last year Erik and I celebrated Valentine's Day (which, incidentally, has the same initials as "venereal disease") by watching *The Shining* with my mom. Like the ill-fated Torrance family, we were also snowed in that weekend—walloped by a blizzard that reeled and barreled east out of North Dakota like my Aunt Carol on a free sample bender at Costco. This year we are again going to see a horror movie, which is a great victory for me because Erik doesn't like to watch horror movies in public, where he feels less comfortable shielding his eyes when the creepy music crescendos and the girl wanders alone up the stairs ("Hello? Anybody up here?"). When we saw *Paranormal Activity* at Point Cinema I suddenly felt the hair above my neck rise; it was actually Erik, lifting a handful of my own hair away from my head into a veil he could hide behind. I only got him to agree to go after showing him an article in *Redbook* about couples' sex lives dramatically improving immediately after engaging in an adrenaline-pumping activity like skydiving, riding a roller coaster, or watching *The Exorcist* together.

In the minutes before we leave, I'm on the phone with Amy, trying to explain why we won't be driving to Wausau to go skiing with the rest of our friends and their husbands next weekend. Part of the reason is that after a few beers, Liz's husband stares at me in a way that makes me want to completely disfigure myself with acid and a dull machete. The other part is that Evelyn has invited us to a dinner party at her house. I'll not only get to see where she lives—which has intrigued me ever since she mentioned the whole "I'm on Medicare and I weld iron" bit—but I'll also get to meet her daughter AND her new boyfriend.

"But the chalet has private rooms for everyone! No sofa sleepers or blow-up mattresses."

"As tempting as that is," I say, trying to sound both disappointed and apologetic, "I can't. We already made other plans last month." I was stretching the truth as far as I could without it snapping back into my face; technically, the ski weekend invitation had arrived earlier. In the mail, with an explosion of confetti and glitter.

"I'll make that sweet potato and rosemary braid you love," Amy sing-songs. "Just for you. And I'll throw in a bottle of Veuve Clicquot." She pauses for effect before whispering, *"There's a hot tub!"*

You can tell Amy has children, because she is skilled in the art of bribery. "Aaaah! Now you're making me feel bad!"

"Do you feel bad because you won't be seeing your best, most awesome friends in the whole wide world, or because you'll miss out on the treats?"

"Can it be both?" I'm actually not as impressed by the fact that the chalet has a hot tub, more a deal-clincher in Amy's eyes than mine. I find hot tubs suspect. Bubbling petri dishes that will only give you a patchy, gray rash that mysteriously travels to different parts of your body, popping up on a thigh in April, your left shoulder blade in August.

Amy murmurs something to one of her children before directing her next sentence back at me. "We missed you at Frankie's New Year's party, too. Everything okay?"

"Yes! Super busy, but what else is new? School, trying to pack up the house, find a new apartment and everything. Blah-blah, it's been kind of crazy." They're a sprinkle of tiny white lies, a dusting of salt on a pretzel. Because teaching has been tiring this semester but manageable, and I haven't given much thought to boxing up my mother's remaining belongings or finding a new place to live since before Halloween.

I don't tell her about Chris or Paul or Alyssa or Evelyn. It's a large omission, but I suddenly don't have the energy to field any questions. Frankie will probably tell her anyway. Maybe she'll tell everyone while they're drinking in the hot tub, developing strange, migratory rashes. Instead, I shine the conversational light back on Amy, asking about the kids and her pregnancy and how long she'll take maternity leave from her job at Oak Park Dental. Despite the fact that they represent things I have on occasion desperately yearned for, felt actual pangs of loss over, I don't mind hearing about her children's sweet shenanigans or her swollen ankles. Amy isn't like some of my friends from work who describe their pregnancies and parenthood as "spiritual" or "the most important, beautiful thing I've ever done." If I were to win any prestigious award—an Oscar, a Nobel Peace Prize, the Bob Hope Humanitarian Award because I eliminated malaria from the developing world—and dropped the trophy on their desks with a proud thud, these assholes would respond by showing me new pictures of their kids and saying, "That's nice and all, but you didn't push a miracle out of your vagina."

As Amy is telling me about her husband's vasectomy, because it is important that her friends know much more about his now-unfertile penis than he will ever guess, Erik comes into the kitchen and clears his throat. He points at the place on his wrist where a watch would be, indicating that we are going to be late for the movie. I tell Amy I have to go, promise that we'll get together again soon, and hang up. I startle Erik when I unexpectedly laugh out loud in the car on the way to the multiplex, after it hits me that Valentine's Day also has the same initials as "vas deferens."

***

I'm thrilled to find that Evelyn lives in one of Madison's eighteen Lustron homes, which were porcelain steel prefab homes made between 1949 and 1950 for returning GIs. "Less than three thousand units were made before the company declared bankruptcy," Evelyn proudly told us when she took our coats and thanked us for the bottle of wine, pleased that Erik and I recognized her home as a historic treasure. I only knew about the unique homes because my mother had briefly dated a Lustron fanatic in the same neighborhood. Unfortunately, the first time he had her over for dinner she discovered he had many more cats than he'd led her to believe—about eighteen more, and that short romance ended up on the discard pile.

"This model is the 'Westchester Deluxe.'" Evelyn continues, leading us into the living room. "It still has the original pocket doors, and you already saw the zigzag downspout pillar accent at the front porch, but the kitchen's been totally renovated, and the metal paneling on the ceilings and interior walls is also gone. Sheet rocked long ago, and thank goodness for that." It's a tiny house, less than eleven hundred square feet, but jam-packed with Evelyn's personality. As we admired the décor, Evelyn excused herself to finish whisking the salmon marinade.

"Quick," Erik whispers, "what are the first three words that come to mind?"

I smile, delightfully overwhelmed by the purple, red, and yellow walls, smaller versions of what must be Evelyn's iron sculptures displayed on any available space, the front bay window hung with massive stained glass panels. You couldn't see their effect at night, but I imagined them in the daytime, casting variegated, jewel-toned patterns all over the room as the sun tracked across the sky. "Exploding. Rainbow. Lesbian," I say, though Evelyn is not a lesbian and the only thing that has exploded is my newfound, irrational desire for a Lustron home of my very own, tucked in by a row of little round shrubs.

My own Grandma Ellis's house had been the complete opposite of Evelyn's, with clear plastic sleeves on the floral-patterned couch and a bowl of hard butterscotch candy that had melted together into one solid lump in a bowl on the shiny glass coffee table. If you went to The National Museum of Interior Design and there was an exhibit called "Old Lady Parlor," it would be Grandma Ellis's living room. Screw up one letter and you get "Old Lady Pallor," which I notice in the mirror with alarming frequency these days. But I digress.

We are the first guests to arrive, and Evelyn asks if we want anything to drink. "Manhattan, martini, Old Fashioned, daiquiri, or Stinger? I thought cocktails from the fifties would be fitting. You know, to go with the house."

"Ooh!" I'm delighted by the concept. "What's a Stinger?"

Evelyn consults a battered bartender's guidebook. "Let's see. Okay, it's brandy and crème de menthe."

"I'm glad I asked. I'll have a daiquiri."

I watch Evelyn carefully measure and pour one and a half ounces of rum and a jigger of simple syrup into a cocktail shaker filled with ice. Next she squeezes half a lime in a citrus press, draining the juice directly into the cocktail shaker.

"No blender?" Erik feigns shock. "No fake strawberry?"

"This is traditional," Evelyn says. "We are 'kicking it old-school,' as they say." She shakes the drink like a pro, carefully strains it into a three-ounce cocktail glass, and hands it to me. "Magnifique!"

I take a sip. I approve. "My students used to call things they love 'amazeballs,' but that's already jumped the shark." I take another sip. "Mmm! It really razzes my berries." I pass it to Erik for a taste-test. "Let me lay this on you, Daddy-O. You're going to flip." For perhaps the first time in my life, my outfit, slang, and drink all conform to the same time period, which is a real Big Tickle.

As Evelyn makes Erik a brandy Old Fashioned, sweet, the other guests begin to arrive. Chris whirls in with air kisses and a massive bouquet of pink tulips, wearing a belted jumpsuit that either came from Barneys New York or a box at Goodwill, and Evelyn's daughter Kimberly shows up empty-handed, wearing a scowl.

Kimberly looks like the kind of person who frequently lodges complaints at customer service departments, who regularly sends food back to the kitchen, who gives out dental floss at Halloween if she turns the porch light on at all. "You totally remind me of my sister!" I say when I shake her hand.

"I hope that's a good thing," she says, not smiling.

"Oh, don't worry, it is."

Evelyn's new beau Carl arrives next, swinging a long baguette in a paper sleeve. "Where's the most beautiful woman in the world?" he asks heartily, sweeping Evelyn into a dramatic embrace. Carl is in his early sixties, with bushy eyebrows that burst from his forehead like tufts of hair stolen from Troll doll pencil toppers. His teeth are straight but coffee-stained, his hair thick and dyed an unnatural shade of brown, neatly parted. Televangelist hair. It doesn't match his eyebrows.

Evelyn giggles and blushes to nearly match her red living room wall when Carl punctuates his Hollywood hug with a pinch to her bottom. She manages to extract herself and make introductions, and Carl squeezes my hand with enough brute force to squeeze the lungs out of a chipmunk. I play it cool, coasting through the pain and waiting for my bones to reset while he pumps Erik's hand. I can't be sure, but I think I see Erik's knees buckle slightly. Next I watch Chris and Kimberly wince as they endure the grip of death. "He broke one of my nails," Chris whispers to me as Evelyn and Carl head to the portable bar, where Evelyn makes Carl a Stinger.

We're interrupted by another knock. "Can someone get that?" Evelyn asks, and I open the front door to find Alyssa on the front stoop with a strange man.

It takes me a beat to get over my surprise. "Uh, hi!" I say, my smile frozen in place, "Come on in."

Alyssa introduces her guest as they slip out of their puffy down coats. "Hi everyone, this is Ben. We're in the same program."

"Hi Ben," we chorus together, like we're at an AA meeting. Ben looks baffled, like even he can't believe he's here. He has a round, trusting face, reddish-blond eyelashes, fine hair the color of sand, and a slight belly protruding over his khaki pants. He vaguely reminds me of a dog we had growing up—Pickles, who would scoot his behind across a carpet like it was nobody's business. Pickles didn't have the sense to come in out of the rain, but if ever you were crying because you skinned your knee or had your heart broken by Tommy Wilson, he'd lay his muzzle on your lap and look soulfully into your eyes as if to say, "I don't mean to be a bother, but when you're done with that, can you let me out so I can roll around on the dead squirrel carcass under the porch?"

Evelyn sails over to kiss Alyssa on the cheek and accept the potted narcissus she'd brought. "They're lovely. Welcome, welcome, please come in! Let me take your coats. Ben, you dropped a mitten. Can I make you a drink?"

Chris marches over to me and crosses his arms, balancing his martini between his right thumb and index finger. We study Ben and Alyssa, who have their backs to us. "Our girl is not ready for a relationship yet," Chris says, his words dripping with disapproval and worry. He takes a sip and stares at them over the rim of his glass.

"I know," I say, "I'm as shocked as you are."

"This is not healthy! I wonder what her counselors would say."

"That it's only going to end badly for Pickles," I say.

"Who?"

I shake my head. "I mean Ben. Sorry." But beneath the happy façade, I am worried. I start to wonder about the statute of limitations as they apply to dating after a suicide attempt. How soon is too soon? Then again, perhaps this is a positive sign. We don't know the back story. Maybe she's known Ben for ages, and he's a supportive, stable force in her life.

"Make mine a double, neat," I overhear him instructing Evelyn. Maybe not.

Fresh cocktails in hand, he and Alyssa join us. They're wearing hopeful, hesitant smiles. I try to keep an open mind. "So Ben," I begin, "You're also a biologist?"

His smile falters, his brow furrowing in confusion. "No, I'm actually a writer."

"Ben had one of his poems published in the *Franklin Review*!" Alyssa gushes.

Now it's my turn to be confused. "I thought you met in the same program?"

Alyssa laughs. "No, we're in the same support circle. Part of the whole group therapy thing."

"Oh, okay!" Oh, not okay.

We transition into awkward small talk about the television shows we're currently watching, and it quickly becomes obvious that Ben and Erik have nothing in common except the fact that they both have prostates. I think. Evelyn puts on some music in keeping with the fifties theme. When he's sure Ben and Alyssa are out of earshot, Erik leans over to whisper, "So should we check Ben for a bottle of Vicodin before dinner?"

"No, but we should check you for a soul."

I follow Evelyn into the kitchen. "It smells wonderful in here! Need any help?"

"Oh, you're lovely. Would you mind slicing the baguette and filling the bread basket?"

I begin to slice while Evelyn checks the salmon. "I think it's ready."

"Did you know?" I quickly ask before she can leave again, tipping my head subtly toward the living room. "About Alyssa's date?"

Evelyn flaps a jaded hand, like what can you do? "I know, I know. I was just as surprised. She asked if it would be okay if she brought a friend, but I thought she meant a girlfriend."

Evelyn's daughter wanders into the kitchen and frowns at the bounty of food her mother spent the afternoon prepping and preparing. "Evelyn, you know I don't eat seafood."

Her mother's face falls. "Oh sweetheart, I'm so sorry! I thought you were eating only seafood. A *pescetarian*, I believe it's called?"

Kimberly rolls her eyes. "Forget it. I'm sure there's something I can eat."

Carl suddenly hollers from the living room like a cave man. "I smell dinner!"

"Have you heard from Paul?" Evelyn asks me, planting a sprig of parsley in the mashed potatoes. "He told me he was coming."

I shake my head.

"Will you make sure I've set the table with eight place settings? I'm so frazzled right now." I check on the dining room table, which is indeed set for eight, and wander back into the living room.

Amidst the escalating bedlam, the doorbell rings. Erik answers it and Paul stomps in, absolutely covered in snow. The hood of his parka is packed with snow and his hair, mustache, and beard are pebbled with melting white chunks. "Did you fall in a snowbank?" Erik asks, taking Paul's mittens and hat, hand extended patiently for his jacket.

"My neighbor," Paul huffs, wiggling out of his parka, brushing snow from his hair and stomping his feet. Snow flies everywhere in wet, white bits. "He aimed his snowblower right at me."

"Your chin is bleeding a little," Erik points out.

Paul investigates with his index finger. When he pulls it away there is a small red dot near the nail. "I thought so. He must have kicked up a piece of gravel."

"Why would he do that?" I ask, angry on Paul's behalf, remembering the baited coyote traps.

"Oh, he's just that way," Paul says dismissively, leaving us to interpret "that way" as we so choose. I pick "subhuman."

Evelyn joins us and claps her hands to get our attention. "Everyone! Dinner is served. Please make your way to the dining room."

Since the living and dining areas bleed into one another, it's only a matter of shifting the herd a few feet to the left.

Once we're seated, Carl asks "for the honor of leading us in grace." The rest of us shrug and glance around the table before tentatively joining hands. Ben and Kimberly, seated on either side of Carl, grimace in pain as he takes their hands. Carl's prayer is epic, covering topics ranging from salmon fisherman to potato growers to utility workers whose industrious dedication to their craft gave us the light by which to see the drops of dressing clinging to the leaves of our salads. For a moment, we think he's finished. Some of us look up. I lift the hands of Evelyn and Chris and say, "Aaaay—"

"Speaking of salads," Carl continues loudly, "we are grateful that this spinach has been triple-washed, and pray that none of us are sickened by the listeria, though this too we know is part of your Greater Plan, dear Lord Jesus Christ. Though I am only getting to know Chris. And Alyssa. And Paul. And Erik. And Kimberly. And Ben. And Jaime, I have enjoyed our time together immensely and thank you for it. And I am humbled, blessed beyond belief to share times both romantic and friendly with Evelyn, the brightest light in my life ..."

This goes on, and my mind begins to drift. My thoughts feel flabby. My *thighs* feel flabby. When did I last exercise? What about this: when was the last time I ate corn on the cob? That's something you don't do very often. Maybe just in August. I look up at the word art elegantly scrawled over the pass-thru to Evelyn's kitchen: *Wine is Bottled Poetry.* You know, my penmanship has really deteriorated over the last few years. *Penmanship is a dying art,* I think. I would love to see some brilliant artist do a full gallery show of nothing but various letters of the alphabet, capital and lower-case, in perfect cursive on giant sheets of recycled penmanship paper, like the kind we used in third grade.

"—and all the unborn children. In Jesus' name, Amen."

I look around, startled. It's over? Is it really over?

"Hallelujah," Erik says, and we all applaud.

"Good grief, that was long," Chris whispers in my ear. "I kept hoping for an orchestra to kick in and play him off the stage." Ben and

Kimberly shake out the hands Carl had been holding, waiting for the feeling to return to their fingers.

"I think God and I both nodded off during the part about Carl's clean colonoscopy."

We dig in to Evelyn's meal, passing the platters around family-style. Kimberly makes a distasteful face at the salmon and takes three slices of bread which—if I do the math—means that once the basket makes its way around the table to me, there will be none left. We eat quietly for a moment, murmuring noises of approval.

"Everything is wonderful, Evelyn," Alyssa says. She suddenly lets out a quick yelp and jumps, her knees knocking the table and rattling the china. I reach out to steady my water glass. Her cheeks go crimson.

"You okay?" Erik asks, raising an eyebrow.

"Yes, I'm fine, it's just this little … nerve pain shooting down my back."

Ben is smiling serenely, his left hand tucked under the table. If you follow the natural trajectory of his arm, you might wonder if isn't resting awfully high on Alyssa's thigh. They share a sly, giddy look, and you'd have to be blind, dense, or a mahogany nightstand not to conclude that he's feeling her up under the table.

"So Kimberly," I ask politely, trying to draw her into the conversation, "Evelyn told me you recently returned from South America."

She nods and finishes chewing before speaking. "Oh, it was splendid."

"It's about time someone rescued the word 'splendid' from the public radio ghetto," Erik adds, agreeably. If you didn't know him, you'd think he was being completely serious.

This trips her up only briefly before she proceeds with her travelogue. "I spent a week in Columbia, two weeks in Peru, three in Argentina, two in Bolivia, and ended in Belém do Pará. I was there for the procession of the Círio of Nazaré. You'll never see so many people fainting in the streets at once!"

"Wow," I say. I have no idea what she's talking about. I listen to Kimberly's descriptions of Cupuaçu, with a name more like a Pokémon character than a food item, and Choquequirao, Incan ruins you can only get to on horseback or by foot, nodding at all the right places, occasionally adding a "huh" or "yes, that does sound spiritual." Every evocative sentence makes me feel wistful and root-bound, increasingly artless and uncultured. A small hillbilly who owns a pet possum and dreams of one day shopping in a real supermarket. Kimberly and Chris begin to share war stories about lost luggage and water purification mishaps, which Evelyn tries to put a stop to with, "Kimberly, nobody wants to discuss diarrhea at the table."

"Evelyn," Kimberly haughtily says, "Nobody even used the word 'diarrhea' until you just did."

"Well, now it's been used twice, so let's move on."

I never called my mother by her first name. It struck me as cold, disrespectful, and bitter. Three adjectives I too will be in danger of associating with if the rift between my siblings and me lasts for decades.

As I finish my mashed potatoes, none of which became airborne at any point in the meal, I overhear Ben telling Carl about his poetry and actually witness the passing of a chapbook. Ben glances proudly around the table, smiling with fake modesty, waiting for others to remark about it.

"Oh, wonderful," Carl says, reaching in his breast pocket for his glasses. "I'm blind as a bat without them," he jokes. I hope he didn't drive here without wearing them. He slips them on, and Ben leans over to recommend a selection of his favorite poems. Carl flips through a few pages, reading silently, mouthing every word. "Very nice," he finally says, in that way you tell someone when you're just being polite. He closes the chapbook and benevolently smiles at everyone seated around the table. "I don't wear my spectacles all the time, because I get headaches. I need the prescription adjusted, but I'm between opportunities with health coverage at the mo—wait, are you a man?" he asks, squinting at Chris.

Chris looks up, mouth agape, forkful of salmon frozen in mid-air. We all pause, horrified, waiting for Chris's response. A creaky sound comes out of his mouth, a kind of long "murhhhhh," and then thankfully, yes Virginia there is a Santa Claus, and a God and a Hari Krishna at an airport in your city, because we are interrupted by a perfectly timed, tinny, far-away, *"Set me free, why don't you babe!"*

"What is that?" Carl asks, frowning.

Chris's blush deepens. He wipes his lips and scoots his chair back. "Sorry! I need to get that," he says, retreating to Evelyn's bedroom for his purse.

"If that's David, I'm going to kill Chris," I say.

"Unless David beats you to it," Erik says. I make a face at him.

Evelyn and Alyssa look at me for an explanation, so I give them the Cliff Notes summary of Chris's abusive relationship.

"Oh dear," Evelyn says, "that is alarming."

"Is that woman a man?" a perplexed Carl asks Evelyn, not even bothering to lower his voice.

Paul, who had been fairly quiet throughout the meal, theatrically clears his throat, and we all turn to listen. "So, can anyone recommend a good lawyer?"

Chapter 17
"We could learn a lot from a dog on a cart."

I like to remember myself during the last year with my mother as selfless, noble, patient ... but many days I felt a mixture closer to resentment, frustration, and acute anger. I seethed inside that my mother had been stricken while human stain Fred Phelps got to keep walking around, pissing people off and eating biscuits and gravy. I raged that I had to bear closest witness to her slow, agonizing death while Gwen participated at arm's length. I was the soldier in the foxhole, sweaty and terrified, and she was the distant politician receiving sanitized, amorphous briefings on the latest casualties.

Clint was a bit more present, though he was "always too goddamn busy" to actually get his hands dirty, so to speak. His infrequent visits, sometimes accompanied by Joy and Hannah, were brief and to the point. But to his credit, he was there for Mom in his own way. His version of helping involved writing a check for her utility bills, while things like caulking windows, shopping for groceries, picking up prescriptions, and mowing the lawn fell to Erik and me. Gwen's contributions included making ridiculous suggestions about alternative therapies and sending a weekly gift: a music box, a lavender neck pillow, and endless bouquets of flowers, which I often purposely forgot to water.

I tried to temper my emotions around my mother, remain neutral and diplomatic when it came to Clint or Gwen, because the last thing my mother needed while she lost her hair and writhed in pain were three warring adult children. Though she never formally acknowledged it, I know she was hurt by the distance between her offspring. But we weren't that family. We didn't organize rummage sales together, we didn't send one another birthday cards. We steeped our resentments like a tea and barely cobbled together a modicum of civility when in the same room. We carried entire *bowls* of chips on our shoulders, with dip.

When it became apparent that Mom would soon need help with household chores, errands, and ultimately daily personal care, I was the obvious choice by default. "Clint has Hannah and works crazy hours, but you don't work summers or have any other … obligations," Gwen had said to me on the phone. She meant children and home ownership, of course. Adulthood. "And you never left Madison."

"Could you be any more condescending?" I'd asked in a rare confrontational moment.

"I'm simply pointing out the obvious." Her tone was clinical, laced with a hint of smug victory. Gwen had left the town we'd grown up in, she'd been to Japan, she lived in a high-rise condo with oversized walls of windows, a second-floor fitness center, and a view of Atlanta's skyline from the rooftop terrace. Erik and I had been saving for a home of our own, but with student loan debt and temperamental used cars plus the cost of fertility treatments and my father-in-law's nursing home, it was pretty slow going. Perhaps if we'd darned our socks instead of buying new pairs, turned down every social invitation, and eaten nothing but lentils and Top Ramen since college we'd have a starter home by now, but you have to live a little, too.

I was jealous of Gwen not only for her ambition and passport stamps and Wolf six-burner range, but because while I was painting Mom's toenails and shuttling her to chemotherapy sessions, I could sometimes feel how much Mom missed Gwen. I heard it in the nostalgic comments she made, I saw it when her eyes lit up whenever Gwen called. *Gwen, Gwen, how proud I am of Gwen.* And isn't that always how it goes? You marry the decent, sometimes boring guy from a good family yet still fantasize about the exciting, handsome asshole who broke your heart in college. Or worse, you pine for the exciting, handsome asshole you never even dated—you just watched him break someone else's heart in a movie on Lifetime.

In the end, I was grateful I'd cashed in every one of my own personal, vacation, and sick days to care for my mother. In the end, I was glad I'd stayed home Saturday nights to play Phase 10 with her and Erik, because in those waning months before she died, Clint and Gwen became almost dear to me again through her eyes. We laughed about how tightly she used to braid Gwen's and my hair, about how we used to ride laundry baskets down the carpeted stairs, about the time Clint and I had a fight and I tried to barricade him in his room, piling chairs and toys outside his closed door only to be stymied by the fact that his door actually swung inward. He'd simply opened the door and laughed at the mountain of debris futilely piled outside his room, and I could only scream in frustration and run away. Mom told me that when we were very small, I would follow Clint everywhere, nearly footstep for footstep, and Gwen would read to me for hours. "I don't remember that," I'd said, quietly. "Why can't I remember that?" While we talked, I wished Clint and Gwen were with us to shade in the details and share more fond memories. I wished they were there so I too could become dear to them again through Mom's eyes. Though I suspected that if they were, our happy memories would gradually devolve into the acrimonious present.

In the end, I'm glad it was me and not Gwen who had to face that demon. Because even as the parent-child roles reversed when I helped Mom to the bathroom or brought her the late-night glass of water, kissing her forehead and turning out the light behind me, my mother still had important lessons to teach me about grace, forgiveness, and dignity.

Gwen will just have to learn them vicariously by watching a movie on Lifetime.

***

Paul is licking his fingers one by one while he stands in line to refill his empty extra large popcorn bucket, so I pass him a handful of napkins. "Hoping for a butter-flavored heart attack?" Erik asks.

"That would be one way to go," Paul answers, tucking the tub beneath an arm to wipe his hands and mouth. There is a small popcorn hull suspended in his beard like a fly trapped in a web, but I don't say anything.

We are standing in the lobby of Point Cinema, discussing the merits and flaws of the movie we just saw: a sci-fi thriller starring Ryan Gosling and James Franco on opposite sides of the law. When we'd first arrived at the multiplex Paul asked if we wanted to see a different movie. "What about *The Dog Builder?*" It was a biopic about a veteran with a prosthetic limb who partnered with an animal rescue group to fit abused and wounded dogs with artificial legs and little carts, becoming emotionally whole again in the process. The climactic scene involved a bomb-sniffing Border Collie who saves an entire airport despite having two bionic hind legs. It was all too much. I immediately shook my head as my throat swelled up.

"Are you crying?" Erik asked me, nearly gleefully.

"Oh my God." I dabbed my eyes. "Trust me, you don't want to watch that movie with me in public."

Paul nodded thoughtfully. "There's something about a dog wheeling himself around on a little cart, isn't there? So much can-do spirit, so much joie de vivre in the face of adversity. We could learn a lot from a dog on a cart."

It seemed we were doing the kinds of things I used to do with my friends, though for some reason, I think of Chris, Evelyn, Paul, and Alyssa more as family than friends. Maybe it's only my frame of mind. Actually, they're even better than family or old friends, because they don't have the baggage or expectations associated with people you've known a long time, who cast you in a certain role years ago and now rolled their eyes any time you attempted to reinvent yourself.

Well, I do have one pure, non-cynical friend who never rolls her eyes at me any time I take up yoga again. Amy. She never passes judgment, she never pokes fun, and she never even talks behind anyone else's back (her husband notwithstanding). She makes me want to be a better person, though I suspect she isn't quite human. More a superhero from the plant kingdom, maybe.

Paul finishes wiping his hands and continues with his previous train of thought about the movie. "I thought the corporate branding everywhere was a nice touch. Reminiscent of *Idiocracy*, but without the laughs."

"I laughed," Erik says, "but I don't think I was supposed to."

I'd suggested the three of us go to the movie because I was worried about Paul. Both Abe and Auschie were still at the vet for observation after their detox—they'd eaten some canned dog food laced with rat poison, set out by Paul's neighbor to put an end to the dogs' crapping in his yard once and for all. The neighbor had disposed of the evidence, of course, but it was clear to Paul what had happened.

"Are you going to sue?" I'd asked after Paul told us the horrible story.

"Yes, we're planning on counter-suing."

To make matters worse, the same horrible neighbor was suing Paul for property damage after he accidentally (on purpose) backed into the mailbox. Over. And over. This same neighbor had routinely called the police during the last year to report Paul for various ordinance violations and misdemeanors—trespassing, animal complaints, noise complaints, vandalism, harassment. The calls gradually escalated in frequency and gravity, occasionally accompanied by reprisals from Paul that only triggered further calls to the police, culminating in the awful pinnacle, the poisoning of Paul's dogs.

"Why didn't you ever call the cops on him?"

"He always beat me to the punch. And I figured when they arrived, I could explain my side of the story. It worked, too. Just CCAP him. Vern Maddox. You'll find all kinds of trouble."

CCAP stands for Consolidated Court Automation Programs. The first of its kind in the nation, it gives online access to certain public records from Wisconsin's circuit courts. Just plug in the name and city of the person in question and *voila!* You could immediately determine whether the guy you met at Starbucks had ever been convicted of a felony, divorced, evicted from an apartment, sued for child support, or been issued a restraining order. Single women in Wisconsin used it with such frequency that it assumed the form of a verb in the common vernacular, like Google and Facebook. *"I Googled him, I CCAPed him, and I Facebooked him. He's clean."*

"I looked you guys up before we met," Paul suddenly said.

"Me too, Paul," I confessed, laughing.

"Civil liberty and privacy concerns aside, you have to if you meet anyone online."

Paul advances to the front of the line and requests a refill on his jumbo tub. He nods when they ask if he'd like butter, staring lethargically while they pump the clear, artificially flavored oil over his popcorn. A sad clown in a bright purple parka and oversized galoshes. I wonder if he would have asked for a refill if he didn't have to return to an empty house. I suddenly feel a violent urge to poison Vern Maddox. A fantasy springs to mind in which I am hired to cater a party at Vern's, and I sprinkle arsenic into his spring pea risotto.

I try to keep Paul talking on the ride home, feeling him out for any unadvisable plans to avenge his dog's attempted murder. The last thing Paul needs right now is time in jail.

"They only got into his yard twice in the last few months," Paul says forlornly. "I usually have them on the leash."

"They're going to be okay. Remember what the vet said? You can pick them up tomorrow."

Erik pulls into Paul's driveway, the headlights sweeping a wide arc over the neighbor's snowy yard, illuminating the scene of the crime. I crane my neck for a glimpse of Vern through his windows, but the house is still. A lamp is on in the front room, and I secretly hope Vern is lying beneath it on the floor, clutching his heart and struggling to breathe. Paul begins to cry, weeping into his greasy bucket of half-eaten popcorn. "I don't know how I'll sleep tonight without Abe and Auschie. I keep imagining them in cages in a dark room at the vet, surrounded by sick and hissing cats, and they're shaking and whining, wondering where I am, and their tummies still hurt—"

"Paul, do you want to stay with us tonight?" Erik interrupts. "We have a spare bedroom."

Paul wipes his eyes with a scratchy movie theater napkin. "Yes," he says, without hesitating. "Can I quick run in and pack an overnight bag?"

We wait for him in the driveway, engine running to keep the car warm. "I hope you know what you're doing," I say

"Getting back in touch with my human decency," Erik says. "I thought you'd be proud of me."

"I am, but this is a little weird."

"What's weird is you being on this side of the argument."

"I'm entitled to change my mind now and then." I feel my sense of healthy boundaries vibrating like an alarm. Bonding with my new family in safe, public places is one thing; inviting them to the house where my mother died, I store my jewelry, and I very occasionally have sex with my husband is another altogether. Then again, I've already been to both Evelyn's and Paul's homes, and I've seen Alyssa and Chris at their most vulnerable. Was I trying to cast myself as the strong, supportive yet distant one in this strange, new play I'd written?

Paul appears again beneath the swag chandelier on his porch, dragging a bulging suitcase. He locks the front door behind him and lugs his bag to the car, motioning with his free hand to Erik, who rolls down the window. "Mind if I throw this in the trunk?"

"No, go right ahead," Erik says, popping the lever.

The car shudders as Paul heaves the bag into the trunk.

"What the fuck did he pack in there, a midget?"

"'Little person,' Erik," I say absently. I aim a vent at my hands and blast my cold fingers with hot air.

Paul rejoins us in the car, slamming the door twice because his scarf caught the first time. "Thanks so much for letting me stay with you. I can't stomach being anywhere near Vern right now."

"I don't blame you," I say sympathetically.

Paul sits in the middle of the back seat and leans forward, fore-arms on each of our headrests. The popcorn hull still floats in his beard. "Hey guys? Do you mind if we hit Taco Bell on the way?"

***

An hour later Paul is tucked into a sleeping bag on the couch, reading *Prevention* magazine. Nancy is curled on his lap, purring. "Did you know," he asks, "that seeing a smile on the face of a loved one cues the same brain waves as being told you've won $40,000?"

"Why not $50,000?" Erik replies, eyes still glued to *The Colbert Report*.

Paul seems honestly stumped. "Good question. I think I'll e-mail the editors."

I suddenly feel like a middle-aged parent, watching television with my husband while our gawky, adolescent son plays a game on his iPad, occasionally shouting, "Nonononono!" or announcing with a spir-ited "Woohoo!" that he's leveled up or scored some new achievement. Our son is usually in his room with the door closed, but I have taken away his solitary computer privileges, and we're together again in the living room, like old times. Soon I will stand and yawn, clap my hands and cheerfully announce, "Time for bed!"

In my fantasies, I view parenthood—even the teen years—with rose-colored glasses. Sure you worry, and orthodontia and college are costly, but just gather the family 'round the flat-screen in your 3-D glasses and your worries shall be washed away. However, I still have vivid memo-ries of being a teenager, hatefully telling my mother I wish she'd aborted me, wasting incredible amounts of time on boys who didn't deserve the attention, and rolling my eyes at every bit of good advice Mom tried to give me. I know it's not like the sitcoms would have you believe.

But sometimes, between the dull routines and violent riptides of life, there are oases of calm. Watching Paul quietly earmark his favor-ite recipes in my *Prevention* magazine, watching Erik laugh at Stephen Colbert, I realize there is a name for the unfamiliar new feeling in my heart. Contentment.

Chapter 18
"Honey, do we need bladder protection already?"

I'm eating a banana at my desk, grading papers, when Emily leaps into my room with an invitation and a huge smile.

"Jesus, you scared me!" I say, putting a hand over my heart like I'm about to recite the *Pledge of Allegiance*.

"Sorry!" she laughs.

"Well, at least you stuck the landing."

"Hey, I'm having a party, and I wanted to invite you! It's an organization party—you know, we all have so much stuff, who doesn't need a little help keeping everything organized?"

Speak for yourself, I want to say. Instead, I take the invitation from her extended hand. It showcases attractively arranged photos of monogrammed desk sets, activity organizers for the wall, stylish diaper bags with secret ninja pockets, nothing with an obvious, immediate use for my own life.

"When is it?" I ask, turning my brain upside-down and shaking it to see if any good, unused excuses might tumble out.

"Next Tuesday night! My house, 6 p.m., and I'll have champagne cocktails and tons of snacks! You eat shellfish, right?"

All I can think of is the excuse Shantell Johnson used today for not having her paper on women's suffrage written: "My uncle's meth lab blew up." Which, in my class, is the new and improved version of "the dog ate my homework."

I give up. I can't keep her at bay forever. "Okay," I say. I wonder if Evelyn, Chris, or Alyssa would be interested. "Can I bring a few friends?"

"Oh my gosh, yes! The more the merrier!" You could almost hear her calculating the bump she'd get in hostess gifts and product discounts.

***

"Do you need anything organized?" I asked Erik as I got ready to leave for Emily's party.

"Ask her if she has a system to organize my pornography collection," he suggested.

"You ask her," I said. After we got married, I actually made Erik throw away an entire laundry basket full of old VHS pornos from the eighties. I always imagined some kid finding them at the city dump, shouting, *"Jackpot!"* and then, *"Crap!"* when he remembered he didn't even own a VCR. Years ago we'd watched a few together in an attempt to spice up our love life, but nothing kills the mood like your husband craning his neck and looking over your shoulder to fast-forward to "the good parts."

I was pleased that Evelyn, Chris, and Alyssa all agreed to come with me, and I picked them up on the way. During the drive, I learn that Chris had indeed fielded a call from David at Evelyn's dinner party, though he insisted they were definitely over, and he was never talking to that man again. I gently admonished him, and Evelyn told us an awful story about a woman she knew whose husband beat her to death. We rode in silence for a few blocks, contemplating this senseless tragedy, until I simply had to try and lighten the mood with a wag of my finger and a stern, "So let that be a lesson to you!" It's like the *NBC Nightly News*—everything so frightening and depressing that you *have* to close with something more upbeat or your entire audience will stick their heads in the oven.

A wreath on Emily's front door features a small, wooden sign that instructs us to *Think spring!* "You never hear anyone say, 'Think winter!'" Chris observes while I ring the doorbell. A swarm of butterflies begins to flap their wings in my stomach when I hear laughter inside and see a shadow approach. Emily flings open the door. "You're here!" She's wearing a white belted shirtdress and a chunky, hand-painted wooden necklace that clatters when she walks. Though we're still three weeks from the official first day of spring, Emily's townhouse is decked with bouquets of red tulips, purple hyacinths in clay flowerpots, and cheerful yellow daffodils in glazed ceramic bowls. Linda Hernandez, chatting with another teacher on the couch, sees me and waves. While I make introductions, Emily's two Dalmatians, Pig and Poke, trot over to greet us. The aptly named Poke immediately sticks his muzzle in my crotch.

"He must smell Nancy," I joke, gently pushing his insistent nose away.

"Poke, get down! I'm so sorry. He's harmless, though." Emily takes my coat and whispers, "Do you have your period? He usually hones in on that like a laser beam!"

I press my thighs together and push Poke away again. Horrified, I feel myself nodding: *yes, I have my period, because my husband's sperm are shaped like little cubes. Now can you please forget any of this happened? And go feed your dog an entire barbecued cow?*

Poke keeps poking until Emily lures him away with the promise of a treat in the kitchen. Pig jumps on Chris over and over, planting her front paws on his chest, wagging her tail and straining to lick his face. "She loves men," Emily explains, and Chris laughs politely and keeps lifting Pig's paws from his silk blouse. I wonder if Chris feels insulted. I refer to Chris with "him" and "he" and "his," though I have to imagine Chris would prefer "her" and "she." It's all a bit confusing. As long as Chris has a penis, I'll probably refer to him as "him." Unless he instructs otherwise. Or she. It's a bit perplexing.

Abe and Auschie, now thankfully recovered from their attempted poisoning, seem so much better behaved than these wild Dalmatians. Then again, they can't jump above the average person's kneecaps, which helps keep the groin-sniffing and blouse-ruining to a minimum.

We find places to sit in the living room and get down to business, fauxdmiring the product samples and passing around a catalog. Emily tells us to help ourselves to the snacks set out in the kitchen. "There's punch!" she urges. "It's non-alcoholic, but there is a bottle of rum next to the bowl for those of you who wish to imbibe."

"What happened to the champagne cocktails?"

"Too much work," she says, shrugging.

I lean over to Evelyn and whisper, "See how awesome *you* are?" I'm referring to her elaborate, authentic fifties cocktails, personalized for each guest.

Evelyn smiles and murmurs, "Oh, not really." My mother was like that, too; she wouldn't accept a compliment if you paid her. When we were in high school, Clint, Gwen, and I would mess with her, intentionally piling on the flattery and laughing at how flustered she'd get: "This chicken is so delicious!" *("Oh my gosh, it's so dry!")*, "Your flowers are the most beautiful on the block!" *("Oh, no! Put your glasses on. Just look at all those weeds!")*, and my personal favorite, an exchange that took place on her fortieth birthday: "Your skin is still as smooth as a teenager's!" *("You idiot!" accompanied by a delighted smile)* Though she blushed and protested vigorously, you could tell she was always secretly pleased. Try this with the next Midwestern Catholic you meet. The results will amuse you.

A few of us wander into the kitchen to browse the appetizers. Avery Morgan, one of the secretaries in the school office, is leaning over the sink, stuffing a brownie into her mouth. "These bars are soooo moist," she groans in pleasure, still chewing. Emily winces at her use of the word "moist."

Avery Morgan is quite possibly the most attractive fifty-eight year-old in Wisconsin. Her youngest daughter married a writer whose first novel featured an author who has a torrid affair with his new mother-in-law. Not surprisingly, it made future family get-togethers more than a little uncomfortable.

Chris and I take paper plates and begin to fill them with hors d'oeuvres: slices of Swiss and Colby cheese, Ritz crackers, raw cauliflower, baby carrots, blobs of dill dip, salsa from a jar and broken tortilla chips. "So Alyssa seems okay to you?" I ask. Chris glances at her in the living room, where she's perusing the catalog for Emily's organizational wares, safely out of earshot.

"She's been kind of quiet, but she seems okay. Why?"

"She made a comment in the car."

"What comment?" Chris bites into a sliced cucumber slathered in dip and folds his arms, the remaining crescent moon of cucumber pressed daintily between his index finger and thumb.

"Some joke about how it's good she doesn't have a car or a garage. If you get my drift."

"Oh, now I remember. What was the context?"

"Something about Ben pulling away, acting weird."

Evelyn joins us at the kitchen island and selects a plate, napkin, and plastic cutlery. "What do you recommend?"

"U.S. treasuries," I joke, silently berating myself for always being so weird and esoteric. "Always a safe investment."

Evelyn doesn't skip a beat. "My entire portfolio is in treasuries. I'm retired, you know." She winks and bites into a carrot, which snaps crisply like in a commercial for ranch dressing.

Evelyn referencing her financial future reminds me of Carl, so I ask how he's been.

"Oh, fine! He invited me to invest in a restaurant he's opening, but I'm not sure I can afford to right now. I've been helping Kimberly pay a few things off, and with the price of gas and groceries going through the roof, I'm not sure. I'd like to save for another trip to Europe in a year or two, and you always want to keep a cushion for medical emergencies. Still, I want to be supportive, and he really is such a savvy businessman. His brother will be the chef. He trained in Europe, Carl says!"

I try, try, try not to shake her and scream, "*Evelyn!*" Instead, I remain calm, nodding and listening with concern. "Well, you know your financial situation best," I diplomatically say, trying to suppress the tic that's threatening to erupt in my right eye. "I'm sure you'll make the right decisions." I drag a mushroom through the dip on my plate and add, "How's his divorce coming along?"

Evelyn sighs and says, "It's a work in progress," which I interpret as *He's going to string me along until he's bored and/or has enough money to open his restaurant and then magically reunite with his estranged wife because she's the mother of his children and would take him to the cleaners in a divorce.*

A better, less cynical person than me would interpret this simply as *It's a work in progress.*

She catches my eye and adds, "I haven't been this happy in a long time."

"Then I'm happy for you," I say, touching her arm.

Linda wanders into the kitchen and makes a beeline for Chris. "I wanted to tell you," she says, "that you have excellent taste in boots."

"Why, thank you!"

After she leaves Chris whispers to me, "Is that the one whose husband has a tiny penis?"

I nod, only a little ashamed that I am terrible at keeping juicy secrets.

I know most of the guests, except for about half a dozen. One of them, a blocky, dour-faced woman who reminds me of a Lincoln Log, keeps frowning at Chris, but he's unflappable as always. He marches right over to her and smiles broadly. "I love your earrings! Where'd you get them?"

She smiles back, flattered and disarmed. "Oh, thank you. My sister got them for me on vacation."

Emily suddenly materializes at my side. "That's my pastor's wife. She was caught shoplifting at a Super Target in Minneapolis last year."

"What'd she steal?"

"Hair clips." She returns to the kitchen to refill the cracker basket.

I sit next to Alyssa on the loveseat. "Are you going to order anything?"

"I'm not sure. It's all kind of expensive."

At this point Poke appears again, anxious to see what my crotch has been up to in the last fifteen minutes. I set my plate on an end table and try to shoo him away. Alyssa laughs. "Excuse me," I say and leave to find the nearest bathroom before my head explodes. Once there I spray myself below the waist with Febreze, which is another proper noun that has become a verb. I *Febreze* the hell out of myself, check my hair and teeth in the mirror, and rejoin the party.

I return to my seat next to Alyssa and ask to see the product catalog. Does my attendance require me to buy something? I suppose so.

"It smells like toilet bowl cleaner in here." Sandy Logan, who teaches band and rear-ended me in the high school parking lot last year, wrinkles her nose and sniffs the air. "Really strong. All of the sudden." Despite having earned two advanced degrees, Sandy regularly says things like "irregardless" and "all of the sudden."

"I know," I say, playing along. I join her in sniffing to determine the origin of this mysterious and off-putting odor. Alyssa starts laughing again next to me, the couch cushion shuddering beneath us.

Chris leans over the back of the loveseat to say, "Honey, do we need bladder protection already?"

"What?"

"Whatever you did in the bathroom, perhaps you did too much of it."

I look down into my lap and am appalled to see that there is a noticeably wet spot where I'd sprayed myself. Alyssa is now laughing so hard she's nearly crying, shaking and turning red, trying to contain it. Chris passes her a tissue he extracts from his handbag, and she blots her eyes.

"I had to Febreze my crotch so the goddamn dog would stop sticking his nose in it," I hiss.

Chris presses his lips together primly. "Well, if you'd shower once in awhile," he says, and marches away to inquire about the pantry organization system, complete with spice flexo-rack in your choice of pink, brown, or blue, now on sale for $49.99.

***

A week later, during an unseasonably warm spell that made the snowdrifts slump and melt from roofs across Madison, forming great, dripping stalactites that threatened to rip the eaves right off people's homes, my phone rings at eleven-thirty on a Wednesday night.

"Hello?" I answer, still swimming up from sleep, my voice hoarse.

I am greeted with soft sobs, then finally, "Ben broke up with me." *Alyssa.*

I sit up, step into my slippers, and pad into the hallway. Erik, awakened by the ringing phone, angrily smothers his ear with a pillow.

"What?"

"Ben broke up with me. He told me he wasn't able to love me the way I loved him, that he wasn't ready for a relationship, that he didn't like it when I wore belts."

"He didn't like it when you wore belts?"

"What does that even mean?" she pleads, sniffling.

"Hon, slow down. Start at the beginning."

Alyssa backs up and tells me everything while I curl up on the sofa downstairs. Nancy settles into my lap and starts to purr, unaware of the unfolding crisis. It was the usual story about two damaged people who had no business trying to love one another.

"I can't go back to therapy. Not with Ben in the same group!"

"Sweetie, can you talk to your doctor and see if there's another group you can join?"

"There's only one group for people with suicidal impulses!" she wails. "Oh my god, how did I get so screwed up," she moans, weeping again. "I'm worthless. I can't do this!"

"Okay," I say softly. I wonder if her medication needs to be adjusted. "Stop. I want you to do something right now for me."

"What."

"Pour yourself a glass of water and take a big sip."

"What?"

"Just do it."

I hear a cupboard slam and the sound of running water, followed by a squeak when she shuts the tap off. "Okay."

"Now take a deep breath, and finish the whole glass before you hang up the phone."

I let her talk, closing my eyes and listening. I will listen as long as it takes. She starts to talk about Ben but she ends up talking about Ryan. About what it feels like to field the call that the man you love is dead. They'd talked about marriage, planned to go to Greece in spring, and now he was shelved in a crypt in Sheboygan.

It was too soon, I tell her. You have to give yourself time to heal. Focus on yourself. It'll be scary, but you have to love yourself before you can even start to love anyone else.

I quote everything my mother ever told me—every ounce of advice, every scrap of wisdom that proved to be true and solid and real over the years. I tell her she'll be okay, that this too shall pass. I make her promise to continue with her therapy, individual and group. I feel horribly unqualified to deal with this. "What are you doing first thing in the morning?" I ask, before a cogent activity even materializes in my mind. It seems like a good idea to get Alyssa to commit to future plans.

"I have lab at nine-thirty. Why?" She sounds apprehensive.

"Want to meet for an early breakfast? I know a great place."

Alyssa considers this for a moment and finally agrees. "Thank you, Jaime," she says quietly. She's calmed down some, though I know she has a long night ahead of her.

"You are stronger than you think," I say. It sounds an awful lot like a lie.

***

I get a chance to test my adage when I check my e-mail a few days later and find a message from my father. Technically, he'd sent it a week earlier, but it had been delivered in my spam folder, tucked beneath a message hawking human growth hormone pills from a sender memorably named "Nocturnal Yellow Finger."

From: Jim and Sharon Stewart <u>andtheirlittledog2@gmail.com</u>
To: J Collins <u>sid_n_nancy@yahoo.com</u>
Sent: Thursday, February 25, 4:36 PM
Subject: hi
Hi kid,

I know what you're thinking—hey, a message from Dad! And, how did he get my email address? You can thank my clever granddaughter for that. She gave me your email! I hope all is well. How's teaching?

Working fairly regularly now, but Sharon's been laid off. Say a prayer for her, if you get a chance...she's been sending hundreds of resumes out, but not much luck.

We're hoping to take an Alaskan cruise this June, if funds allow. Getting older now, not enough time to do all the things you want. Seize the day, after all!

I had surgery on my rotator cuff last October, and now I'm taking eye drops for glaucoma. The medication makes my lashes nice and long—thinking of applying it to my bald spot. Also beginning to develop arthritis. Look at me, I'm turning into one of those people who write letters about their health problems. I'm falling apart, I guess.

Sure miss you, wish we could get you and that husband of yours to come visit in Portland. Write when you get a chance. I'll try to be better about keeping in touch.

Hugs,
Dad

All those years spent pretending I wasn't desperately waiting for him to toss a few emotional crumbs my way, to actually build a relationship with me ... at some point I stopped waiting, and now here he is again. It's not unlike pining for a lost love who decides to pop back into your life long after you've moved on. I read the e-mail again, mentally cataloguing the take-away points to share with Erik later:

1) My father is facing more frequent physical reminders of his own mortality—a possible reason for his attempt to reach out to me?

2) Hannah gave him my personal e-mail address. What prompted that?

3) We both named our e-mail accounts after our pets. I am strangely bothered by this.

4) He signed it with hugs. Which makes me want to sign my response, Bitter and wary, Jaime.

I read it again to tease out any hidden meaning. It's an awkward message, nearly self-conscious, even somewhat conciliatory. Now the ball is in my court. Do I delete and forget? Forgive? Respond politely? Tell him thanks for playing, better luck next time?

Maybe I'll know what to do when I can answer this question: Am *I* stronger than I think?

Chapter 19
"You're not going to die first."

Erik and I are sitting in the parked car with Nancy, spying on the potential buyers touring my mother's home. Because I've left the curtains open, I can see them standing around the kitchen table, talking to the realtor. "They've been in there for over an hour. What's taking so long?"

"Maybe they found your vibrator collection."

"Maybe they found your sense of humor."

To kill time while we waited, we drove around Madison, scouting potential new apartments. There was a duplex I liked, one of two units in a stately old Victorian painted blue with maroon accents on the spindles and gingerbread trim. Yellow and violet crocuses skirted the foundation shrubs, looking jaunty and hopeful as they poked through the patchy remains of our last snowstorm. I could already imagine myself drinking coffee on the second-level balcony, a songbird perched on the railing, serenading me cheerfully. But it was in a neighborhood Erik called "questionable," and it lacked a garage or covered parking. Erik preferred something in the western suburbs, with modern fixtures in the bathrooms and a fireplace that turned on with the push of a button. Our last apartment had been run-of-the-mill, with fluorescent lighting that buzzed and clicked in the laundry room and mysterious black stains on the carpeting in the stairwell, but it had been affordable, and an easy commute to work for both of us. When we first moved in, I'd gotten permission to paint the walls; my mother had helped me paint the living room a soft cocoa and the bathroom a cool gray, with white trim. We'd made it nice, cozy. You could almost overlook it when my upstairs neighbor did step aerobics at four-thirty in the morning.

Watching strangers stand around the table at which I'd eaten oatmeal for breakfast, I am struck by a wave of frustration and exhaustion. There is also a feeling of panicky dread; things are irrevocably changing faster than I can keep up. "Why can't we just buy a house?"

"We could, but it would wipe out our savings. How much debt are you comfortable with?"

"We'll get some money after Mom's house sells. And I can start selling plasma."

Erik studies me carefully. "Are you serious?"

"About selling my plasma?"

"No. About buying a house."

"Maybe. Yes." We discuss what kind of down payment we might have, after Mom's house sells, and how financially stretched we'd be if one or both of us suddenly had to replace a vehicle or limb. We itemize the things we could do without: Showtime, a landline phone, meals prepared by professionals. I'm buoyed by the new possibilities before me, though they feel nebulous and undefined. Like looking at online photos of a Tahitian resort. I can just as easily imagine myself shopping for flooring at Lowe's as I can sipping a Mai Tai on the beach. Both seem like nice ways to spend a Sunday afternoon, but with dim prospects of actually happening.

"It's a major commitment," Erik warns.

"Interest rates have never been lower," I counter, parroting a commercial I'd heard on the radio the day before. I am daring it to happen.

The prospective buyers finally leave, armed with sales sheets and umbrellas they snap open on the porch. The temperature hovers right above freezing. Wet clots of snow begin to fall, melting instantly into the pavement. It's always peculiar to return to the house after strangers have been through it, judging your furniture and frowning at the lumpy linoleum near the stove. You are compelled to see the house through their eyes, noting new imperfections and odors where this morning there had been none. You even feel sorry for the wobbly railing near the stairs, because you know they criticized it. Today, they've left a note scrawled in boxy cursive, on the back of the realtor's card: *Thanks for letting us dream!*

I read it aloud to Erik.

"Didn't they see the pink bathtub?" he asks. "That's really more of a nightmare."

Later I open my mother's closet and stand in the weak glow cast by the interior light. There are still dozens of dresses, slacks, and blouses on hangers, shoes for every occasion resting on a tiered tree. I turn and analyze the rest of her bedroom. Though Clint and Gwen had already picked through our mother's belongings, taking the most valuable and attractive furniture and meaningful mementos, there is still so much left. In the attic. In the basement. In the garage. In every room in the house. Garden tools, books, side tables, blenders, chairs, bird feeders, teapots, shower curtains, furnace filters and bulletin boards. A catalog of my mother's life thick enough to stop a bullet if worn close to the chest. Overwhelmed and anxious, I ask Erik what we're going do with it all.

"Start packing."

"I know, but then what?"

"Garbage. Yard sale. Goodwill. Storage unit. Does it matter? It's just stuff, and we don't really need any of it."

It's just stuff. His complete lack of sentimentality makes me stiffen. I feel something dark and inky bloom inside of me, an anger slowly staining my organs as it spreads. "If I die first, would you do that with my things? Just box up my life and throw it away, drop it at Goodwill? Maybe dump my ashes down the garbage disposal?" I bring my hands together and dust them briskly. "Well, that's that! What time is *Pawn Stars* on?"

Erik sighs heavily, always the rational one. "You're not going to die first."

"Of course not," I agree. "You gorge on triple Thickburgers with extra bacon and smoke like a chimney when I'm not around to guarantee *I'm* the one who will be widowed and die alone."

"I'm not having this argument again." He walks out of the bedroom, and my anger only mushrooms, at Erik and at myself. *Fight with me,* I want to scream. *Stop being so patient, so rational, so clinical!*

"Why not?" I yell recklessly. "We know our lines so well!"

See how quickly I can now turn a bright, hopeful conversation into a painful, toxic one? It's a neat little trick they don't tell you about in the books on grief management, and I've gotten so good at it.

Right now, I want to shout after him, he is the last person I want to buy a house with. I'd rather get divorced than watch another person succumb to cancer. I'd rather die a horrible death all alone than box my mother's life up and watch her disappear forever.

***

That night, I sleep on the couch for the first time in years. I stare at the green glow cast by the technology stacked in our entertainment center, finally falling asleep some time after three. Erik finds me downstairs in the morning, a hurt look on his face. "We never sleep apart," he says, like a wounded little boy. I tell him he was snoring, that I couldn't sleep, that I didn't want to wake him with my tossing and turning. The real reason is this: I'd simply wanted to be alone with my sadness, giving it space to spread out, because there wasn't enough room for all three of us in the queen-sized bed.

***

People are usually on their best behavior when you first meet them, but gradually the demons and frailties begin to emerge as the relationship progresses. It's like the opposite sides of a balance scale. As one side sinks with your deepening knowledge about this new person, the other side, holding their insecurities and dysfunctions, rises. You learn that they are incredibly generous, always offering to pay for lunch, but they also have a bad habit of canceling plans at the last minute. You learn their address, where they went on family vacations as a child, that their favorite ice cream is rocky road—but also that they gossip, are obsessed with money and appearance, and are closet racists. Eventually, you have to decide whether to stick it out or cut your losses. Where you make the call depends on what they mean to you, and perhaps how long you've known them.

Look at my students. On the first day of school, even the most sullen among them, Dylan Rodriguez, was bright-eyed and bushy-tailed. Notebooks were clean and unmarked, waiting to be filled with brilliant or industrious prose. Pencils were sharpened and unchewed, erasers plump and whole; no one could even fathom making a mistake that would warrant their use. I too began the new school year optimistic, sleeves rolled up, confident that this year my students wouldn't sleep or whisper through class, this year I'd have more than three parents show up for conferences, this year I'd inspire in my kids a love for learning that endures and transports. Today, seven months into the school year, I broke up a fight between Dylan and Ryan Nelson, sending them both to the principal's office. Ryan's notebook is intricately doodled with rotting zombies and skulls with huge, gaping eye sockets, and Dylan's erasers are still plump and whole, because he rarely writes anything at all. Yesterday, Breanna Derozier and Cody Price were suspended for explicit sexting, exactly one week after the best poet in my class, Jordan Nichols, was expelled when a drug-sniffing dog led one of our school resource officers straight to the baggie of pot in his locker. Though there are still two months of school left, we are all counting down the days until we don't have to see one another on a near-daily basis.

I am now beginning to see how this formula also applies to my new family. Take Evelyn, for example. Initially, the kind of strong, independent older woman I aspired to be, now a lonely older woman so desperate for love that she lets her daughter and new boyfriend take complete advantage of her. Last night I received an anxious call from her. She'd loaned Carl $20,000, he'd grown more and more distant since then, and now he won't return her phone calls. I didn't chastise her, ask her how such a smart woman could fall for this blatant con man, because I saw the way she looked at him. I saw the hope and excitement in her eyes. You always think, *Oh, I'll never marry the wrong person or get pregnant out of wedlock or cheat on my wife or fall for a scam when I'm elderly or vote Republican* and then it happens, and you can't believe it. You become the jaded, scuffed-up person who tells cocky, young idealists, "You say that now!" and you can't believe how arrogant and naïve you once were.

"So what are your options?" I asked her. "If it's technically considered a gift, can you take him to court to get it back?"

"I don't think so," she said, sounding much older than she actually was. She sounded confused, bewildered that this had happened, that it was happening to her. She sounded like my father-in-law in the months before he was admitted to the Pheasant Ridge care facility. He'd find himself in the neighbor's garage, fumbling with their lawn mower, and wake from whatever cognitive haze he'd been in, baffled and lost, living a sadder version of the Talking Heads song: *Well, how did I get here?*

"Do you want me talk to him?" I asked. I'm not a very confrontational person, but $20,000 is a large chunk of money. "Or maybe we should get the police involved. See if he's done this kind of thing before, if he can be prosecuted."

Later that night, after I spoke with a brusque female officer who took down the details and gave me a vague assurance they would do everything they could to get Evelyn's money back, Erik joined me in the kitchen. He'd heard most of my phone call and quietly said, "You know, you can't bring back your own family back by saving any of them."

What could I say to that? He was right, and I knew it, but it was so much more than that. Part of it was that I felt like a broken shard from a smashed vase, and I only wanted to spend time with the other broken pieces because maybe we could glue ourselves together and hold water again. Erik wasn't a broken shard. He was a whole vase, forged from some space-age unbreakable polymer. He bounced when he fell. I shattered into sharp little pieces waiting to slice into the next person unfortunate enough to walk into the room barefoot.

Or as Frankie would say, I'd cut a bitch. And then feel really bad about it.

Chapter 20

"But I love her!"

Chris calls me the following Friday night, frantic. He's barricaded in his bathroom, and I can hear pounding and yelling in the background. It's David, and they had another fight, after which Chris locked himself in the bathroom. "Have you called the cops?" I ask.

"I really don't want to get them involved again," Chris whispers into the receiver.

"Chris! You have a restraining order out on this man. Use it!"

I hear more pounding, and a muffled man's voice, pleading. "We can't call the police," Chris hisses. "There are drugs in the house!"

Oh, for Christ's sake. "Whose drugs?"

"David's. Just a little bit of pot. Anyway, he's the one with the restraining order, remember?"

I'd been watching a movie with Alyssa at her apartment, and she pauses the DVD when I get up from the couch and wander into the kitchen. Kevin Bacon's face freezes into an unattractive, twitching mask on the screen.

"Call the police," I instruct. "Please."

"He's already on probation, and they'd throw him in jail!"

"Don't you think that might be the best place for him?"

"No," Chris says, nearly whimpering. "He can't go to jail. They'd eat him alive!"

"This is so insane and unhealthy," I say, more to myself than Chris, rubbing my eyes.

"I'll go back to therapy. We both will." Bargaining and denial. Two of the stages of grief. Can't wait 'til we hit anger.

I guess what they say is true. An addict has to hit his or her own personal rock bottom before giving up their drug of choice. Chris thought he'd hit it. *I* thought he'd hit it. Turns out he only bounced off the side of the cliff during the fall.

"I need you to talk to him. You're so rational and levelheaded."

I laugh out loud. "No, I'm not. Just ask Erik."

"You are! I can't do this alone. I need your help. Someone sane to talk him down. He won't listen to me."

"Is he being violent? Is he threatening you?"

"No. I only want him to leave, but he won't. He just needs help."

Don't we all, Chris. Don't we all.

I brief Alyssa on the way to the car. "Are you sure this is a good idea?" she asks, trotting to keep up with me, keys jangling.

"No. It's probably a terrible idea, but Chris needs us, and I don't know what else to do." Alyssa seems troubled by this, so I add, "If it's ugly, we're calling the cops." If Erik knew about this, he'd blow a gasket and call the police first thing, because he has more sense than the rest of us combined.

I'd only been to Chris's place once before, when dropping him off after lunch on State Street one Saturday. He lives near the "questionable" neighborhood with the stately Victorian I adored in a ramshackle brick house divided into four apartments. Some of the windows are flecked with stained glass, and the cement front steps are cracked and crumbly, illuminated in a weird yellow light from the special bug bulb screwed into the grimy wall sconce. It's probably up to code only in his landlord's imagination. A young man in jeans and a navy hoodie is smoking on the porch, the orange ember at the end of his cigarette glowing brightly with every inhalation. He unfolds himself and slinks away as we approach.

"I did a whippet behind this building one year in college," I confess to Alyssa. "My first and last ever, during the Mifflin Street Block Party." I don't know why I'm telling her this; perhaps to establish some street cred, give myself the aura of toughness before we go inside like straight Cagney and Lacey to deal with whatever mess is unfolding near Chris's bathroom.

"Which apartment is he?" she asks, focused not on a poor choice I made in college but on the badly labeled intercom near the mailbox. Two of the boxes overflow with pizza delivery fliers, bills, and magazines.

"Apartment two, first floor."

We enter the foyer and I hear music, mostly thumping bass, coming from Chris's apartment. His door is unlocked, and I carefully turn the knob. The music crescendos as the door swings open, and I'm surprised when I recognize it as Chicago's "Feelin' Stronger Every Day." A song completely at odds with the situation. The living room is hazy and cluttered with books. The coffee table is set for two, with plates, wine glasses, silverware, napkins, and an empty bottle of wine. They had dinner together? I see David slumped on the hardwood floor with his back against the bathroom door, crying and smoking. He doesn't seem surprised by our sudden presence and greets us with a tearful, exasperated, "She won't come out!" Like we're on the same team, like he's tattling on a mischievous sibling. Clean-shaven and well-dressed, with warm, brown eyes and neatly clipped fingernails, he doesn't look like the kind of man who would abuse a habit, let alone a person.

I take a deep breath and say, "It's time to go home, David,"

His face sours and he angrily stubs his finished cigarette into an ashtray on the floor next to him. "What do you know about what time it is?" His words are slurred, his eyes glassy. "You shouldn't even be here. This is between me—" he points at his chest— "and Chris." He points at the bathroom door.

"Jaime, is that you?" Chris shouts from the bathroom. "David, I can't take this any more! Please go home!"

I cross my arms and stand my ground while Peter Cetera wails behind me. "We've called the police. You have less than ten minutes to leave." I'm bluffing, of course, but it works. Alyssa also crosses her arms and stands next to me, my trusty, depressive sidekick. A sober fear works its way into David's face as he processes this. He seems to respect the seriousness of his situation for a minute, then proceeds to fall apart all over again.

"But I love her!"

"If you loved her, you wouldn't hit her," Alyssa says. *Her*. I suddenly realize why Chris loved David so deeply, why he was so unwilling to let go despite the abuse—David was one of a handful of people that saw Chris as a woman, the way Chris saw himself. *Herself*. It occurs to me how little I truly know about the people who answered my ad, who have formed my experimental new family. I know the basics, like Paul's favorite TV shows and Evelyn's tendency to over-tip servers and that Alyssa played the flute in high school and sprinkles nutritional yeast on her popcorn, but this didn't mean I *really* knew them. I could feel the scales tipping, the more I paid attention. *"You know what cancer taught me?"* I remember my mother softly saying, *"Cancer taught me to be present in every moment. To pay attention to every detail. Also, if you can help it, never get it."*

"Come on David, it's time to go." I don't extend a hand to help him up because he scares me, quite frankly. Also, he doesn't deserve a helping hand. Instead, I clap them briskly. *Chop-chop, party's over!* He scrambles to stand, sloppy and loose, and has to steady himself against the wall, head down, before he's ready to face the world.

"Do you want us to call you a cab?" Alyssa asks, deftly stepping out of the way as he stumbles in her direction.

"I can walk," he insists, his words deliberate, defensive, and angry. We stand perfectly still and watch while he lists and pitches across the living room as if he's on a ship in turbulent water.

Once he's gone, I turn off the stereo. "Go to the window and make sure he's leaving," I tell Alyssa, who sprints to the front bay window and spies. *Thank God he didn't have a weapon,* I think. I carry pepper spray, but two young women and a diminutive man in heels and pantyhose are no match for one crazy guy armed with a gun. *What was I thinking?* The dangerous potential of the situation suddenly hits me like a roundhouse kick to the gut.

"He's leaving," she reports, and Chris unlocks the bathroom door. My sleeves feel funny, like they're conducting a mild electric current, and I look down to see my hands are shaking.

"I can't believe we did that," I tell Alyssa, adrenaline sizzling through my body. "Chris, are you crazy? Why did you let him come over?"

"I'm sorry, I know, I'm weak!" His cheeks are streaked with mascara, his curls askew.

Alyssa examines him. "Are you okay? He didn't hit you, did he?"

"No, I'm fine."

"We should have called the cops," I tell him firmly. "Next time I will."

"But don't let there be a next time," Alyssa clarifies.

"Chris, I don't know what to do here. You need to stay away from him. Or you'll be just like that woman Evelyn told us about. Beaten to death by the man who claimed to love her."

"Chris, this is serious," Alyssa adds gently.

Chris sits carefully on the edge of the couch and puts his face in his hands. I crouch beside him, joints popping, and touch his arm. "Hey," I say softly, "we care about you. We don't want to lose you. But this is as involved as I can get here. The rest is on you."

"I know," he says. "I know. I'm going to get help."

"Is there anyone we can call?" Alyssa asks.

Chris shakes his head sadly. And therein lies the problem. The reason Chris answered my stupid ad in the first place. It's also the reason I posted the ad, and now it's the reason we're here tonight instead of Chris's parents.

"This is another fine Tony's Pizza you've gotten yourself into," I mumble under my breath.

Alyssa looks at me. "What?"

"Never mind."

***

Back at home, I fall onto the sofa in an exhausted heap. The house is dark and empty, a vaguely hostile note on the kitchen table: *Went out for awhile. Be home late.* Not, *Playing darts with the guys, be home by midnight, love you!*

My Friday nights were usually spent with Erik, but the last few have been dedicated to search and rescue missions on behalf of Paul, Chris, Alyssa, or Evelyn. Maybe this was all a horrible idea. Things were getting messy, out of hand. I know I'm losing myself in the care and feeding of my new "family," neglecting my marriage and other friendships, but I'm not sure how to find my way out of this. It's like a wonderful dream that has gradually twisted into a horrifying landscape of naked PowerPoint presentations and orgies featuring the Ichabod Crane lookalike who works at your local Starbucks. I close my eyes and listen to Nancy crunching kibble in the kitchen. I tell myself I'll feel better in the morning. Everything looks brighter in a fresh coat of sunshine.

***

I wake up the next morning still on the couch, confused first as to where I am and then mildly hurt that Erik didn't wake me when he got home.

"How was the movie?" Erik is reading the paper in the kitchen, a mug of steaming coffee in hand. He's already showered and dressed—the remote, critical parent. I am the disheveled, disappointing stepchild.

"Why'd you let me sleep on the couch?" I sit up and slide my feet into my well-worn slippers, swimming up from my sleepy disorientation into the day.

"I tried to wake you, but you were dead to the world."

Dead to the world. If that's not a depressing way to be described first thing in the morning. As I pour myself a mug of coffee, my cell phone rings. I check the caller ID. "It's Large Marge."

Large Marge is our realtor. Her real name is Paula. With a peach-fuzzy chin, smoker's cough, and a beefy set of jowls tucked in by a thick, no-nonsense gray perm, she looks and sounds exactly like Large

Marge from *Pee-Wee's Big Adventure*. More lumberjack than realtor. "I've got great news for you!" she says in greeting. I wait for the great news: the sixth mass extinction event is not already underway, unemployment rate drops below zero, *Jersey Shore* cancelled, your mother discovered alive and well, running a bed and breakfast in Hawaii. Instead, she says, "We've got an offer on the house!"

Chapter 21

"Only you know the answer to that question."

"Most people are a little more excited when they receive an offer," Large Marge says, confused and annoyed by my apprehension.

"Oh, I am, I am!" I insist, scrambling to feign enthusiasm. "There's just so much to do before we can move." My mind begins to frantically leapfrog from task to task: *sorting through Mom's things ... packing ... labeling ... giving, selling, storing, tossing ... losing her all over again ... finding a place to live ...* Large Marge starts talking about how we're in the driver's seat, we can set the closing date and counter-offer if we like, and a bunch of other things I only half-hear. Erik is eagerly eavesdropping; occasionally I look over and he meets my gaze, brows raised expectantly: *Well?* I put him off with a lift of my hand—I'd tell him when I got off the phone.

I tell Large Marge I have lots to discuss with Erik, and we hang up. "So?" he says.

"The buyers are offering twelve thousand less than asking, but Paula thinks in this market, we might not get anything higher," I dutifully report. We'd been listed for six months, fielding only one offer that was so ridiculously low it was barely in the same room with serious. It had begun to feel like we would be stuck in my late mother's home forever, and the new, sudden possibility that I might be waking up in an entirely new house in a month or two both exhilarates and terrifies me. You get complacent, just sleepwalking through life until you step on a landmine or a skydiver drops to the earth right in front of you, doing a violent somersault into his deflating parachute. You need time to get used to these kinds of surprises.

"Let's do it," Erik says. "Get on with it already. We'll start going through things today. Set up a yard sale, maybe the first weekend in April. Start house-hunting tomorrow. If we have to rent for awhile, I don't even care."

There it was again. Erik Collins and his full-steam ahead, take no prisoners or souvenirs, never-look-back approach to life. I wonder how he'd be if we got divorced—if he'd burn all the old photos and mementos, throw his ring off a bridge, move to Sacramento, start dating a yoga instructor and forget I ever existed. Actually, she wouldn't be a yoga instructor—more likely she'd be a budget analyst. Someone he met in his work as a city planner. Someone ambitious, proficient at retirement planning and good with dogs.

But I can't blame him. It must have pushed him right to the edge to have to live in his dead mother-in-law's house for the last year and a half, taking a shower in the pink tub every day and hearing the novelty doorbell play the first eight notes of "Here Comes the Sun" whenever anyone rang it. It was more than many men would have patiently endured.

"It still has to pass inspection and they need final loan approval," I say, in part to slow Erik's relentless forward motion. But it doesn't matter, because the train has left the station, is now picking up momentum. In an hour, I will be packing a box with photo albums, marking it *storage*. Memories to be sorted through at a later date.

"Are you going to call Clint?" Erik asks, rinsing his coffee mug in the sink.

In answer, I return to the living room and lie down on the floor. I throw my arms out, horizontally crucifying myself, death by Stainmaster. Nancy weaves around my shoulders and steps over my head, delighted by my new prone proximity. Her furry, flabby belly grazes my cheek.

"Okay," Erik says, "but you have to call him sometime today. He's going to want to weigh in on the offer."

***

"We got an offer on the house."

"Jesus Christ, it's about time," Clint says. "How much?"

I tell him.

"Are they fucking kidding me? That's not even eighty percent of assessed value!"

"Paula thinks we should take it. She says the market is still terrible, and it's actually not a bad offer." I like that in this conversation, Paula and the buyers are the scapegoats. I am only the messenger's messenger, though they too have been killed for the message from time to time.

"Tell Paula to tell the *buyers*" he says, spitting out the word *buyers* as if they were sore-covered syphilitics instead of a nice young couple looking for an affordable starter home with a fenced-in yard, "that we'll go six thousand less, and no lower. If they don't like it, they can stuff their offer straight up their twats."

"Okay, I'll tell her. Six thousand less." I ignore the rest of his commentary. It was the first conversation we'd had since Thanksgiving. I think it went surprisingly well!

Twenty minutes later I relay the G-rated version of the message to Large Marge. I wonder briefly how I'd been appointed to deal with the realtor. I don't even like calling to order pizza for delivery, and I'm the one entrusted with the role of communication liaison when a major financial and life decision is being made? How I wished I could pick up the phone and call my mother, ask her what to do.

Erik and I start in the kitchen, working quietly while we sort through utensils and match plastic storage containers with lids. We're sitting cross-legged on the linoleum, waiting for the children we never had to dance around us, tapping our heads: *"Duck, duck, duck, GOOSE!"*

"By the way," Erik says, breaking our silence, "Chris called. He said to thank you for last night."

This catches me off-guard, and I scramble to explain my whereabouts. A kernel of panic pops in my stomach. "Yeah, last night was fun. David came around again, and Chris locked himself in his bathroom. Alyssa and I managed to talk them both down, though."

Instead of responding to my explanation, he moves along to the real conversation he wants to be having. "I spoke with Frankie and Liz, and they're worried about you. We're all worried about you." He's looking at me like I'm a crazy person he's trying to talk off the bridge, a bomb he's trying to disarm, speaking calmly and carefully.

"What are you talking about?"

"You're getting a little wrapped up in these people's lives, don't you think?"

"It was Frankie's idea that I do this!" I scowl at him and look for an exit. "You talked to Liz and Frankie? Jesus, what are you, planning some kind of intervention?" I get up and defensively rummage through a random drawer. I don't even know what I'm looking for. "And when did you talk to them, anyway?"

"They've been calling you, but you're never home to get or return their calls."

"I have a cell phone."

"So use it!"

I sigh and rub my forehead.

"You could have been hurt last night," Erik says.

"I could be hurt on the drive home from work every day."

"Jaime, would you listen to yourself? My God!" I'm alarmed when I realize how angry Erik is. "I went along with all of this because I figured maybe this is what you need right now. And I don't exactly have family falling out of my ass. It's just us. You and me. But I'm okay with that. I know we'll find a way to fill life up. Thing is, I need 'just us' to be enough for you, too."

I glance down at the ice cube tray in my hands. It's metal, with one of those levers you pull to break the ice, leaving a pan of wildly sized shards. "What if it's not?"

I look up to gauge his reaction. He looks so small and dejected sitting on the kitchen floor, shoulders slumped. I should go to him, lean down and wrap my arms around him, bury my face in the stubble on his neck and whisper, *I didn't mean it. I don't know what I'd do without you.* Instead, I stare stupidly, mutely, at the jumble of dusty Tupperware.

"Only you know the answer to that question."

***

Erik is hauling boxes to the garage when I sneak upstairs to dial my mother's old number. I feel like a junky stealing away to shoot up. I don't breathe while I listen to her outgoing message: *"Hi, you've reached Claire Stewart. I'm not available, but if you leave your name and number, I'll call you back as soon as I can. Thanks, and have a great day."* There is a long pause before the beep, because she'd pressed the wrong button when she tried to hang up. I don't leave a message. I never do. Just a series of hang-ups that collectively, one day, will be enough to trigger the replacement of my mother's voice with an automated message that her voicemail box is full. Soon after that, her contract will expire, like any old package of lunch meat. Another umbilical cord severed, and you're almost on your own, kid.

Not ten seconds after I hang up, my phone rings in my hand, startling me. It's Clint again. Maybe he wants to clarify his twat-stuffing instructions, and I nearly greet him with this. Instead, I say, "Miss me already?"

"You have to come to the hospital," he says in a rush, his voice electric with fear. "There's been an accident."

Chapter 22
"Why would anyone not want to get married?"

"Hey, what was the name of that guy we knew in college—the one we called 'Spooky Tooth?'" Frankie sounds delighted, ready to burst into laughter on the other end of the line. "He's here right now! At the grocery store, one aisle away from me! And his tooth is still spooky!"

"Hannah's been in a car accident," I blurt. "We're on the way to the hospital right now."

Her good humor abruptly vanishes. "Oh my God. What happened?"

Hannah and a few other kids were being driven home from a sleepover by one of their mothers when a young kid in a Ford F-350 who'd only had his driver's license for two weeks sped through a red light, T-boning the much smaller Hyundai Accent in the middle of a busy intersection. Hannah had been sitting at ground zero—directly behind the front passenger seat. The impact of the crash had fractured her pelvis, as well as both bones in her right forearm. There were internal injuries, and she was being closely monitored in the ICU.

"Is there anything I can do?" Frankie asks anxiously. "Will she be okay?"

Erik is driving, and he extends his right hand for me to hold while I talk. The gesture is both an olive branch and an oxygen mask dangling from the airplane ceiling, and I gratefully accept it. "Yeah. I think so. But she's going to be down for the count for a long time." It's been a long, emotionally taxing morning already. I can feel my fear snowballing, picking up unpleasant debris with every passing hour. You never plan to spend the weekend in the hospital, much less select it as the setting for an impromptu family reunion. You never plan to field a phone call telling you that your only niece, the one innocent, adored link between you and your estranged family, has lacerations on her liver, and won't be playing soccer again for awhile, unless she's using a pixilated avatar.

Frankie insists on joining us at the hospital, since she's known Hannah for most of her life. When Hannah was little, she'd call her "Fankee," a nickname I still use from time to time. Frankie is also a damned decent human being and a better friend than I probably deserve.

"Joel Witzel," I say, turning around to see if the cop parked at the top of the hill would pull out after us and flip his lights. He stays put.

"Who?"

"Joel Witzel was Spooky Tooth."

***

"She's going to be okay," Erik reminds me after we find a parking space at the hospital. I'm racing ahead of him, frantic, and he takes long, brisk strides to keep up. The on-duty nurse looks familiar; perhaps she's the same one who manned the front desk on Christmas night. Today, instead of Christmas garlands, the main desk is decorated with pastel eggs and paper cutouts of cartoon bunnies. There is a basket of bright plastic eggs nestled in a bed of garishly green Easter grass on the counter, between a jumbo bottle of clear hand sanitizer and a box of tissues. The nurse directs us to the ICU, where we are led by another nurse to Hannah's curtained room. I pause for a moment to summon whatever remaining resources of strength I can scrape together before pulling the privacy curtain aside. Clint and Joy are there, holding vigil. Though there is no love lost between Joy and me, I don't like seeing the pain and worry in her eyes. Clint is sitting by Hannah, holding her hand. He looks sick, old, and frail, like he should be wrapped in a blanket with a thermometer sticking out of his mouth. Though he appears temporarily harmless, I can feel my guard rise the minute we nod in awkward acknowledgement of one another. I wish once again for the kind of brother I could fold into an embrace.

Oh, Hannah. Packets of clear fluid drip into an IV plugged into my niece's forearm. Her right arm is sheathed in a plaster cast. Though she's covered in a thin blanket, I can tell by the lumpy outline of her torso that her hips are likely encased in some sort of mobility-restricting apparatus. She looks so small in the hospital bed, sleeping or perhaps knocked out by painkillers, her fine, straight hair tucked neatly behind her ears, as if someone had been lovingly stroking her hair earlier. My vision blurs with tears.

Joy greets us with, "She only broke her pelvis in one place, thank God."

Clint clears his throat. "The doctors say she'll need surgery to screw in a metal plate and stabilize her hip, and she'll be checked in for a week or two, depending. She'll need rehab to walk again."

At this point I nearly lose it. "Oh, God."

Clint continues, holding up one hand and raising his voice to put the brakes on my potential meltdown. "But she's young and strong. They say she'll bounce back, good as new. It would take longer if she were older, not as healthy."

"What else?" I ask, panic still nibbling at my heart. "What about the internal bleeding?"

"The doc says most pelvic injuries come with internal bleeding. Nothing torn, but she's a bit banged up. What'd he call it?" Clint turns to Joy for clarification.

"Minor abrasions," Joy answers.

"Right. Minor abrasions." He is trying desperately to be brave and remain calm. There is no evidence of Clint's combative demeanor; no sarcasm, no rage, no insulting, derogatory language to describe the doctors or nurses or even the insurance company. This nearly scares me more than Hannah's battered, bruised body, but it illustrates his profound love for his daughter.

At this point, Hannah opens her eyes. "Mom," she says, her voice thick and slow from the medication, "it hurts." Clear, fat tears begin to well in her eyes and spill down her cheeks.

"Hi sweetheart," I say, gently touching her unbroken arm. I feel frustrated, helpless, lost.

"It hurts so much," she repeats, weeping. She reaches for her mother, not me, reminding me of my place in the pack. As her aunt, I am not the one she looks to first when she's in pain and needs comforting; my job is to buy the sushi rolls and show her how to use chopsticks, to send roses on her sixteenth and eighteenth birthdays, to keep secrets about crushes.

Two nurses, one young and one old, interrupt us to check the IV drips and draw blood. "I can't move my legs," Hannah tells them, still crying.

"I know, honey," the older nurse says. "But can you wiggle your toes?" Her hair is salt and pepper gray, cut in a short, easy style they used to call "wash and wear."

Hannah closes her eyes, concentrating hard. We see the blanket twitch near her feet.

"There you go." The older nurse turns to Joy and quietly says, "We're going to have to cath her now."

Hannah's crying is the music that plays us out of the room, and I feel my heart break with every note. In the hallway, we just stare at the well-shined floor for a moment, dazed and raw. You can still hear Hannah wailing over the nurse's soothing reassurances. Clint abruptly turns and hugs me—something he hasn't done since college? High school, maybe? At first I'm shocked, and I feel myself freeze and pull away, sure it's a joke. Had he tripped and accidentally fallen into me? The distance between us is so deep it nearly feels perverse. But soon I relax and allow myself to hug him in return. I rest my head on my long-lost brother's chest. My prodigal sibling. He smells like laundry soap and campfire, and something more. Something familiar. Something *familial*.

And then it hits me. I thought I'd come for Hannah, but I'm actually here for Clint.

***

Like an encore performance of Christmas night, I follow this trip to the hospital with coffee, though this time it's fair-trade and being served in a proper diner, in real ceramic mugs. Clint, Joy, Frankie, Erik, and I are crammed elbow-to-elbow in a booth at Bluephies. Erik and I are sharing a plate of beer and bacon waffles, Frankie is devouring her breakfast jambalaya, and Clint and Joy pick at their respective halves of a cheesy pork and mac sandwich. Even though my stomach hasn't seen a solid food item yet today and Clint and Joy skipped both breakfast and lunch, nobody felt much like eating until Frankie insisted on it. "You need to eat something. Fortify yourselves before you head back to the hospital."

"I hate this place," Clint grumbles, taking an angry bite from his pickle spear. "Full of pretentious yuppies."

The old me would have said, "Now *there's* the Clint we all know and love!" but the new me simply says, "It really sucks that Man's Breakfast closed already." Apparently, business really trailed off after a customer had a heart attack and died in the parking lot before the paramedics could arrive. I don't mind Bluephies, which bills itself as both a restaurant and vodkatorium. With over ninety kinds of vodka behind the bar, it's a popular happy hour destination for some of the teachers from work. It's also a popular brunch destination for people who drive Volvos and subscribe to *Utne Reader*. We overhear a woman one booth down placing her order with the waitress: "I'd like that without tomatoes, and could I sub gluten-free toast? And could I have pepper jack instead of feta cheese? Is the cheese organic? Are the fries baked or deep-fried in the same oil you use to fry the meat? Also, there's a bit of brown plastic or something, a speck of dirt it looks like, floating in my water."

"A hundred years ago, a person like her would be dead by now," Clint says, loudly.

"Strangled by her servants?" I ask.

"No, starved to death."

Most of our conversation revolves around Hannah and her prognosis, and the fact that Clint wants to sue for what are sure to be exorbitant out-of-pocket medical expenses. It wasn't yet fully clear, but texting may have been a possible cause for the driver's inattention. Clint used to be one of those guys who complained that the whole country was going straight to hell because everyone was sue-happy; we were litigating ourselves to death. He echoed buzzwords like "frivolous lawsuits" and "tort reform," and nothing pissed him off more than the idea that an appointed judge might be "legislating from the bench" somewhere. But now he's found a new target for his fury, and he would even hold his nose and vote for a socialist, go vegan for a month if either activity came packaged with swift, violent retribution for the kid driving the F-350.

We learn that the other passengers walked away from the accident with only minor sprains, bruises, and cuts. Poor Hannah would be lucky to be walking by Labor Day, let alone jumping to spike the volleyball when her team reconvened next fall. I hope I'm wrong; I'm a pessimist by nature, something I'm trying to remedy. Clint is angry by nature, but at least he's not directing it at me for the time being.

The accident has made Joy detached and withdrawn, her normally prudish, judgmental distance now a sad one, and I begin to actively worry about her until she turns to Frankie and asks if she and her boyfriend plan on getting married. If anyone were to stumble upon a personal question that Joy has yet to ask floating in some distant galaxy, or perhaps hiding under a rock in the Amazon, you may want to laminate it, bottle it, roll it in bubble wrap and ship it to a museum, because only the Amur leopard is rarer.

"Um, I actually don't want to get married," Frankie says. "Hey! Is there barbecue sauce in that sandwich?"

"Why would anyone not want to get married?" Joy asks, unable to even comprehend the existence of a woman who wouldn't want to fold her husband's underwear every Saturday or assume responsibility for remembering the birthdays and anniversaries of a whole new batch of relatives.

If Erik hadn't been sitting by my side, I would have joked, "I can think of a few reasons," but again, I wisely keep my mouth shut. Once in awhile, I make the thoughtful, adult decision.

Frankie politely says, "It's an arrangement that makes sense for Ed and me." She feels no need to elaborate, to bring her motorcycle or Ed's children and ex-wife or her pursuit of a master's degree in sustainable small-scale agriculture into the conversation.

Joy sighs, troubled. "I don't know what I'd do without my family."

"Me either," I say, subtly defending child-free, gay, and nontraditional families everywhere.

"I called Gwen," Clint announces. "She's taking the first available flight here."

I wipe my mouth and meet his gaze. He's looking steadily, almost defiantly, at me in a way that says, *Check your ego at the door. There are more important matters at hand than your inability to defend yourself from the Ice Queen.*

Incredibly, I hear myself saying, "Does she need a place to stay?"

"She'll stay at our house."

Even though just the notion of having Gwen as a houseguest makes me want to arm myself and buy space in an underground bunker, I'm oddly miffed. Who made that decision, I wonder—Gwen or Clint? I feel out of the loop. The runt of the litter. The smallest and wobbliest of three eagle chicks, pecked and ultimately pushed out of the nest by its two stronger, bigger siblings.

I take a breath. *One ego to check; please keep it safe and don't mix up the tickets.*

"I also called Dad."

I hear a long wheeze, like a balloon deflating, and then I realize it's coming from me. "Don't you mean 'The Sperm Donor?'" I ask, quoting Clint.

He doesn't take the bait. He's all business right now. Brusque obligation, duty, responsibility, appearances. "Hannah's his only grandchild. I thought he should know."

"Is he coming?"

"I don't know. He said he'd try, but you know what that probably means."

"Well, what did he say? What were his exact words?"

"He'd try to make it, thanks for telling him, how awful, he's just heartbroken, blah blah."

I press again, desperate for clues. "You had to have said more than that! When's the last time you even talked to him?"

"What do you want, the fucking transcript? Jesus Jaime, it was a three-minute conversation!" Clint lifts a finger to beckon our waitress and asks for the check before finishing his thought. "If he comes, great. If not, that's great too."

And the subject is dropped.

After lunch, Clint and Joy head straight back to the hospital. Erik, Frankie, and I plan to join them, but first we take a detour to Barnes & Noble. I want to pick up a few books for Hannah. A salesclerk with a thick red ponytail helps me build a stack of the latest releases popular with the tween demographic. I know she probably won't feel well enough to read for awhile, but she's going to be bedridden for weeks, and there's only so much bad television even a fifth-grader can take. When I was Hannah's age, I was stealthily reading Stephen King, dog-earing the sex parts and passing the books around with my friends. I decide to buy her a whole set of classic Judy Blume books, tucked in a special, sturdy box. I'd read and loved them all in my younger days. I remember telling the neighbor girl—Kelly was her name, we were maybe eleven at the time—that I'd just read *Then Again, Maybe I Won't*, and she went, "Wooooooo! That's a naughty book!" and I crossed her off the Stephen King exchange list. If she couldn't handle a seventh-grader grappling with an inconvenient yet completely natural biological response, there was no way she could deal with a guy angrily jerking off on the bed of his married ex-lover while she and her son were trapped in a car, terrorized by a rabid Saint Bernard. If I were to suggest to Kelly that even Mr. Rogers probably had a nocturnal emission in his day, she'd end up drooling and rocking in the corner, humming the *Love*

Boat theme song. Kelly's family was blissfully intact, her parents seemingly asexual, two beige cheerleaders in the bleachers with a bucket of nachos and their sensible shoes at every one of our softball games. She still believed in Santa Claus in the fifth grade and had an innocence I both envied and wanted to smash. No family is as perfect as it seems, though, nobody gets through life unscathed. Years later I learned that Kelly's older brother, once our school's idolized, reigning champion of life, was diagnosed with schizophrenia and disappeared. He was found beaten to death in Vancouver weeks before our last class reunion, and it was all anyone could talk about. Kelly hadn't been there, of course.

Back at the hospital, there is a man reading the paper in the waiting area. An older man, around sixty, with a trim, white beard and an earring in his left ear. Something about the way he shakes the newspaper to straighten out the wrinkles, the way he crosses one ankle loosely over the opposite knee to seem bigger than he actually is, strikes me as familiar. When he turns the page, I get a better look at him. Brow furrowed in concentration, thinning blond-white hair, ruddy, red complexion.

His belly is bigger, his body somehow melted and softened by time, like a wax figure left out in the sun too long, but there is no mistaking it. The man reading the paper in the hospital waiting area is my father.

***

"Dad?"

Though I haven't called him that face-to-face in over a decade, he immediately recognizes and responds to the name. A smile spreads over his face, revealing a perfect set of straight dentures so white they're nearly blue. "Jaime!"

I can feel Erik and Frankie freeze next to me. How many late-night conversations have we had about my father and the gaping hole he left in my life when he left those many years ago? Early on, you needed a suspension bridge to cross that gorge, but time is the incredible shrinker and healer of wounds. Now I could easily step over it. No—*gloss* over it, is more like it, because you don't think about your father abandoning your family every waking moment in days filled with dental appointments and brownie recipes and office gossip and oil changes and ugly sweater parties. After awhile, you have to get on with things. You run after life before it takes a left at the next block and leaves you behind. *Hey, wait up!* (Unless you're made of less resilient material, and then you might end up on A&E's *Hoarders*.) But most days, you have bigger things to worry about. It's like you lost your big toe in a freak escalator accident; after the initial pain subsides, you forget about it until the weather warms and you're wearing flip flops again and you remember: *Hey, I lost that little piggy, didn't I?*

Hannah will heal from this accident, too. I feel this with every nerve, bone, and cell in my body. And one day, after the pain dissipates or fades into the general background noise of aging, she might forget there is a plate screwed into her hip unless it's about to rain. *Oh, right— that happened to me, didn't it?*

This is what I think when I see my father's face for the first time in more than ten years. How this was something that happened to me, and I got on with life. Still, there is the little matter of forgiveness. There is still the little matter of his absence warping me into a new, cynical shape, impacting every one of my decisions to this point, if only subconsciously.

Even my marriage to Erik. See, he was the obvious choice because though there were no guarantees, I believed down to my core that he would never leave me the way my father left my mother. And if you've ever wondered how women can marry men who confess to love them just a little bit more, now you know.

Chapter 23
"Putting a dead bird on your pillow was guidance?"

"Hi Dad," I repeat, bracing myself when he stands to hug me. It feels like hugging a stranger. Some random, older man I met at a gas station.

"I was lucky to catch a flight right away. She's my only grandchild," he says, in quick, defensive explanation to a question nobody asked. His earring twinkles in the late afternoon sunlight streaming in through the hospital's wall of windows. I wonder if he's waiting out here because he knew we were coming, or because he was working up the nerve to go in alone. The prodigal grandfather returns to pay his respects.

"Erik," he says, offering a hearty, manly hand to shake. "Good to meet you."

"Howdy," Erik says gruffly, like a cowboy, and I give him a look. Nobody knows how to act right now. We are characters in search of a script.

After Erik and my father finish shaking hands, Frankie extends hers and introduces herself. "Frankie?" he asks. "Is that short for something?"

"Frances," she reluctantly admits. "I was named for Frances Farmer."

"Beautiful gal, that one. A bit crazy, though. Well then," he says, clapping his hands into a hearty, nearly jolly clasp. "Did you kids eat lunch?" he asks. "I had a sandwich at the airport in Portland, but I haven't had a thing except those three peanuts they give you on the plane." *I hope you can forgive me for abandoning you and your mother those*

*many years ago. I'm different now, see? I make jokes! Peanuts on airplanes . . .
am I right or am I right?*

"We just ate lunch," I say. "With Clint and Joy." *What makes you
think we'd even want to eat lunch with you?*

"Is Gwen coming?" he asks, hopeful. *I'd like to make up for years of
neglect by awkwardly bonding with all three of my children at once—more bang
for the buck.*

I nod. "Yeah. I don't know when, though." *The apocalypse could
happen at any time.* I ask about his current wife.

"Oh, Sharon's great. She still hasn't found work, though." He
married Sharon three years ago, and what I know about her could fill
a thimble. I do know she's got two grown children from a previous
marriage, she had a hysterectomy this past spring, and together they
spoil a jittery little Maltese named Hicky. The latter two details had
been prominently featured in last year's Christmas letter. "Your stepbrother Wayne will be finishing his online degree in mortuary science
this May," my father adds.

"He's not really my—"

"Say, do you think we can go back and see Hannah?" he urgently
adds, getting to the heart of the matter. "I came all this way. I'd like to
be there for her. You get another pass at things when you're a grandpar-
ent, and life is just so short." He seems embarrassed, fumbling for the
right words and then rushing to expel them before he could change his
mind.

There are so many ways I want to answer this, so many things I
need to say, but instead I leave it at, "Sure. Let's go see if she's awake."

When he leans down to pick up his jacket, I notice a cursive tattoo on his forearm. Three names: *Gwen, Clint, Jamie.*

My name is spelled wrong. It's perfect, really. *Holy spririt, rain
down!* I start to laugh—quietly at first, and then I'm really into it, bent
over, belly aching. "What's so funny?" Erik asks. Frankie and my father
look at me, puzzled.

"Nothing." Nobody's buying it, so I try again. "I guess I'm just
like Mom. Bad timing for a case of the giggles."

***

Later, after we've been in to see a doped-up Hannah, I ask Clint if he'd like to take a walk. "You look like you could use some fresh air."

He looks miserable, actually. He nods in a detached way. "Yeah. I guess so. Okay."

Erik goes home to feed Nancy and prep for a meeting with some regional planning commission, but I really know he's going to masturbate because he rarely gets that much time alone in the house. Frankie hugs me and also heads home, promising to call later because I still need to tell her about my crazy new family. Clint looks at me curiously as she says this, and I roll my eyes and shrug dismissively: *it's nothing.* We button and zip our spring jackets and walk out of the hospital into a light April drizzle. The ornamental trees planted in neat rows around the parking lot are heavy with reddish-brown buds, the grass below them thick and green. A few dandelions even bloom cheerfully in the warmer microclimates near the building itself. Clint seems uncomfortable at first, but our footsteps soon settle into a companionable rhythm.

"When's the last time we took a walk together?" I ask, pulling my hood over my rapidly frizzing hair.

"Never," Clint says.

"Probably trick-or-treating when we were kids." I smile. "Remember that hobo costume Mom made for you when you were nine?"

"God! That's the main reason I can't drink coffee to this day. I came home and puked my guts out while you and Gwen stole the best candy in my bag."

Mom had slathered Vick's VapoRub over Clint's chin and cheeks, pressing coffee grounds into the sticky ointment to give him a five o'clock shadow. I'd gone as a fairy that year, with gossamer wings made of pink nylon stretched over a wire frame. Clint threw my wand over a fence bearing a *Beware of Dog* sign, and I cried through most of the neighborhood. But I smile at the memory now, because he was right; I had stolen the best candy from his bag when he wasn't looking. All of the Reese's Peanut Butter Cups.

We talk about Hannah for awhile, about her upcoming surgery and the long recovery ahead. "I have some things I can bring over that she might be able to use. Mom's shower bench, the tub handles, that raised toilet seat thing."

"That would be great," Clint says, with no sarcasm or animosity. "The doctor says her prognosis is good. They have a team of people working on it."

"I like that word. 'Team.' Like it's a game we're going to win."

"Damn straight, we're going to win," Clint insists.

What I don't say is that Mom had a team, too. But she lost.

We watch an elderly couple clutch one another as they navigate the parking lot to the hospital entrance. They're wearing matching blue raincoats and sturdy galoshes, shuffling along in tiny, careful steps. The woman is wearing a clear plastic kerchief knotted beneath her chin. "Why do old ladies wear bread bags on their heads when it's raining?" Clint asks.

"They have to protect their old-lady perms somehow."

"God, I hate getting old." I look at him from the corner of my eye. There are wrinkles around his eyes where a few years ago there had been none, partly because as Clint once told me, sunscreen is for pussies. A few more gray hairs sprout above his ears, and his stomach is less six-pack/more beer gut, but he still has the broad chest of the football player he was in high school. He could still throw a spiral or win a local hot dog eating contest.

"Yeah, what are you, eighty? It's a good thing I'm bringing over the tub handles and the raised toilet seat."

He smiles, but it's small and distracted.

"Hey, I almost forgot. Did you see Dad's tattoos?"

"He has tattoos now? Christ, what a cliché."

"That's not the best part. They're our names. Clint, Gwen, and Jamie, and he spelled my name wrong."

"Oh, for fuck's sake. What a douche nozzle."

I shrug, smiling at my brother's eloquence. "He feels guilty, I think."

"A little late for that."

"Well, better late than never." I'm oddly proud of myself for my optimism. "Listen," I cautiously add, "I want to apologize. For Thanksgiving."

"I don't want to talk about it. Let's forget it, okay?"

"Okay. But can I ask you something?"

"Depends what it is."

I rephrase my question into a sentence, nearly an accusation, because otherwise it sounds too desperate. I say it quickly, before I lose my nerve. "You seem like you hate me sometimes."

Clint looks surprised. "I don't hate you."

"Okay, then why are you so mean to me? It's like you enjoy hurting me. And no smart-ass quips, please."

He sighs as if wrestling with an unpleasant truth. "Do you want to know what it is?"

I nod, a little afraid.

"You need to stick up for yourself. Why don't you stand up to me? Honestly, sometimes it's hard to respect you."

"I'm not a wrestling opponent, I'm your sister. I don't want to be constantly defending myself when you act like a jerk. Do you know how exhausting that would be?" I pause, searching for the right words. "After Dad left, that role fell to you, like it or not. I looked up to you, and I remember the guidance you gave me." I'm embarrassed to say this out loud. I sound trite and I feel naked.

"Putting a dead bird on your pillow was guidance?"

"Well, when we were a little older. You seemed so brave, so confident. I wanted to be like you."

"Why?" He stares at the approaching sidewalk, honestly puzzled and even uncomfortable, and for the first time I see his insecurities.

"You're my big brother." We walk quietly for awhile, lost in thought, giving the glue time to dry on the cracks. Eventually we circle back to the hospital.

Clint breaks our silence. "Dad didn't even send a card."

"When?"

"For Mom's funeral. He couldn't fucking be bothered."

"Well, they were divorced. I don't know if that's the protocol."

"She was still the mother of his children."

We reach the main doors, but before we go in and the atmosphere changes, I ask, "So would we go to Dad's funeral?" I'm stalling to make this moment last, because who knows when the next good conversation I'll have with Clint will be. Something awful has happened to a person we both love, but it had the effect of humanizing my brother, if only temporarily. He's still the same offensive, belligerent person he was last week, hard to love and harder to like, but today, he is a heartbroken and frightened father. He is my only brother.

"That is a good goddamned question," he says, and the sliding doors part before us.

Chapter 24
"Typically played by girls, though not always."

Gwen is beaming at us. "Everyone, I'd like you to meet Anthony. Anthony, this is my father William, my brother Clint, his wife Joy, my sister Jaime, and her husband Erik. Don't worry," she giggles, "there won't be a quiz later.

Erik and I glance at one another, eyebrows raised. Smiling? Gushing? Giggling? Gwen? It's nearly nine at night. Early spring moths fly in dazed, foolhardy loops around the streetlights, and the air is fresh, hung with the smells of green things waking and growing. We are sitting around a table set for six at the Roman Candle Pizzeria, which Gwen suggested as a meeting place after she'd had a chance to check in at her hotel and freshen up. She didn't mention she'd be bringing a guest, which was probably the reason she'd ultimately declined Clint's invitation to stay with him and Joy. "Nice to meet you," everyone says, exhausted, trying to keep up. Who brings a date to her niece's accident?

Erik flags down a flustered-looking waitress. "We'll need a seventh chair and another place setting, please."

"Why couldn't we have ordered pizza back at our house?" Clint grumbles while we consolidate our plates and cutlery and water glasses to give Anthony some room.

Joy sighs. "Because the house is a mess, and it's a longer drive for everyone."

My phone vibrates in my purse. It's Chris: *Where r u?*

I surreptitiously text back: *Roman Candle. Willy St. Where are you?*

Chris: *David. Fighting. I know. Dont yell.*

Me: *WTS!*

Chris: *Sorry!* Then, a few seconds later: *What does WTS mean?*

Me: *What the shit!!! If he kills you, don't come crying to me*

Erik gives me his cool cucumber look. He's irritated, but trying not to let it show. "Who are you texting?"

"Chris. He's fighting with David again."

"Call the cops."

"It might come to that." I keep typing: *My niece had an accident. Eating dinner w/family now. Call you later?*

Chris: *Oh no! Is she ok?*

Me: *She will be, in lots of pain. You ok?*

My phone falls silent, and I stuff it back in my purse. I'll deal with him later.

"Stop texting at the table," Clint commands. "It's rude." Our father just looks at us, bewildered, his role long since usurped because the son became the father years before the latter rolled back into town.

"Sorry." I quickly change the subject. "So Gwen, how was your flight?"

"Long," she says, overdramatically. "Anthony had to sit next to a crying baby on the second leg, but he was such a good sport about it."

Anthony shrugs. "I don't mind babies. He was really cute, actually."

"I think Anthony's more maternal than me," Gwen says, still smiling.

Erik writes this on a napkin and slides it over to me: *A cockroach is more maternal than Gwen.* I discreetly spit my gum into it and crumple the napkin into a ball.

"So how did you two meet?" Joy asks, being polite.

We learn that Anthony owns four coffee shops, one of which Gwen visits every morning. He co-chairs local fundraisers for the Special Olympics and PAWS Atlanta. He is an avid mountain biker and completed his second half-marathon last month. He makes his own nut butters and an excellent seafood paella.

How did this man make it past Gwen's defenses? Gentle demeanor, liker of babies, maker of nut butters ... He has these perfect, expressive brown eyes and an architectural, nearly graceful nose. He'd be intimidatingly handsome, but one of his teeth is slightly crooked, and he has a long, yokel-y laugh that sounds staged. It's something you nearly have to endure, but Gwen doesn't seem to mind.

After Gwen determines that we now know all we need to know about Anthony for the time being, she gets serious. "How's Hannah?"

Clint fills her in. I watch Gwen absorb the details and prognosis, nodding intently. In supple leather flats, faded jeans, and a cashmere V-neck the color of oatmeal, she looks softer. Happier and relaxed. Like she's just returned from a long vacation in the Caribbean. We make plans to return to the hospital first thing in the morning.

"So how's school?" Gwen suddenly asks me. Word choice is an interesting thing, isn't it? Instead of asking me how *work* is, Gwen asks how *school* is going, because school is the more dismissive option and implies to anyone within earshot that I still haven't grown up.

"Fine," I say. This seems inadequate, so I add, "Same old, same old."

"Well, that's specific," she says crisply.

"You know what they say about those who teach," Clint says.

"Don't even start," I interrupt. He gives me a smug, self-satisfied look: *you know it's true, but I'm glad you're finding your voice.* Before he can launch into a tirade about tenure and merit pay and property taxes, I head him off at the pass. "Last week I had a sub one day because we had a staff training thing scheduled. My kids convinced this poor woman to let them all out early for honors band, which doesn't even exist. Tanner Vandenberg told her he played the skin flute."

Joy cocks her head, smiling quizzically.

Erik clears his throat and explains, "It's a traditional folk instrument adapted by many cultures. Typically played by girls, though not always."

"Oh," she says, and Anthony looks eagerly around the table, politely waiting for a signal that it's okay to laugh.

Our father does, heartily. "Jaime, you've got yourself a live one here."

Clint rolls his eyes. "It's a blowjob reference," he clarifies to Joy, who flushes deep red. A woman sitting behind him spins around to scowl at us.

"Are you ready to order?" our waitress says, suddenly appearing with pen and pad in hand, a life preserver ready to haul us back to dry ground.

***

After our pizzas arrive and we divvy up the slices, I notice Clint frowning over my shoulder, concerned. "There's a tranny outside, staring at us through the window."

Just then my phone vibrates again. *I'm so, so sorry. I'm outside.*

You have got to be kidding me.

I wipe my mouth with my napkin and stand up. "Excuse me. I'll be right back."

When I get outside, I'm first confronted by a tall panhandler who smells of sauerkraut and armpits. If he were a cartoon, there would be flies buzzing around his head, perhaps a cloud of dust floating around his shins. "Can I have a dollar?" He opens a wrinkled plastic shopping bag and shows me what's inside, as if trick-or-treating. The bag contains a small plastic piggy bank, a travel first-aid kit, and a cracked protractor, the kind you use in geometry class.

"Sorry, I don't have any money with me."

"You're eating here, so you must be rich."

Chris teeters over to me in a pair of herringbone-patterned pumps. He fishes a five-dollar bill from his purse and hands it to the vagrant. "Here Ernie, go buy yourself a sandwich."

"God bless you. It's kind ladies like you who make the world a better place." And Ernie shuffles off to pester a couple unfortunate enough to have chosen the outdoor patio area in which to dine.

"Chris, what's going on?"

"David is threatening to kill himself. He's locked in his apartment, I think he took some pills. Now he won't answer my calls. I'm sorry, Jaime. I didn't know what else to do." His voice is strained, his face drawn with anxiety.

I press my face in my palms for a second before I look up, in full, confident teacher-mode. "Here's what you're going to do. You're going to call 911. You're going to report the whole situation. Names, addresses, blood types, the whole thing. And you're going to repeat after me. David is no longer my problem, because we are not dating."

Chris dabs his eyes with a tissue. "This is so difficult."

"David is no longer my problem, because we are not dating."

Reluctantly, he repeats the mantra, not believing a word of it.

"This is only difficult because you're letting it be." I cross my arms. "Call the police right now. I want to watch you do it."

"Not the po-lice!" Ernie shouts, hop-shuffling down the street, screeching like a siren and swinging his bag like a bolo, one man's small yet meaningful contribution to urban noise pollution.

Chris grimaces at his pink cell phone as if he were instead holding a fistful of sand I told him to rub in his eyes. But he dials the numbers, and dutifully follows my instructions before hanging up and bursting into tears. I hug him. "You're going to be all right. Now I want you to call Evelyn or Alyssa. They'll take it from here," I say, trusting in this innately. "Okay, sweetie? I need to get back to my family."

We embrace once more, and I turn around to see my entire family watching through the window. When I return to the table, there are six eager faces waiting for an explanation. I sit down and shrug. "Keep Madison weird, right?"

***

Our father and Gwen are each staying for three days, though their time here overlaps because Dad arrived earlier. During their visit, we settle into a rhythm of activity anchored by regular visits to Hannah in the hospital. Our father stays in a cheap Best Western on the other side of town but spends most of his time attempting to awkwardly bond with us. On his second afternoon here, he helped Clint spread a mountain of mulch in his backyard, sweating and really getting into it to make up for years of not being around to repair decks or spread mulch. He was limping later at the hospital. "I told him to lift with his legs," Clint explained nonchalantly, absolving himself of any responsibility for our father's sprained muscles.

Erik and I dutifully take that Monday off to spend more time with Gwen and our father while they're here, something I never imagined I'd ever be thinking, let alone actually doing. In the morning, Erik drives my father and Anthony to buy souvenir cheese at Fromagination, a generous, sure-to-be uncomfortable errand I'll be paying dearly for later, so Gwen can help me sort through more of our mother's things. We start in the garage, going through boxes of holiday decorations. I open the garage door for some fresh air, and it creaks and squawks as it shimmies up.

"We should have an old-fashioned garage party. Sit in some lawn chairs facing the street, drink beer and wave at people when they drive by."

"Or not," Gwen says, because she was born without a sense of humor.

"Do you want these ornaments?" I ask, holding up a paper tray of baubles.

Gwen shakes her head. "I never get a tree."

"Do you still celebrate Christmas?" I ask, smirking. I carefully balance the box of ornaments on the "donate" pile.

"Jaime, just because someone doesn't put up a tree doesn't mean they skip Christmas," she archly replies. "In fact, this year Anthony and I spent it with his family in North Carolina. We rented a cabin in the Blue Ridge Mountains. "

I suppress the first snotty response that comes to mind ("How lovely for you"), because I'm really trying here. We work silently for a few minutes, sorting through the debris that remains after a life ends. I'm trying not to attach meaning to everything, but my nostalgia rescues a few things from the trash heap: an antique potato ricer, my mother's gardening gloves, an old red tricycle I remember finding tied with a green bow under the Christmas tree when I was four.

"What do you remember about Dad leaving?" I ask Gwen, wondering if the tricycle had been our mother's or our father's idea.

"Why do you want to remember any of that? You were always so morbid."

"I guess to see if I remembered it wrong. Do you remember them fighting?"

"Yes. My room was right next to theirs." She works efficiently and quickly, her ponytail bobbing as she tosses old boxes of rose fertilizer, mouse traps, and rusty cans of wasp spray into an industrial black trash bag.

"Were you ever pissed that Uncle Harry and everyone didn't seem to care? Did you ever feel left out?"

"Why waste time or energy worrying about it?"

I don't give up. Instead, I dig deeper: *my closure has to be in here somewhere.* "Isn't this weird, though? We don't see Dad for years, and he just shows up like this, almost out of the blue."

"I saw Dad last Easter. I flew him and Sharon to Atlanta."

After my initial shock subsides, an explosion of self-righteous jealousy makes the vision in my left eye go temporarily white. But perhaps this was Gwen staking claim on half of our original family while the rest of us shared glazed ham and scalloped potatoes and awkward silences we filled with complaints about Brett Favre. That's the thing about families. Somebody somewhere is usually feeling left out.

There are three bicycles behind a stack of boxes—mine, Erik's, and Mom's, and I rummage around the cobwebs behind them until I find the tire pump. I inflate the tires, dust the seats with a rag, and wheel two of them out, one at a time. I flip out the kickstands and park them in front of Gwen. "Want to go for a bike ride?"

She smiles.

***

It's a good day for biking—clear, sunny, light traffic. We head south toward Lake Monona, legs pumping, no particular destination in mind. Seemingly overnight, the trees have fully leafed out, and shadows from the green canopy flash across our faces. My thighs begin to burn, and I know that sitting in any unpadded chair tomorrow will be torturous, but with the wind in my hair and the occasional bug in my mouth, I feel thirteen all over again. We have no helmets ("Don't forget your brain buckets!" Mom used to say), because we are risk-takers. We flirt with danger. We live on adrenaline and hazard.

Also, I couldn't find the helmets.

I play with the gears, making it harder and then easier to pedal. I worry about the chain falling off and having to walk the bike six miles back home. When the bike lanes disappear, Gwen and I slalom around lampposts and parked cars and pedestrians with jogging strollers and shiny Golden Retrievers. She leads for awhile, and then I leapfrog ahead.

Before long, we find ourselves near a tangle of woods south of La Follette High School. We coast, slower and slower, coming to a full stop at a bench near a trailhead for a walking path. It's funny, but it almost feels as if we've been pulled here. Reeled back through the years like the Steely Dan song. We flip out the kickstands and stand astride our bikes. There is something familiar about this park, this weedy blot of nature in the city. "Hey, didn't we used to play here when we were kids?" I ask.

Gwen frowns down the shadowy path, which is swallowed by a mass of unruly Viburnum bushes and red twig dogwood. She doesn't acknowledge my question. Instead, she offers me her water bottle. "Let's head back. The guys will be home soon."

"Can we take a break for awhile? I need to rest my legs." I take a swig of water and pass the bottle back to her.

She fidgets with the cap. "I guess we can sit for a moment."

We park the bikes near the bench and sit. A jay caws raucously in the thicket behind us, the air heavy with the fragrance of blooming honeysuckle and lilac. Gradually, my memory of this place begins to rise like water filling a rain gauge, and with it, a feeling of guilty unease.

I was nine, and Dad had just moved out, taking his Doobie Brothers cassette tapes, Lenny Bruce poster, and our last innocent summer with him. We lived on this side of town then, in a bigger, ramshackle house that filled with echoes after he left. One afternoon, riding home from school on my secondhand Huffy with the duct-taped banana seat and pink and white streamers flowing from the handlebar grips, I found myself in this same spot. There had been no public bench here then, no city garbage can or signage for the walking trail which was then only a ribbon of flattened weeds littered with used condoms, broken glass, and empty beer cans instead of the smooth, clear mulch highway it is now. Back then, these woods were little more than an overgrown, abandoned lot. Just a tangle of scrub trees and brush, mostly invasive buckthorn and garlic mustard.

It was early September, and school had barely started. I remember parking my bike so I could pick some Black-eyed Susans for Mom, to cheer her up. I'd been wearing my Sony Walkman, listening to The Bangles, and I remember the sudden symphony of crickets that greeted me when I took off my headphones and dropped them in the plastic basket on my bike. As I began to tromp through the ditch picking my bouquet of wildflowers, sleepy late-season bumblebees trundling around me, I heard a twig snap in the underbrush and froze. A beat later, I also heard a voice: "Stop! I don't want to!" A girl's voice.

I quickly dropped into a crouch and duck-walked down the trail a few yards until I saw movement in the woods: three kids clustered together, partially obscured by leafy branches. Two boys and a girl. Rivulets of sweat began to trickle down my back. Mosquitoes hovered and landed. I blew them off my shoulders and squashed them into my ankles. The kids in the woods were touching one another, doing something improper. Something I'd seen in a magazine Brad Engell brought to school. Something Stephen King may have written about, and I felt a hot, sickly rush of excitement until I realized that the girl looked an awful lot like my sister Gwen, wearing the same baggy blue sweater she'd been wearing at breakfast that morning. I leaned into the prickly, spidery weeds for a closer look, losing my footing as the edge of the trail dropped into a hidden embankment. I wildly grabbed at a tree limb to steady myself. The skinny branch broke with a dry crack, and all three heads spun in my direction. I slipped and sprinted back down the trail while one of the boys shouted: "Get back here!" I heard shuffling, angry footsteps behind me on the crispy mat of leaves, more twigs snapping. An electric terror began to pulse in my chest: what if they caught me? What if they did to me whatever they were doing to the girl in the woods? I remember my shock that the girl could have been (was?) Gwen. My older sister who had become a complete stranger to me in the blink of an eye. How had she ended up in those woods, with those older boys?

Shaking, I hopped on my bike and pedaled furiously home, flower petals raining behind me, my lungs on fire, ready to burst. My mother was in the kitchen, canning tomatoes, and I raced past her, taking the stairs two at a time. "Slow down!" she shouted after me. I pulled down the attic ladder and climbed, drawing it up behind me. I spent the rest of the afternoon hiding in the explosively hot attic, reading my comic book collection, trying to erase what I'd seen with old *Archie* comics, water-stained issues of *Tales from the Crypt,* even a weird little comic about the life of Pope John Paul II. I stayed there until Mom called me for dinner, and I reluctantly climbed down. Gwen was already at the table. She wouldn't look at me, but anytime I looked down at my plate, I felt her studying me from the corner of my eye. "You're kind of quiet tonight," Mom said to both of us. Though I inhaled my food so I could be quickly excused, I left the table with more dread than chipped beef in my stomach. It had been Gwen. I was sure of it. That was her voice saying, *"Stop! I don't want to!"*

And I'd done nothing. I'd done nothing but run, leaving something awful to happen to her.

How had she ended up there, with those two older boys? Had it been consensual? Had it started willingly only to twist into something dark and forced? Thanks to my cowardice, I'll never know. Three days later, Clint got in a fight with two boys at school, earning a black eye and an in-school suspension. It didn't occur to me then, or perhaps I only subconsciously connected the dots, but now I wonder: had those boys bragged about what they'd done to our sister? Clint and Gwen seemed closer after that—as if they'd joined a secret society from which I'd been banned for life. A distance developed between Gwen and me. Soon, Gwen got on the fast track to success and never looked back, leaving for college a few years later.

It was one of those things you see as a child and convince yourself that you haven't actually seen at all so you can continue attending piano practice and slumber parties and track meets with the rest of the kids who pretend that they too have never seen such things. You pack it into a box, tape the seams shut, and bury it deep in a closet in your mind.

Sitting on this bench with my sister, I wonder if she too remembers. We are silent, watching wispy clouds glide across the sky. "I'm sorry we're not closer," I say. My voice sounds peculiar and vulnerable. I want to say so much more. That there is nothing to be ashamed of. That it wasn't her fault. That it can be so frightening, so perilous to be a girl. That I was a stupid, scared little kid, but I should have done something. That I was wrong, with my fair share of the blame.

Many things can break a family—fear, grudges, jealousy, secrets. But many things can also rebuild it. Forgiveness. Hope. Laughter. Love. We are adults now, on the other side of the world from childhood, with only the photos and memories and passport stamps to prove we'd been there. It's just a place we traveled through, confusing and fraught with danger in places, but mostly quite wonderful. It doesn't have to define us.

Gwen looks at me and smiles sadly. "Me too."

Maybe it's as simple as this: to *have* a good sister, first you have to *be* a good sister. It can't hurt to try.

A butterfly floats into view, beating its orange and black wings determinedly against the breeze. I point to it and announce, "First Monarch of the season." It looks like it's flown a great distance to get here. We watch it disappear over the tree line. It's time to go. "Want to head back?"

"Sure," Gwen says.

The ride home is downhill, and we coast most of the way.

Chapter 25
"She always had the best sense of humor."

It's another gorgeous spring day, sunny and 68 degrees, the sky a bright blue tarp stretched above us. I volunteered to drive my father back to the airport. His flight leaves this afternoon at 3:40. We make uncomfortable small talk for the first few miles, about Gwen and Clint and Hannah and how the city of Madison has changed since the mid-eighties. We both agree that having a cavity filled would be more pleasant than a few hours spent in the company of Joy, and for a moment it feels good to be on the same page, with a shared irritation.

Though I haven't told him, I'm taking a detour on our way to the airport. We pass the Majestic Theater and Camp Randall stadium and the Vilas Park effigy mounds and endless warehouses and storefronts until we reach a block of pale green trees tucked behind a stone wall. As I turn into the main drive of the Peaceful Valley Cemetery, my father gives me a wide, nervous look. He doesn't say anything yet. He's still appraising the situation. He doesn't know me, not really; we're still polite enigmas to one another, and I can feel him wondering if I'm going to go ballistic on him, rant and rave and cry, running through his options if I did.

But I say nothing while I steer the car quietly down the paved, winding road, which is sprinkled with a smattering of soggy seedpods in places. Rows of mausoleums and granite headstones march neatly away from the road, a small city with buildings of varying heights. One other person is in the cemetery—an older woman in a wide-brimmed hat tidying up a gravesite, hand-pulling weeds. I rarely come to my mother's grave, because I am too keenly aware that she is nothing but a sealed tin of ashes beneath me. There is no decomposing body, which is a relief, but she's just not *there*. Instead, I feel her at the Pheasant Branch Conservancy, where we used to walk the trails. I feel her at Devil's Lake State Park, where she helped us build sand castles on the beach when we were younger. I feel her when I smell clean sheets, every time I hear a Cat Stevens song on the radio.

It takes a moment to orient myself, but I quickly remember that her grave site is four down from the oak tree with what looks like a giant bellybutton poking from the bark, three rows from the arbor vitae hedgerow. We park and walk wordlessly to her plot, which lies between a Korean War veteran and three members of the Winkler family: Mother Helen, Father George, Daughter Karen. Her marker is unobtrusive and simple. A small, gray rectangle of rock speckled with flecks of black and red and brown.

Claire Stewart
1956 – 2011

I'd planted a few perennials around her headstone last fall—day-lilies, daisies, a pair of variegated hostas, the green shoots of which push up from the earth, reaching for the sun. Like me, they'd made it through the winter. We stand side by side, contemplating her grave site. Together again. My living father, my dead mother, and me—the baby of their long-dissolved union, the last-ditch effort to glue them back together. Or maybe I was an accident. My mother never really said.

"Mom told me never to bring flowers, but instead to plant them. She said that way she'd really be pushing up daisies."

He smiles at this. "She always had a quirky sense of humor."

I suddenly feel cruel and misguided for bringing him here. What had I hoped to achieve? He'd spent days nervously contemplating the shallow end of the pool in a pair of inflatable wings, dipping a hesitant toe to test the water temperature, and now I'd dragged him to the deep end and rudely pushed him in.

"I didn't know if I should go to the funeral," he continues, his voice halting and timid. "I felt maybe it was best if I just stayed away."

"A card would have been nice. Or a call. You were together what, fifteen years?"

"I'm sorry. I just, Sharon, and Wayne is living with us and ..." He trails off, thinking about his new family, this whole new life on the other side of the country. His ridiculous earring glints in the sunlight, part of his costume for the whole new life.

You know how people always say, *If you're going to cheat on someone, at least have the decency to break up with them first?* Well, my father took that advice to heart. One night he said to my mother, "I haven't cheated on you, but if I stay, I'm going to." So she let him go, because she had dignity and she was no fool. There was no begging, no walking in on him screwing his girlfriend on her side of the marital bed, no mysterious late-night run of hang-ups on which to pin our loss—at least none that I was aware of. There simply came a day when he no longer lived with us, and Clint was the one mowing the lawn every weekend. Maybe it would have been better if there'd been a big, ugly scene. At least then we would have catharsis and a woman's house to vandalize instead of this dark vacuum, this giant question mark in our lives.

It was bigger than his wandering heart, of course; as an adult, I can look back analytically at all the myriad reasons he left. His house painting business was faltering, he'd never really experienced his own childhood, he was always restless, even while sleeping. Beneath it all ran the uncomfortable truth that ultimately, he loved Mom much less than she loved him. Nobody told me this or acknowledged it, but you could nearly taste it in the air. The recipe was off; the cake had come out uneven, off-balance. Years passed before she stopped wearing her wedding ring, and she never had a bad word to say about him. I won't go so far as to say she pined for him the rest of her life, but you could tell every man she dated after our father was being measured against him. "He was too short," she'd say after an unfortunate date. *Your dad was so much taller.* Or, "He had no sense of humor." *Remember how your dad could get me laughing?* It made no sense at all to me. But when you're a kid, you don't see adults as much more than food- and money-dispensers. People who drop you off and pick you up and yell at you to get off the phone, with no hopes or desires or regrets of their own. As I got older, after I fell in and out of love a few times, it began to come into focus, like those 3-D dot-matrix pictures they used to sell at the mall. Stare at it long enough and you'll see the tiger, about to devour you.

"She did a good job raising you," he says.

"Alone. She raised us alone." My voice comes out harder than I'd meant it to. When I turn to see the effect my words had on my father, I'm surprised by how wounded he looks. A direct hit to the heart with a guilt-tipped arrow. You could almost feel sorry for him.

"I did love your mom once, a great deal. But people change. That's one thing they don't tell you when you're standing at the altar, making those wild promises. And there we were, two dumb, young kids who had no idea what we were in for. I knew that if I stayed, it wouldn't be fair to either of us."

"We're grown up now, and I think we turned out basically okay, but you should know how lost we were without you. Me and Clint and Gwen. We weren't little, maybe, but we still needed our dad." When he moved out, we were no longer adorable, entertaining babies and toddlers; we were gangly, sullen adolescents, uncomfortable in our own skins. We were easier to leave. Acknowledging this out loud feels like putting my full weight on a leg that had been broken and badly set years earlier. It's functional most of the time, but any time you put pressure on it you feel a jolt of pain and remember the bone snapping like it happened yesterday.

"Would you rather I stayed and pretended? Would you rather it got ugly?"

"Depends on the day you ask." In truth, I wouldn't go back and change my childhood, because it made me the person I am today, even if there is a little bite to me. I learned early on that nothing comes easy. That life was full of disappointments but also love and laughter, if you knew where to look. By the time I got to college, I was ready for whatever they threw at me.

"Jaime, I can't ask you to understand. I can only give you my side of the story. She was wonderful and good, your mother. But a little too good for me."

A robin flies into a nearby shrub and begins to sing.

"I never stopped loving you kids, you know. Even if we aren't close, I think about you every day."

On one hand, I find this incredibly hard to believe. On the other, he's trying. His being here after all these years, his mid-life outreach campaign and graveyard confessional—pat as it sounds—demonstrates this. I quickly catalog the initial responses that come to mind: sticking a finger down my throat and gagging ... rolling my eyes ... or being the adult and doing what Mom would have done. Forgive him, let go of the anger, focus on tomorrow instead of yesterday. I realize how much courage it must have taken for him to suck it up and face us again, knowing one or more of us might give him a well-deserved earful. And I can appreciate that. I check my phone for the time. "We should get you to the airport."

We talk some more on the drive there, about everything and nothing. I learn we are both afraid of heights and addicted to Nutella. We both flunked our driver's test the first time and we have the same smattering of freckles on our arms. He tells me that Erik and I should come to Portland for a visit. I tell him that it would be fun, and we'll try, though I'm really just being polite. We share DNA, but I don't really see us sharing much more. That would require a bit more time and effort on both our parts.

"By the way," I say, accepting his hug at the security checkpoint, "you spelled my name wrong on your tattoo."

Chapter 26
"It's just finger-painting with five-year-olds."

Gwen and Anthony stop by the house to say good-bye before heading back to the airport. It's raining today, steady and slow but warm. I offer them coffee in our mother's kitchen.

"What kind is it?" Gwen asks.

"Folgers, I think."

She sucks in a breath through her teeth, and Anthony urgently clasps my forearms. "Oh, my dear, dear girl. One day, we need to have a long conversation about coffee."

"That reminds me, Anthony," I say, fetching something we found in the cupboard during our cleaning, "I have something for you." I press an ancient jar of Sanka into his hands. The instant crystals have long ago solidified into a hard, brown lump, and the expiration date reads 7-1-92.

He laughs. "Thank you so much. It's just what I've always wanted."

"Keep me posted about Hannah," Gwen says. "Clint isn't always the best when it comes to keeping in touch."

"Well, we're not too hot either," I say.

"You have a point there."

A silence descends as we contemplate our failure to communicate, but before it becomes awkward, I add, "I promise to let you know how things go."

"God, I'm dreading the pile that will be waiting for me when I get back to the office." She changes the subject because their flight leaves soon, and we are at risk of actually entering uncomfortable, emotional territory. Well, there's something we *do* have in common: a legacy of conflict avoidance. Gwen looks expectantly at me, waiting for me to nod, acknowledge this statement in some way.

"The life of a lawyer," I finally offer.

I know so little about my sister. I don't know her hobbies, her favorite restaurants, how she spends Sunday mornings. Where do you even begin? Is there a form we could fill out and return to one another? So much has been lost. I can't shake the feeling that it's more my fault than I want to admit. How often did I pick up the phone to call Gwen in the last five years? Once, maybe twice a year out of some reluctant yet deeply innate feeling of obligation? The realization shocks me. I avoided her, because it was the easiest way to maintain my own feeling of self-worth. No phone call meant I didn't second-guess my own choices. No phone call meant no feelings of inadequacy, no wishing or hoping or envy or bitterness. No phone call meant, ultimately, no sister. And we fade to black—resentful enigmas who willfully threw their past away, losing so much more than just each other.

The doorbell rings: *Here comes the sun! Doo-dee-do-doo!*

A quick peek out the side window reveals Paul standing on the front porch with a carton of eggs, wearing striped overalls over a KISS concert tee. I open the door and greet him. "Paul! It's so good to see you!"

"I brought you some eggs." He passes the bumpy carton to me. Two rubber bands hold the lid shut because some of the eggs are massive. Double-yolkers.

"That's so nice of you!" I say. "I've been in the mood for an egg salad sandwich lately."

I hand the carton to Erik, who contemplates the gigantic eggs on his way to the refrigerator. They are nearly the size of softballs. "Those poor chickens," he muses. "What did you call it? The hole where the eggs come out?"

"The cloaca," Paul explains. He'd be a great keynote speaker for a ladies' auxiliary meeting.

"Oh, my achin' cloaca!" Erik says, his voice muffled because his head is in the refrigerator. He's doing Ernie from *Sesame Street*, though I have no idea why.

"Sorry," Paul says, "I didn't know you had company." He wipes a few stray raindrops from his face with a blue handkerchief.

"Paul, this is my sister Gwen, her boyfriend Anthony. Guys, this is my friend Paul." They all shake hands: *Nice to meet you, nice to meet you.*

"Well," Paul says, clapping his hands, "I wanted to stop by to drop off the eggs. Remember, crack them in a separate bowl, because you don't want any surprises. Gallus Gallus Domesticus fetus is not good eats."

Anthony looks mildly horrified, but in a delighted way. Like he'd enjoy a person like Paul in his life. Paul tips an imaginary hat our way and heads back to his van. I make a mental note to call him later, hear how his court date went.

After he's gone, Gwen asks, "How do you know Paul?"

"A local grief group," I say, and she nods in understanding.

"I never really thanked you for staying here with Mom," she says, and I can tell she means it. "It couldn't have been easy."

I don't snipe, *That's an understatement,* or *Easy for you to say.* Instead I say, "I was glad to do it. Thank him." I nod my head in Erik's direction, because he's the reason I'm still here and not living under a bridge somewhere.

"Erik, you are Superman."

"That's what I've been trying to tell her!"

"Well, we should head out. They usually want to take their time when they pat Anthony down."

He theatrically shrugs and poses for us like a model. "And who could blame them?"

"You do look vaguely terrorist-y," I say, only because Anthony seems to have a good sense of humor.

"I think it's my eyes," he says, batting his lashes.

There is a moment of uncertainty after Anthony hugs me and shakes Erik's outstretched hand—do I hug my sister or wait for her to make the first move? Who will be the one to water the garden after seasons of neglect? I will, I decide, and offer Gwen a tentative hug. She embraces me in return, without hesitation. I haven't hugged my sister in so long. At first it feels alien and awkward, but as we relax, it feels more like hugging a friendly acquaintance. *Gwen is my family,* I think. She smells like lavender shortbread and feels more substantial and forgiving than she looks. Anthony has been good for her. I should send him a thank-you note. I wonder again if this is all a persona she's trying on for Anthony (*Your Fabulous New Girlfriend!*™), or perhaps the residue from a book she'd found in the spirituality or self-help section of a bookstore, but I stop myself. Give her the benefit of the doubt.

"I'll ship those boxes to you," I say, referencing some of the items she'd set aside when we went through Mom's things. Souvenirs from childhood. Things to hold on to, remind us how far we've come. She thanks me, and we follow them onto the porch as they leave. "Wait," I say, and Gwen turns around. "What's your favorite restaurant?"

She laughs. "Why?"

"Just wondering."

She thinks for a moment, smiling and cocking her head at me. "Bacchanalia."

"Maybe we'll take you there sometime," Anthony adds, and they dash down the walk, dodging raindrops.

Erik and I wave while we watch them climb into the rental car and back down the driveway. The house feels cool and cavernous after they're gone. Emptier, somehow. "Hey, Anthony forgot his Sanka," I say. Erik tucks it into one of Gwen's boxes. Before he can turn around, I come up behind him and wrap my arms around him. I rest my cheek against his back. *Erik is my family.*

"You're more than enough for me. You know that, right?"

He picks up my right hand and kisses it. "Yes, but thank you for saying so." He turns around and we hug. "Want to fool around, or drive around and look at houses?"

"Drive around and look at houses. I didn't shower today."

***

There's something both sad and hopeful about the end of the school year. You say goodbye to "your" kids, nervous that their next batch of teachers will dislike them or poke a knitting needle in their ears to unhook every lesson you tried to impart on questioning authority, thinking for themselves, being innovators instead of regurgitators. But you can't worry for long, because you have another crop of incoming students who read three years below grade level. There is always more work to be done.

The week before the last day of school, I run into one of my future students in the high school principal's office. His name is Damien Farley, and he spends more time here than he does in the classroom. Part of the problem is the crowd he's gotten sucked into—a ragtag band of older boys who fancy themselves gangsters. Juggalos who drink Faygo and vodka in vacant lots, daring one another to accost any lone person unfortunate enough to walk through their "turf." Other teachers talk about Damien as if he's a lost cause destined for prison, but I know his family. Though she's a little rough in her parenting approach, his mother cares, actually comes to conferences. And I know his potential: he's a talented artist, capable of earning at least a solid C average. When Damien was little, he even played T-ball for the local team that Clint used to coach: this skinny, bobble-headed five-year-old wildly swinging the bat and scampering around the bases, all legs and arms and noggin. You wanted to wrap him in a bear hug and feed him a whole pizza, take him to an amusement park and buy him cotton candy.

"Hi, Damien," I say. I pause for a second before checking my mailbox. "Any plans for summer?"

He shrugs listlessly. "Probably just hang out."

"The Rec department is offering a few summer art internships. Eight to noon Monday through Thursday."

"It's just finger-painting with five year-olds." I notice he's wearing black eyeliner, and one of those long wallet chains you could jump rope with.

"I think you'd like it. You'd be good at it, anyway." Though he remains slumped in the chair, arms crossed and feet splayed out like a tough guy, his eyes light up ever so slightly. He's starting to reconsider his own potential.

"Maybe."

"Looks like you'll be in my class next year."

"I guess so."

I wait until he looks up and meets my gaze. "I expect great things from you," I simply say. He doesn't need to hear that it's no good, the crowd he's hanging with, that he's going to burn out his options, that if he screws up once more he'll be suspended, amount to nothing, be lucky to one day land a job swabbing vomit from Tilt-O-Whirl cars at the county fair. Chances are he's heard it all by now, anyway. Everyone comes down hard on a kid like this, but the punitive approach doesn't seem to be working. Isn't the definition of insanity doing the same thing over and over again while expecting different results? Why be so predictable, anyway?

He screws up his face, puzzled, but also encouraged. "Yeah?" It's a small blue flame of encouragement. Not enough to light your way at night, not nearly the forest fire of self-esteem and ambition this kid needs, but it's something.

"Absolutely. You are going to be my star pupil," I say with conviction. One of the secretaries behind the counter is eavesdropping and smiles at this while she types.

He tries not to show it, but the tiny smile playing on his lips tells me this pleases him immensely. "You're some kind of comedian."

"And you're better than this." I pat his shoulder and make my way down the hall to the key room. "Great things, Damien," I say for emphasis, leaving him with that for the summer.

Damien.

What kind of lunatic names their kid *Damien*?

Chapter 27

"Why don't dogs wear glasses?"

"Hi. What's your name?" A young boy, maybe five or six, is standing in front of me smiling, his hands planted on his hips. His mouth and chin are stained purple.

"I'm Jaime." I smile and glance behind him. "Where's your mom, sweetie?"

"In the car."

"Your mom is in the car?"

"Ethan, there you are!" A frazzled-looking woman jogs into the canned goods aisle. She glances at me and offers a wan smile before crouching to reprimand her son. "You can't run off like that. A stranger will snatch you!"

"It's okay, I'm not really—" but she quickly steers her son away, and the end of my sentence (—*the snatching type*) fails to materialize. Erik and I are grocery shopping, and children seem to be in season. They are everywhere, clapping their sticky hands at me, hiccupping and drooling and laughing and singing. "Thank you so much for your help," one mother says indulgently to her toddler, who is putting every random can or jar she can reach into their cart. "We couldn't do this without you!"

Another mother pushes an older boy in her cart. "We. Are. Farmers!" he sings, swinging his feet, and she happily finishes the jingle: "*Bum-bah-dum-bum-bum-bah-dum!*"

Today, there are no screamers, no meltdowns in the checkout lanes. Only joyful little cherubs and their adoring parents, buying macaroni for art projects, cookie dough for an after-school treat. I push my cart faster, but I can't escape them. I'm not yet feeling weepy, but a deep, familiar longing envelopes my heart. An insistent ache to be wrapped in the tough yet bird-like hug of a four-year-old, to laugh at his quirky questions: *"Why don't dogs wear glasses?"*

"Slow down," Erik shouts after me, "You're going to forget the orange juice again."

"Sorry," I say. "All these cute kids." I turn it into a joke. "There's no escape! Aah!" It sounds much more manic than I'd intended.

"Well, that one's kind of ugly," Erik says, trying to make me smile. His eyes light up when he thinks of a way to distract me. "Hey, let's see if Rick and Renae want to meet for a drink. What do you think?"

I pause, focusing on the display behind him. Cling peaches are on sale, limit three cans per customer. I shrug. "Sure. Why not."

***

Rick and Renae are one of the few couples we socialize with who have no children. Renae has told me on more than one occasion that kids are not for her. She doesn't want any, no way, no how. We even shook on it, in a strange kind of deal: *All right then, you don't have kids if I can't.* Over the years, attending the baby showers and fielding calls heralding the joyful news had just worn me down. *Congratulations! I'm so happy for you. Yes, it's so exciting. How wonderful, wonderful for you.* Eventually, I stopped feeling left behind and even weirdly betrayed. I stopped crying in the shower and instead tried making a cynical peace with things. I rationalized and justified.

I always believed that Erik would make a playful, loving father, in part because he's still a big, goofy kid at heart. His favorite movies include *Wall-E* and *The Iron Giant*, and he's so fun and easygoing with our friends' kids, lifting them up to ride his shoulders when they're tired of walking, effortlessly able to coax giggles from fussy babies. And I find him incredibly sexy when I watch him patiently assembling a puzzle on the floor with Liz's boys. I imagine us carving jack o'lanterns with our son, going to our daughter's school play, even hosting crowded family dinners when we're in our sixties.

But I don't imagine Erik dealing with the middle school principal, calling the insurance company about denied claims, making dinner that doesn't come in a bag or box. I don't imagine him dealing with the logistics of parenting while also working full-time, stumbling into the office on twenty minutes of sleep, worrying about daycare politics and highly contagious viruses. That would be me. *Maybe having a child would demolish our marriage,* I'd think. *I know I'm not giving him the benefit of the doubt, but what if it feels like having two children instead of one and one night I find myself kneeling over him while he sleeps, ready to smother his snoring face with my pillow?*

Eventually, my rationalizing turned up the darker questions: what kind of world would my child grow up in? Would tigers become extinct in the wild, the oceans little more than acidic deserts, food shortages and rolling blackouts? Do I just want a child to satisfy some ego-driven, biological need or achieve the next culturally endorsed milestone? Does the earth really need my genetic progeny in an already crowded field? *Maybe it's for the best ...*

Given enough time, I can overanalyze anything.

But. *But*—trying to squash my desire for a child also meant giving up a bit of hope. A chance to make things right in the world, to have the family I always wanted. To be a better person. To see if it's true that as a parent, you love more selflessly, completely. And then I'd think, well, that's putting an awful lot of responsibility on my hypothetical child's shoulders, and I was right back where I started. My brain trying to beat my heart into submission.

In many ways, Renae reminds me of my friend Amy—generous, thoughtful, easy to laugh. However, there's one key difference. Every year, Renae goes bear-hunting with her father and three brothers, with stale doughnuts for bait and a pack of barking hounds that run their quarry up a tree until Renae arrives to shoot the terrified animal down.

In college, Frankie dated a guy who once went bear-hunting. "When the bear was strung up in a tree and skinned," he told us, "it looked like a man hanging there. All that exposed muscle, two legs, two arms. Totally creeped me out."

So now, when all our other friends are busy with their kids' activities or can't find a babysitter, our dinner options dwindle to post-nasal-drip Rick and his wife Renae, who is sweet and kind and kills bears and doesn't seem to notice that they look like skinned people hanging from trees.

***

In line to pay for our groceries, I text Renae: *Drinks tonight? 7 pm?*

Instead of receiving a text in response, my phone rings. Renae. "Can't meet for drinks," she says in a voice both coy and ebullient, and I brace myself because I've heard this tone before. I know what's coming. "I'm pregnant!"

Of course you are! is what I think, but instead I say, "Congratulations! I'm so happy for you. Yes, it's so exciting. How wonderful, wonderful for you." She tells me when she's due, about how Rick cried tears of joy when he found out, how she's scared and thrilled and craves guacamole. She says nothing about never wanting a child.

Erik and I are quiet on the drive home until he says, "Do you still want to go out for a drink? Just you and me? Tornado Steak House? Adults only, no kids allowed."

"I don't know. I'm kind of tired. Let's just go home."

As I put the groceries away I start to feel restless, wishing we had gone out after all. I pick up my phone and call Evelyn, in whom I have confided my feelings about parenthood.

"I found out another friend of mine is pregnant. The one who shoots bears."

"Hmm," she says. "How do you feel about that?"

I rip open a bag of pita chips. "Happy for her, but I hope she never loses the baby weight and won't sneeze again without wetting herself." I peel back the protective plastic wrap from a tub of hummus and sample it with one of the chips. "Does that make me a bad person?

She laughs. "No. If you're a bad person for saying it, I'm just as bad for laughing."

"How are you holding up?" I ask, referring to her situation with Carl. I load another chip.

"I'm broke, and I'm embarrassed, which are no fun at all. You know, they say with age comes wisdom, but when the heart wants what it wants, there's no telling what good sense you throw out the window."

"You can say that again." I finish chewing and swallow. "Sorry about the crunching. Chips and hummus. I was starving. God, I'm so rude."

"I don't care. Eat, eat. You're too skinny anyway."

***

Two hours later Erik and I are lying on the couch together, watching a mindless action movie, all car chases and explosions and completely implausible romance. I'm barely paying attention, but it's the kind of movie where you don't really have to. "Do you think Renae will take their kid bear-hunting?" I ask Erik during the second shootout.

"Probably."

"I guess I'll buy her some of those camouflage onesies," I say glumly. "You know, for the shower."

We quietly watch the movie for a few minutes, and then he pulls me closer and kisses my forehead. "Honey, I like our life."

After a beat I add, "Me too." I'm pretty sure I mean it.

"Let's focus on more interesting things."

"The fact that airlines deliver luggage better than Taylor Lautner can deliver his lines?"

"No," he says, kissing my neck, running his fingers through my hair. "This."

Chapter 28
"Fingers crossed!"

I think we found a house. Three bedrooms, two baths, open concept kitchen and living room, paved patio under a pergola, room for a garden, and a man cave for Erik. It's at the top end of our price range, but it's in a quiet neighborhood with mature trees, miles from the nearest check-cashing store. A place we could be comfortable in for awhile. Whoever lives there now has a near-obscene fondness for wallpaper borders, and the bathroom fixtures are hideous gold-plate straight out of 1986, but those are easy fixes. I'm actually getting excited thinking about laying fresh Contact paper in the cupboards, picking out paint swatches, becoming a real, live homeowner and finally learning what the word "escrow" means.

We accepted the buyer's offer for my mother's house, and if we time this right and our offer for the new place is accepted, we just may avoid a brief period of homelessness. "If that happens, you're welcome to live in our garage for a few days," Clint said to me, smirking. We could sleep on his old orange couch, store our milk and lunchmeats in the beer fridge, pee in a bucket, play a little ping pong if we wanted. I told him to be careful, because I might call his bluff.

Hannah is home now, recovering from her surgery. "My hip is numb," she told me the first time I visited post-surgery, carefully showing me her scars. "There aren't any nerve endings there anymore." We gazed at her hip in wonder.

"Well, you're titanium down there now," I replied. "You can hip-check any guy who messes with you into next week." I've been over to see her three times since she's returned, bringing books and her favorite lobster macaroni salad. I even brought Abe and Auschie with me one night (with her parents' pre-approval, of course), and Hannah absolutely fell in love with them. Another night we played a marathon game of Monopoly with Joy, who handily kicked our asses. Hannah is still confined to her bed or the living room couch, still in a world of hurt and constipated from the painkillers. Coughing hurts, sneezing hurts, sitting hurts, moving hurts … but her bones are healing, the deposits of calcium phosphate hardening, marrow multiplying at a cellular level even now. She starts physical therapy next week.

Tonight Erik and I are at home together. He is finishing up some work on his laptop, and I am watching trashy television, digesting and marinating on the other end of the couch instead of taking a leisurely after-dinner stroll around the block because I ate too much spaghetti. It is early summer, mere weeks before the one-year anniversary of my mother's death. I've been preparing myself for this day for the past few months, both dreading and anticipating it because once you pass this first black square on the calendar, the rest aren't so scary. You can remember how you spent that first year, which gives you a benchmark to measure against. An instructional manual of sorts, even if it's been poorly translated from Mandarin and includes the phrase, *Special area for deformed, please to slip down and fall carefully.*

"Do you know," I say to Erik during a commercial break, "there is no other human being who knows me as well as you do and still not only loves me, but likes me? That's a pretty big deal."

"Yep," he says, the keyboard clattering away. The screen gives his skin a ghostly glow.

"Hey, what do you think about adopting?" He tosses this out like a casual survey on whether I prefer Ragu or Barilla marinara sauce, still staring intently at his laptop.

I grin. "A new attitude?"

He shakes his head.

"A stretch of highway?"

"Try again."

"A forty-year-old member of the KISS Army?"

He laughs. "Seriously. Ted at work just adopted a rug rat. Cutest little bastard."

I'm smiling, wide and goofy, because I can't help myself. Me, somebody's mother. Wouldn't that be something?

***

"Hey Marge." I close my eyes and shake my head. "I'm sorry. *Paula.* I don't know where my mind is these days."

"Oh, can I relate," she says. "Just wait 'til you hit menopause."

I laugh. "I can wait."

We are ushered into a cool, high-ceilinged conference room at Paula's office, about to sign the offer for the house. It is the one-year anniversary of my mother's death.

"I don't want to visit the cemetery," I'd told Erik earlier, so instead, we packed a picnic lunch, with plans to visit Lake Kegonsa State Park after our appointment. I'd just been to the cemetery, and now I have new, complicated memories of that place. It's too soon to return. And I'd prefer to be somewhere Mom enjoyed. Somewhere she thrived and laughed, a place where dragonflies landed on her shoulder and she collected milkweed pods for an art project with her catechism students.

Paula says things like, "Sign here," and "again here" and "now at the bottom" and flips endless pages of tiny print we nervously scan. I feel as if I'm about to go scuba diving blindfolded, waiting for my tour operator to push me from the boat. There is no telling what we are agreeing or not agreeing to. I want the house, and I don't even care if the inspection reveals dry rot or an Indian burial ground beneath the pergola. It's become primal for me. I already know what color I want to repaint the kitchen, have looked into the types of perennials that will grow well in the shady backyard. I have officially become a realtor's wet dream.

"I'll fax it in today," Paula assures us. She promises to call the minute she hears from the sellers. "It's a good offer," she says. "Fingers crossed!"

Later we unwrap our sandwiches—provolone, lettuce, and tomato on mustard for me, salami, cheddar, and horseradish for Erik— at a picnic table at Lake Kegonsa State Park. While we eat, we watch parents push their children in swings on the playground. A few teenagers lazily toss a Frisbee in a clearing near the parking lot, dropping the blue disc more than they catch it. They give up after it hits a parked recreational vehicle with a sharp clunk, nearly hard enough to leave a dent. A hairy man in nothing but cutoff jean shorts steps out of the RV to frown around the parking lot, and the kids take off, laughing.

We sometimes came here when I was younger. Gwen would spread her towel, oil her arms and legs, and read *People* magazine on the beach next to Mom, who would be engrossed in a book about strong frontier women beneath her floppy hat. Dad would bury Clint and then me in the sand. Afterwards he'd flip Clint from his freckled shoulders into the lake, right next to the floating buoys tethered together with nylon rope, cordoning off the deep end of the swim area. There would be an excess of splashing and whooping, a break in the action only to expel water gone up the nose or down the wrong pipe. I would pretend-swim in the shallow end, walking on my hands beneath the water's surface, legs floating behind me, shouting at our mother: "Mom! Look! I know how to swim! I'm swimming! Are you watching?"

"Yep, I'm watching," she'd absently reply, nose still in her book. A bag of Doritos would be passed around. There would be a container of washed grapes in the cooler, cans of Miller Lite and Dr Pepper, and sensible sandwiches on whole-wheat bread. There was an unblemished and intact childhood—at least for that afternoon. We'd get sand in the car on the ride home, our towels damp, our eyelids heavy, Dad humming along to Tom Petty on the radio. When we fell asleep that night, we never dreamed we'd look back on that day with such longing.

At least I didn't.

I lift my face to the sky, wondering if I'll receive some sort of cosmic sign from my mother; a chickadee that cocks her head and stares at me too long, a single red flower bursting from a crack in the sidewalk, a sudden swirl of wind in answer to my open heart. Even *two monarchs doing it!!* Instead, I hear my mother's warm voice in my head: *Honey, don't be dippy. I follow a totally different calendar now, and I've got better things to do than possess birds and mess with the weather. Johnny Carson's having a dinner party tonight!*

After lunch, Erik and I follow the boardwalk into the marsh. We startle a family of mallards, who scurry into the water and paddle away from us. I memorize the day—how the sun bronzes Erik's hair, the ratcheting of a wren in the bushes, the glossy green of the rushes bending and shushing in the breeze. Because sometimes, you don't recognize a perfect day until it's gone.

Chapter 29
"You did it!"

"Who told him he could bring fireworks?" Erik is asking me in our new kitchen, peering out the window at the driveway, annoyed. I am busy tearing open bags of chips, pouring them in an oversized plastic bowl. I say nothing, because I was the approver of Clint's request. But when he asked if he could bring a few fireworks, I hadn't expected him to bring enough to ring in the Chinese New Year. I reach up to touch the scar by my ear, from that long-ago bottle rocket Clint aimed at my head. It's not easy trying to transition from overly accommodating to perfectly assertive overnight.

"He's going to set those trees on fire," Erik mutters, and marches outside to initiate a conversation with Clint, ostensibly about the wisdom of setting off eight hundred dollars' worth of fireworks so close to both our new house and our landscaping.

We are throwing a housewarming party. Always the one to push me from "maybe" to "all right," Frankie insisted on it. "I want to meet the tranny," she'd whispered, excited, and now she's sitting on a lawn chair in my new backyard, doing exactly that. Chris isn't a circus freak, I told her. Chris came with her new boyfriend, Ian, who owns a dog grooming business on the west side of Madison. I'd suggested that Chris get a dog to help her heal after the final-FINAL breakup with David, and she'd adopted Miles without imagining it would lead her to the first healthy relationship of her life. So far.

Miles, an elderly Chihuahua mix with bug eyes and a white muzzle, is playing with Abe and Auschie, occasionally lifting his leg on one or the other, to Chris's embarrassment. When this happens, Chris wobbles over, heels aerating the lawn, to scold Miles and redirect his attention to the bonanza of dog toys cluttering the patio.

I carry the bowl of chips and a tub of sour cream and onion dip to the patio, juggling them as I slip out the sliding glass door. "Need any help?" Alyssa asks, fanning herself. Hannah is lying next to her on a chaise lounge, texting a friend.

"You're sweet, but I think I've got it under control. Did Evelyn say when she was getting here?"

"No, but she said something about an appointment today."

I crank open the umbrella to give us some shade from the searing sun. Next spring, I'll plant a vine or two at the base of the pergola, see what that does to make our outdoor living space more comfortable. "I can't believe July is almost over," I muse. I can't believe I have an outdoor living space. I turn to my niece. "You feeling okay, Hannah?"

"I'm fine," she says, still texting.

"This summer did go by fast," Alyssa agrees. "Two more days and I'm off to California!"

"We're going to miss you."

"I'm going to miss you, too." Instead of returning to school in fall, Alyssa is going to take a break and do the traveling I wish I'd done at her age. First to California to meet up with a friend from high school, then on to Alaska and Australia. They're starting with the A's.

"Will you come back to school?"

"Eventually. But I need to do this first. Get my head sorted out, see the world."

"I am insanely jealous. Have I told you that?"

"Come with us!"

Oh, to be young and single again. I consider the possibility of tagging along for a brief, shining moment: finding my passport, booking the tickets, boarding the plane, filing for bankruptcy, being left for the budget analyst who is good with dogs. "Not with this new mortgage. Here's a tip: postpone responsibility as long as humanly possible, because once you sign up for that cruise, it's basically non-refundable."

"Tip taken." She laughs lightly, not really believing this. She's embarking on an adventure; why bring a distant mediocrity—joint checking accounts, Roth IRAs, term life insurance—into the picture?

"I wish I could go," Hannah says wistfully.

"You will someday. Are you hungry? I can make you a plate."

She shakes her head and leans down to grab one end of a rag-toy to play a gentle tug-of-war with Abe, who digs in and really pulls, stronger than he appears.

Chris joins us on the patio and hisses, "Your brother won't stop staring at me."

"Have you seen his wife?" I say, feeling only a little guilty. "Who could blame him."

Chris puts an arm around my shoulder and squeezes. "I love this girl." We watch Frankie laugh with her whole body at something Ian has said to her. "Isn't he handsome?" Chris asks, selecting a ham and pickle roll-up skewered by a tassel-topped toothpick.

"Dreamy," I confirm, and she kisses my cheek before popping the appetizer in her mouth.

"Who brought these?"

"Paul did," I say. "Did you hear he's got a sort-of-girlfriend?"

"No!" Chris dabs a blot of cream cheese from the corner of her lip. "Do tell!"

"He met her at Zumba. She's a Montessori teacher. Paul says they don't tell kids they did a great job, or that they're good or whatever. Instead, you're supposed to just say, 'You did it!'"

"Why?"

"Something about kids not associating achievement with their self-worth." I search for the rest of it and end with the unsatisfactory, "Conditional love and whatnot." I cringe at my use of the word 'whatnot.'

"Paul does Zumba?" Alyssa asks.

"It's his new thing. He's lost what, five pounds already?"

"I'd pay to see Paul doing Zumba," Alyssa says, grinning. I'm pleased to report that Paul won his court case against his horrid neighbor—a cash settlement covering the dogs' veterinary bills and then some, for pain and suffering. Vern was also slapped with an animal cruelty charge. Unfortunately, Vern shows no signs of hemorrhaging to death or moving anytime soon, so Paul is also investigating his housing options. He's mentioned moving in with his sister a few times. I could see him bartending at The Grumpy Troll, explaining permaculture growing systems and the difference between biodynamic and organic wine to his patrons. But I know he'd miss the funky vibrancy of the city—the dreadlocked buskers and their loyal yellow dogs, the patchouli-scented head shops on State Street, the eclectic selection at Four Star Video Heaven, homecoming gigs for Mama Digdown's Brass Band, the Barrymore Theater, now host to acts like Ani DiFranco instead of movies like *Deep Throat*.

I hear a car door slam in the driveway, and the dogs start barking, racing to greet the latest guest. "Oh, I think Evelyn is here!" There's a twinkle in Alyssa's eyes as she says this.

Paul stops erecting the badminton set and runs to meet her, and the rest of us follow.

Evelyn is standing next to a borrowed pickup, doing a swimmer's stretch. There is a huge metal sculpture in the bed of the truck, all iron gears and sharp angles and industrial curves. It's a dragonfly, I realize. Six feet tall, red with rust, and substantial. It will weather any storm.

"You did it!" Paul says, lifting his fists to shake imaginary maracas in celebration.

"Evelyn, it's beautiful!"

"I'd hug you, but I'm all sweaty. I had four guys help me load it in the truck."

"Oh, who cares," I say, wrapping my arms around her. "It'll wash off." I circle around the truck, amazed. "I can't believe you made this!" I wipe a few tears from my eyes.

I know Evelyn had bigger things to worry about than welding metal these last few weeks; she hasn't gotten her money back from con man Carl, but at least her daughter Kimberly has moved out, pursuing further spiritual enlightenment in Djibouti or some other such country you've heard of maybe once in your life. But her eight-year-old granddaughter arrives next Tuesday for a weeklong visit, and Evelyn has been excitedly planning activities: a trip to a water park, the American Girl

doll benefit sale at the Madison Children's Museum, even a cookie dec-
orating class, which Hannah may join them for, if she's feeling up to it.

The men form a brigade to hoist the sculpture onto the driveway,
glad to have an excuse to flex their muscles and testosterone. Chris
stands to the side, a manicured hand resting anxiously on her chest
while she frets over the proceedings. "Be careful of your back, Ian!"

"I remember you saying your mother liked dragonflies," Evelyn
says to me, explaining her artistic direction. It's possibly the most
thoughtful, and definitely the largest gift I've ever received, other than
living through this last year.

Somehow, we'd boxed the rest of my mother's things up. Many
of the boxes ended up at Goodwill, the rest in a rented storage unit
from which we are slowly transferring them to our new house. There
are things I've set aside for Hannah, and all of the photo albums are
already safely displayed on a shelf in my new living room. Taking our
final walk through Mom's house before turning over the keys to the
new owners left me with mixed emotions. On one hand, it felt artificial and staged; doesn't nearly every popular sitcom end its run with
that final tour of the bar or apartment, one last meaningful look back
before turning off the lights? I was keenly aware of this with every self-
conscious step I took. On the other, this was the last place I'd spent
time with my mother. We'd shared so many memories, both awful and
tender, in those rooms. But you have to move on. You can't cling to
everything. You can't live in the past. People have tried, and it doesn't
end well.

"Goodbye, wobbly ceiling fan," I said. *Beneath which a hectic night
was spent ministering to my mother, who shivered when she was hot and sweated
when she was cold. Beneath which we laughed so hard at an old, unsent letter
from Clint to a high school girlfriend.*

"Farewell, hideous bathroom," Erik said. *In which I helped my brave
mother—too wracked with pain to feel embarrassed—insert prophylactic painkillers because she couldn't keep her meals down any longer. In which I simply
flossed and brushed and washed.*

"*Adios, yellow kitchen countertops.*" *On which I cut and sorted pills like a second-rate drug dealer. On which I chopped carrots and celery for chicken soup when Erik had the flu.*

By the time we reached the front door, I was ready. If the walls could talk, they might have stories to tell, but I wouldn't be around to hear them.

***

As we're admiring Evelyn's handiwork, a Toyota Corolla pulls into the driveway: Amy and Liz, with the newest addition to the Kimmel family: Baby Surprise, now formally named Stella, just shy of three months on the planet. She's bundled in a pink and brown blanket, sleeping, and wakes when Amy unbuckles her car seat straps to give me, the first person she sees, the stink eye. Amy passes her to me, and I gingerly cradle her head. "It's nice to meet you, Miss Stella." As Erik puts on some music and the party shifts into a new gear, Stella grips my index finger with strong, tiny fingers. "Watch out for the Stanley Kowalskis of the world," I whisper to her. "They may be handsome, but they're no good, I tell you. No good at all." She screws up her face and burps at me, appraising me coolly with bright blue eyes.

We make small talk for a few minutes, about the drive here, about the new house, until I notice Amy, Liz, and Frankie exchanging subtle looks. "What?" I ask bluntly.

"I left Steve," Liz plainly says, her expression impenetrable. I can't tell if she's thrilled or broken about this.

"Oh my God," I say, shifting from side to side while I hold Stella. We study her, waiting for tears, the heavy sigh, clenched fists, any kind of external reaction to mark the end of her marriage, but instead there is a kind of grateful and quiet acceptance.

"Well, it was a long time coming."

"What about the boys?"

"They're taking it surprisingly well. They're only four, so to them, it's like an adventure, so far anyway. Bunk beds at Dad's, glow-in-the-dark stars on the ceiling at Mom's. I don't know, maybe it hasn't sunk in yet."

"Oh sweetie, I'm so sorry." I truly am. Even though Steve and Liz were mismatched, it's not going to be easy cobbling a new life together with joint custody arrangements, connected for the rest of their lives by their identical common denominators. I imagine Luke or Liam posting an online ad one day, maybe fifteen years from now: *new family wanted for Christmas dinner. Stepmother a nudist, stepbrother insane.*

Paul's finished setting up the badminton set, and an impromptu game begins: Ian and Alyssa against Paul and Joy. She shrieks every time she misses the shuttlecock, which strikes me as uncomfortably funny. She's all elbows and poorly timed lunges, swinging wildly, fiercely competitive. It's a side of Joy I've seen once before, during our Monopoly game a few weeks ago.

I refresh drinks and give the tour. "Nice wallpaper," Liz says, sipping her homemade mojito.

"It's going down next week."

She poses next to the waist-high border in the kitchen, hand extended to absently caress it like Vanna White, a plastic smile on her face. "I particularly enjoy these pink teacups." Her voice is a lilting, showroom monotone; she's imitating someone, some comedian or news personality, but I can't put my finger on who it is.

Amy laughs, shifting from side to side in an attempt to calm her fussy daughter. "Say, would you mind if I fed Stella in your bedroom?"

"Not at all!"

Later, after the sun slides toward the horizon and stretches long shadows over the lawn, some of my coworkers arrive, after they've spent the day doing yard work or attending their own family picnics. Linda Hernandez, Emily Garrison, Avery Morgan, Nate Halstrom. I feel vindicated to finally invite Emily to a party of my own, and she doesn't show up empty-handed; she brought us a beautiful potted orchid.

Evelyn has assumed control of the drink-making at my kitchen peninsula, whipping up authentic cocktails our grandparents used to drink. It's getting hot in the house, but not hot enough to crank the air conditioning, so I open a few more windows and turn up the dining room ceiling fan, which begins to wobble alarmingly over the buffet of snacks spread on the table. *Beneath which my friends and family ate guacamole at our housewarming party.*

Around eight p.m., as people are making motions to leave, Clint marches around, whistling to get everyone's attention. "Fireworks show in the driveway!" There is a cigar clamped in his mouth, his left eye squinted above the pungent smoke. It's a new hobby he picked up when we weren't looking. Hannah angrily fans the air in front of her face any time he comes near, coughing emphatically. He passes out sparklers and lights them; I watch my guests transform into children, burning their names in the night sky, waving them as if at a concert. Paul conducts an invisible orchestra with his.

Slowly, we congregate in the driveway, where Clint has arranged a small arsenal of explosives. "The neighbors should love this," Evelyn says to me, one eyebrow raised.

I feel my anxiety tick up a notch. "Clint, are you sure this is safe? That looks like an awful lot of fireworks."

"It's fine," Clint says, leaning down to light a long fuse. "I have it under control." A horsetail of blinding pink and green sparks shoot up from their cardboard canister, and the assembled crowd "oohs" and "aahs." Miles goes bananas at the cracks and explosions, whining and shaking and barking. Chris picks him up and holds him close to her chest, caressing him and murmuring reassurances. She and Amy retreat to the house with their babies. Clint lights a few more, which spiral up into the sky and explode into electric carnations. Clouds of acrid smoke begin to drift over our subdivision. Some of the kids in the neighborhood abandon their sidewalk chalk art or games of H-O-R-S-E and wander over to watch. They huddle at the end of the driveway, leaning against scooters or clutching basketballs against their stomachs.

"Can we play with a few sparklers?" one of them shyly asks me.

Lawsuit, is the first word that comes to mind. I crouch down to their level. "Guys? I would let you, but first your mom or dad needs to say it's okay." Their shoulders slump in disappointment.

"But she did!" the youngest, a girl around seven, insists. "My mom said it's okay!"

"Did she really?" I say, smiling, raising one eyebrow. What is this kid, telepathic?

"Yes!" I maintain eye contact, still smiling, until she frowns and confesses with a dejected, "No."

Erik is getting nervous. "That one's awfully close to the pines, don't you think?"

Clint ignores him and bends to light the fuse. There is a deep WHUMP! you feel in your chest, followed by a hot pink sideways jet of sparks. "Oh shit," he says, nearly calmly, while we watch a gorgeous weeping Japanese Maple, the anchoring shrub in our neighbor's east foundation planting, take a direct hit. It doesn't quite go up in flames; rather, the delicate red leaves slowly evaporate along an advancing line of bright orange, leaving behind black, skeletal veins that curl and crumble into dust.

"Clint, we haven't even met them yet!" I yell. I anxiously scan their windows, wait for someone to run out of the house, brace myself for the inevitable confrontation, but nothing happens. Nobody's home. Still, I can see the headline now: *THERE GOES THE NEIGHBORHOOD! CLODHOPPERS BUY 736 CAMDEN AVENUE.*

"Settle down, I'll take care of it!" Clint roars at me, agitated.

"You settle down!" I shout back, channeling my inner eight-year-old.

While Erik scrambles to unreel the hose, someone appears beside me. Ian.

"Those are expensive trees," I say, wincing.

"We'll take up a collection."

"No, *Clint* will be the one paying for this," I clarify.

We stand together, watching Erik and Clint hose down the neighbor's landscaping. Ian shakes his head, bemused. "You don't have to like him," he says, "but it's okay to love him."

I turn to him, distracted. "What?"

"My shrink gave me that pearl of wisdom. I have a brother too," he explains.

I nod. "That about sums it up."

"Ah, your burning bush has been extinguished," Ian announces, and I laugh. I like Ian, and I hope things work out for him and Chris.

More guests say their goodbyes, leaving only the diehards to spray their arms and legs with mosquito repellant, crack open a fresh beer, and return to the buffet to pick over slices of hardening cheese. Another badminton game begins: Paul, Erik, Evelyn, and Clint, who promised to send me a check for whatever the neighbor valued the tree at. Paul's ringing phone draws him from the game, and I step in to replace him as Erik's teammate. Despite the fading light, we find our rhythm and get a good volley going. Back and forth, over the net. A few bats begin to swoop through the yard, chirping in Morse code and sending Alyssa scurrying into the house. Hannah, trapped on the chaise lounge, watches them miserably. "Did you know," Paul says to her, closing his phone, "that one brown bat can eat up to three thousand mosquitoes in one night?"

"Yeah, I heard that."

This is my family, I think.

My coworker Nate and his girlfriend are the last to leave, and do so reluctantly. It's nearly ten p.m. Erik and I pack the leftovers and store them in the fridge. While I pick up discarded cups and paper plates, he carefully builds a flammable nest in the fire pit at the edge of the patio: crumpled newspaper, dry twigs and kindling, a pyramid of heartier logs stacked on top. We nestle into matching Adirondack chairs and watch the flames come to life, tidy and crackling. I warm the soles of my shoes against the grate.

"Fire is funny," I say to Erik, the hypnotic glowing embers soothing me into armchair philosophizing. "It kills hundreds of people a year, but without it, none of us would probably be here. Civilization as we know it wouldn't exist."

Erik nods in agreement and gets up to stir the embers. He feeds two more logs into the fire, which spits and pops in approval.

I look up at the night sky: a violet canvas speckled with brilliant white. There are more stars where we live now. Or maybe we just have a better view.

Before he sits back down, Erik turns to me and says, "I think I'm going to get a beer. Do you need anything?"

I shake my head and smile. Right now, I have everything I need.

THE END

Acknowledgements

First and foremost, I have to thank my husband Jason: without you, I would be far too lonely and uninspired to write. Also, without your kind and keen eye, this book would have had far too many bad puns and jokes about skin tags. Nobody wants to read that shit. My family and family are (nearly) nothing like the dysfunctional oddballs I've created in these pages—if word got out about how hilarious, supportive, and awesome you all are, everyone would try to kidnap you. To my agent Laura Blake Peterson: I am so grateful for your unflagging cheerleading and belief in my writing.

I also owe an incredible debt to my early readers: Stephanie Elliott (aka "Manic Mom"), Trish (Swishy) Garner, Mary Hennessy, Michelle Ralston, Lucinda Vette, Nikki Kallio, December Gephart, Julie Nitz-Basler. Your constructive feedback helped make this book better, and your friendship makes my life better.

Thank you to Jim Thomsen for his editorial magic, and to Sarah Hansen at Okay Creations for an awesome cover.

Thank you as well to my sisterhood of authors, whose support and camaraderie keeps me sane: Eileen Cook, Danielle Younge-Ullman, Lisa Daily, Jenny Gardiner, Gail Konop-Baker, Jen Lancaster, Sarah Pekkanen, Julie Buxbaum, Allison Winn-Scotch, Lesley Kagan, Therese Fowler, and all of the wonderful authors in the Girlfriends Book Club. The list could actually fill the page, because the writers I know are among the most selfless, generous, and helpful people on earth.

To all of the book clubs, libraries, and readers who took a chance on me with *Driving Sideways*: thank you, from the bottom of my heart. You remind me daily why I do this.

Coming Spring 2013:
MANDATORY RELEASE

Recently paralyzed in a car accident, thirty-year-old Graham Finch spends his days managing a caseload of unruly inmates and his nights attempting to stave off loneliness with one painfully awkward date after another ...

... until his former high school crush Drew Daniels walks through the prison gates one hot summer morning. On the run from a painful past, Drew is a new teacher at Bone Beach. Graham, smitten all over again, tries to squash his unrequited love with a new relationship. But when the heart wants what it wants, can you really redirect it?

Amidst escalating violence at work, Drew is forced to confront her secrets and find a way to forgive past sins. Graham must also learn to make peace with his own past. Together they realize that if you're going to save yourself, sometimes the best way to do it is by saving someone else first.

Set in a medium-security men's prison near the dunes of Lake Michigan (and inspired by the author's work in such a place), *Mandatory Release* is an honest, funny, and gritty love story about broken people who work in a dangerous place, finding hope where they least expect it.

***

Chapter 1

So when do you suppose it's a good time to tell the woman you've been flirting with for a month online that you're actually in a wheelchair? And probably won't be running the Full Moon half-marathon with her like she thinks? I used to run half-marathons. Back when I was married and had much less limited mobility.

That's what I am now. A single guy with "limited mobility." I am also a liar, if your definition of lying includes the selective withholding of information.

I wish I could tell you that I was paralyzed during a prison riot. That I was stabbed in the spine with a shank made from the sharpened end of a toothbrush. And that I'd rescued my entire unit, and ended up something of a local celebrity. Maybe even getting a few endorsement deals out of it, pitching used cars or furniture. I could tell you that's how it happened, but for some reason, I don't want to lie to you. I want us to get off on the right foot. So here's the unfortunate truth, which is much less sexy than a prison riot stabbing: it was actually a car accident. My ex-wife was driving us home from a wedding. I probably don't need to tell you we were both drunk. Or that she swerved to miss a family of raccoons crossing the road and the car tumbled down a ditch and gracelessly ejected me into a field.

Basically, I lost my dick to a family of raccoons. Bet you've never heard that before.

So now I'm glib when I should be reflective. I'm caustic where I should be smooth. I'm half when I should be whole. And I'm being perfectly honest about my feelings here, which is something I've supposedly had trouble doing. Just ask my ex-wife.

Anyway, right now I'm on a first date with the marathon runner I met online, and she doesn't know any of this. Her name is Margie and she's an accountant. With a name and occupation like that you'd think she wears pearl earrings and Isotoner slippers, right? But she's got five tattoos and rides an Indian. No, I don't mean "East Indian" or the catch-all name rednecks give American Indians. I mean the motorcycle. A Scout, no less.

She doesn't have a sidecar.

We're at a restaurant called O'Clancys, and its German proprietors have definitely done their part to keep the knock-off movie memorabilia industry alive. To give you a feel for the joint, think Groucho Marx meets Vin Diesel. Everywhere you look there's a framed B-movie poster or black and white publicity shot of an actor who hasn't done much since the early nineties. We're sitting beneath a clapperboard that looks as if it may drop onto Margie's head the next time a server marches by.

I tap the plastic-covered menu against the table and clear my throat. "The Caesar salad is good here." I've said the exact same thing to two other women I've met here in the last six months.

Margie smiles tightly. She doesn't look up from her menu. "Is it?"

I know I'll be ordering the perch, like I do every time I eat here. And if this date goes anything like the last two, Margie will next place her menu on the table, sigh deeply, look me in the eye and say, *"Why didn't you tell me you were in a wheelchair?"* The next thing out of her mouth will be either, *"You could have told me; I wouldn't have judged you"* or *"If you can't be honest about something this big, I don't see a future for us."* At least these were the responses I got from the last two women I went on dates with.

"The perch is good, too." Another lie. The last few times it's been kind of bland and rubbery, about as appealing as a baked eraser. But I keep ordering it because I like perch, and I keep hoping that one of these times they'll get it right again. My job and physical situation have conspired to turn me into a glass-half-empty kind of guy, except in two key areas: dating and perch. Because despite the dim prospects for both, I keep coming back for more.

Margie doesn't respond. "Take on Me" by A-Ha dribbles from the speakers overhead. *Take me on, Margie,* I think.

I've discovered that the best way to proceed in this kind of situation is to pretend nothing is wrong. I mean, how else would I get out of it? We're talking major tightrope-walking over a moat of lies. A Mariana Trench stuffed with lies. She's uncomfortable, and by now I'm extremely uncomfortable that my disinformation campaign has gone so far. As I have in the past, I tell myself that I'm only screening for women with a good sense of humor.

And like before, of course I don't believe myself. Because while I occasionally do dabble in self-deception, even I know when I'm truly and completely full of shit.

So let me ask you again: how do you tell someone you've connected with, someone you really like, that you're not everything they think you are? After a few conversations it becomes too late. You both enjoy one another—or at least, the illusion of one another—too much. What are you going to say, "Oh, by the way, have I mentioned I'm a midget?" or "Gee, sorry I didn't tell you earlier, but I've got a port wine stain the size of Rhode Island on my face. I grapple with chronic infections of the asshole, too." And by then, you like them, and they like you. Your Truth Window has closed. So you either carry on the ruse or end everything immediately. And if you carry on the ruse, they're going to want to meet face-to-face at some point. Then, you have two unappealing options. You can either do the "I have something important to tell you" speech before you meet (which, I've found, isn't always effective). Or, you can tell them during the date. Unfortunately, I think my "during" window has already closed, too.

Margie plays along, pretending nothing is out of the ordinary. But I can literally taste her discomfort. It's a bit steely, like old Cointreau with cranberry juice. Our waitress senses it, too. I make a mental note to leave a bulky tip as compensation for this table of awkwardness.

I order the perch, and Margie orders the walnut-crusted chicken. The period between ordering and the delivery of our meals is always tricky. But I take heart in the fact that none of my previous dates (the ones where I neglected to mention the whole wheelchair thing, anyway) even lasted this long. Adrenaline simmers in my gut while I wait for her to say something. It's the kind of feeling you can get addicted to, if you're not careful.

While we wait, I tell Margie an inmate story. At first I'm tempted to tell her the one about the guy that intricately fashioned an entire chess set from his own feces, but we're eating. Instead I tell her about a guy that ate an entire computer keyboard, letter by letter. She smiles politely, and I notice that she blinks a lot. She's got kind of a tic thing that she does, where she continually opens her eyes really wide, but just for a split second, as if to clear them of some debris.

Or maybe this is how she always reacts to what must at first seem like an optical illusion. The waitress appears from stage left, our meals balanced in each hand. She swoops in, and steaming plates clatter in place before us. It feels like a rescue. I smile at her: slight gap between her teeth, black pigtails, eyes spaced too far apart, breasts small but perky. They make me think of nectarines. "Careful, those plates are real hot!"

I wonder how many times she says that in the course of one shift.

Margie asks for another iced tea, and then we're alone again. I rub my hands together to indicate how psyched I am to dig into my perch, painfully aware of the uncomfortable weight my false brevity carries. I've become a one-man show playing to a hostile audience.

We listen to "99 Luftballons" while we chew our meals, and I watch a couple laughing and sharing entrees across the aisle. *You could have that*, I think. *If you stopped lying.*

The silence at our table is palpable. *Think. What did you two discuss in your e-mails? In your six phone conversations?* An idea burbles up as I glance at a poster for *The Godfather II*. "Have you seen the latest De Niro movie?"

She shakes her head and chews, her eyes darting around the room between blinks. I notice that she chews very quickly. Almost as quickly as she blinks.

"I didn't much care for it," I answer for her. "I found it bloated and predictable."

Her left eyebrow shoots up, as if to say, *Well, you're certainly bloated, but definitely not predictable.* I spear a chunk of perch and dredge it through some tartar sauce. Is fish supposed to be gray? I wish I'd gotten the fajitas.

"Yeah," I continue, ignoring her eyebrow. "His films are so pandering lately. So formulaic. Whatever happened to taking risks? Whatever happened to *Taxi Driver? Raging Bull?*" I chew a mouthful of breadstick and add, "He's really been coasting with his last few roles."

She blinks at me again and shovels a forkful of rice into her mouth. It's a look I take to mean: *Coasting, huh? You would know.*

The discomfort level has inched up, but I take it in stride. No pun intended.

Think think think. Ask her about her family.

"So how's your mother?" During one of our earlier conversations we'd bonded over our mutual family dysfunctions and misfortunes. She told me about her mother's multiple sclerosis, and I told her about my brother's Asperger's syndrome. He's a meteorologist and can pinpoint wind speed, barometric pressure, and humidity with ninety percent accuracy in twenty seconds.

There's really no comparison. But it was all I could come up with at the time.

She shrugs and extends a see-sawing hand to indicate "so-so."

A weightless feeling begins to rise in me; maybe she won't say a thing about my chair! *Maybe she hasn't even noticed.* But she shortly dispels this notion by saying, "Graham, you know, this is probably the biggest physical feature anyone I've met online has ever attempted to hide from me." She begins ticking bad dates off on one hand. "I mean, there was the guy who was a foot and a half shorter than he claimed, and the one who wore a toupee. And one guy who was probably sixty pounds heavier than his online profile would have led me to believe. But this is really a bit more than a toupee, isn't it? This is getting into a freaky place I don't really want to go."

For a split second I think she's the most incredibly insensitive, dis-criminatory-against-the-disabled person I've ever met. This segues quickly into smutty shock: is she referencing what sex with me would be like?

Then I realize that she's indicating my failure to disclose what's become of my legs.

"Honest to God, I waited this long to say anything because I didn't know quite what to say. It was just so . . . so *bizarre*." She crumples her nap-kin, tosses it on her plate, and gives me a look of contempt that I thought only my ex-wife had mastered. "Running a marathon? Give me a break!"

My cheeks are hot. "You're right," I say. "And I'm sorry. I should have told you."

"Damn right, you should have!" With this she scoots back, her chair squawking angrily. By the time I think of my follow-up, she's already four strides away.

Desperation. I toss out one final question, though what good it will do me now is of dubious value. "Would you still have gone out with me if I told you?"

She pauses and turns around, gripping her purse so tightly I fear her knuckles will snap in half. "You need help."

And then she's gone.

Up until the end, it wasn't half-bad for a first date. Though I would have much preferred hearing The Question over the angry dia-tribe. The Question I am still amazed I even have to answer: *"Why didn't you tell me you were in a wheelchair?"*

But I don't really have a good answer to this.

Because sometimes in my mind, I'm not.

***

Be sure to "Like" the author's Facebook page (https://www.facebook.com/JessRileyAuthor) for the latest updates on **Mandatory Release**, scheduled for release in spring 2013.

19005812R00161

Made in the USA
Charleston, SC
02 May 2013